THE COMPLETE COLLECTION

MASTERS OF THE HOTEL BENTMOORE

SHELBY CROSS

Copyright XXXXXXXXX by Shelby Cross. All rights reserved.
ISBN-13: 9781475138894
ISBN-10: 147513889X

Visit http://shelbycrosswriter.blogspot.com for updates, news, and more.

Cover and Interior: Streetlight Graphics

Dedicated to my Husband

Table of Contents

Michelle

"MICHELLE, I AM MR. Dean. I will be your host for your stay at the Hotel Bentmoore."

"It's nice to finally meet you, Mr. Dean." Michelle Langley's hand came up to shake Mr. Dean's. Mr. Dean accepted the gesture of cordial introduction, but frowned. He was not used to women shaking his hand at the Hotel Bentmoore, at least not within the confines of the lower floor. Above, where guests mingled side by side, hotel staff brushed shoulders with wealthy patrons, and everything looked as proper and as elegant as a hotel should, women would sometimes nod his way, smile as they caught a glimpse of him walking past...if they didn't know who he was, they would sometimes assume he was just another guest, and shake his hand to introduce themselves to a handsome, self-assured man.

But within the walls of the lower floor, it was a different story. Women stripped before him, knelt before him, spread themselves open when ordered...they regarded him with reverence, obedience, and most of the time, complete submission.

They did not shake his hand.

But Michelle was smiling at him as she took his hand, genuine, hopeful, innocent and--Mr. Dean thought--rather naive, given the place she was in. There was a tiny kernel of nervousness in her eyes, but that was to be expected. It was usually the anticipation and the fear of the unknown that made the women nervous, at least at first.

Eventually, with some strict training and consistent discipline, they all came to know what they could expect from his hand. But the nervousness never completely went away--it just turned into a better respect and understanding of him, the man, Mr. Dean. Their host.

In fact, Mr. Dean was expecting more fear behind the eyes, not this tiny shred of trepidation. Perhaps he was too used to his reputation preceding him, he thought.

Michelle gave his hand two small shakes, and when she was done, her smile grew wider. Her hand was small and warm inside his own, but slightly damp. She was more nervous than she looked, Mr. Dean realized. She was sweating. She hid it well.

"I understand you are a friend of Monique's," he said, trying to get the conversation going. Michelle's eyes lit up.

"Oh yes, she and I are good friends. She's told me how, um, how *satisfied* she's been with the service at this hotel. I decided I would just have to visit and see for myself." She ended the sentence with a small nervous giggle.

Mr. Dean grunted in response. Getting new guests through referrals was nothing new; many of their long-time clients had come to them through referrals. But it was important to discover exactly how much information had been shared, so that no secrets of their clients were revealed. And it was also important to go over exactly what it was the new guest was looking for during his or her own visit, to ensure complete satisfaction.

Monique Hooper was a regular guest of Mr. Dean; she had been visiting him exclusively for almost two years now. But she also came with an established list of expectations, and those expectations varied little from visit to visit. Mr. Dean had no idea if Michelle shared the same predilections of her friend. In fact, he'd been given very little information about Michelle at all, a fact he found most irritating. He had only heard about this new guest the day before, and from Mr. Bentmoore himself.

"I've got a new guest for you, Dean," Mr. Bentmoore had told him, swiveling around to face him behind the ornate desk. All the hosts had their own offices, but they were small and scantily furnished. Mr. Bentmoore's office was grand and elegant, with a large claw-foot desk taking up the center of the room.

"Young woman by the name of Michelle Langley," Mr. Bentmoore had continued. He sat in his large leather chair, looking calm and matter-of-fact, but his eyes were buried in a pile of paperwork. "Twenty-three, straight, no husband, owns her own business. She heard about us from her friend, Ms. Hooper. Ms. Hooper's been an exclusive guest of yours for a while now, I believe?"

"Yes," Mr. Dean had answered absently, furrowing his brows. "She and I get along well together...but Monique told this woman about us?" His tone was one of surprise. He had always thought Monique kept her regular visits to the Hotel Bentmoore a secret. "Do we know what, exactly, she said to her friend about us?"

"No, and I couldn't ask, of course. That would be prying. But whatever it was, it was enough that her friend has booked a stay with us this weekend, and has asked for you, personally, to be her host during her initial visit. I told Michelle with absolute confidence you will take care of all her desires, and make sure her stay with us is a happy one, from start to finish."

Mr. Dean said nothing to this. He tilted his head, looking somewhat concerned.

"This woman, Michelle--did she give you any idea what she wants from the visit? What she specifically has in mind?"

"No, actually, she didn't. Of course, she expects the full treatment, everything our reputation assures—complete fulfillment. But Michelle was somewhat vague on the specifics of what she's looking for."

Mr. Dean frowned. "So what you're telling me is we know *nothing*?"

Mr. Bentmoore sighed. "Frankly, Dean, I got the impression this woman isn't sure *what* she wants. She doesn't sound all that experienced with sex, or men in general, to tell you the truth. I think she's looking for someone to 'show her the way,' as it were." Mr. Bentmoore began to straighten out his pile of papers, avoiding Mr. Dean's incredulous stare, a fact Mr. Dean noted with alarm.

"But then…why is she being given to *me*? Why not Shern, or Cox? Or even Sinclaire? All of them know how to handle a woman like that better than I do."

"True," Mr. Bentmoore said, smiling down at his papers. "The others have much more experience dealing with the, ahem, *inexperienced* women. But Ms. Langley heard about you specifically from Ms. Hooper, and insists you be the one to…initiate her. Obviously, Ms. Hooper told her something that caught Michelle's interest." Mr. Bentmoore leaned back in his chair, looking up at the ceiling…still not looking Mr. Dean in the eye. "I told her that *all* our hosts are very adept and knowledgeable, fully able to satisfy her needs. You will, I am sure, figure out how to do that."

Mr. Dean's eyebrows went up. There was something going on here, he knew, but he couldn't quite figure out what. One thing was for sure, he didn't like feeling cornered.

"Mr. Bentmoore, I don't know if I am the right host for this guest. Perhaps she should be given to someone else this first time, and once she figures out what she needs, if I am still the right person to give it--"

Now Mr. Bentmoore looked at Mr. Dean sternly, his expression implacable. "She has asked for you, and so she will get you. I know this might be difficult for you at first, Dean, going in blind, but you'll just have to figure her out. Talk to her first. Get her to open up a little. I'm sure it will be fine."

They stared at each other for a moment, Mr. Bentmoore looking at Mr. Dean expectantly, and Mr. Dean contemplating his options. At last, Mr. Dean gave a little shrug.

"Yes, Sir," he replied. "I'll do my best."

"Of course you will," Mr. Bentmoore agreed, in a tone that said he considered the matter closed. "I'm sure you'll enjoy our new guest immensely."

But now, standing in front of the new guest, Mr. Dean wondered again if, perhaps, the woman would have been better served with a different host. She certainly did not seem to be the kind of guest Mr. Dean usually attended to.

Michelle was a small woman, short and petite: she barely came up to Mr. Dean's shoulder. Her skin was a dark crème, even and flawless. It looked very soft, and, to Mr. Dean's practiced eye, very fragile. She wore a royal blue cashmere sweater over her lithe torso; it clung to her thin arms and softly rounded shoulders, before narrowing in at her flat, tiny waist.

Michelle had surprising ample breasts. They stretched across the material of her sweater, looking proud and evenly rounded. Mr. Dean wondered if she was wearing a padded bra. Probably; there was no way a woman that small could have such generous breasts.

The sweater curved around the top of her narrow hips, the ribbing clinging to the material of her pants. Her pants were black, the kind Mr. Dean thought of as women's career-slacks, straight-legged and creased. While he knew they were very popular among the high-executive businesswomen, Mr. Dean hated them. They made women look like they were trying to dress like men, when they should be showing off their curves and highlighting their femininity.

Michelle's hair, a rich luxurious brown, was done up in a soft twist, but a few wisps fell lightly across her delicate nape. Wide, almond-shaped eyes looked at him openly. Her soft lips, shiny with a thin layer of gloss, curved up a little, smiling again in nervous hope. Mr. Dean exhaled slowly. He felt like he was on unexplored territory, and would have to tread carefully. He didn't much like it.

All the hosts (and hostesses) of the Hotel Bentmoore had reputations for what they were good at, what they could handle best, and what they preferred. One of the things Mr. Dean was known for was being the "ass man."

He trained women in all things anal, and had a vast collection of anal dildos, butt plugs, vibrators and toys kept inside the wardrobes of the activity rooms he frequented. But he was also known for being the serious host, the no-nonsense disciplinarian. He was not a Master Sadist, like Mr. Sinclaire, but he was a Dominant, and did very well with women who felt the need to submit to a strong, controlling, and unbending male figure. He was meticulous, persistent, and very, very strict.

This woman did not look like she wanted to experience the feel of a strict hand on her derriere. She did not look like she even knew *what* she wanted. In fact, she looked almost confused about what she was doing there at all. But she had come on the recommendation of Monique Hooper, a fact Mr. Dean kept in the forefront of his mind.

Monique Hooper was definitely not the shy or confused type. She had been clear with Mr. Dean from the very beginning about the kind of discipline she craved, and Mr. Dean had always been quite happy and adept at delivering it to her. Could it be that her friend, Michelle, was looking for the same treatment, and simply did not know how to say so?

"Let's sit down and talk, Michelle," he said. "I'd like to get a better idea what it is you want from your visit to the Hotel Bentmoore, what it is you're looking for. I need to know how I can best please you." The woman dutifully obeyed, planting herself in the chair; but Mr.

Dean took note how she anxiously smoothed down her pants, and kept her eyes lowered to her lap. Perhaps she was more submissive than she looked?

"You are very nervous. Why?"

"I've never done anything like this before," she said, her voice high.

"You've never come to place like the Hotel Bentmoore before? Most of our new guests have not."

"No, I mean, I've never done *this* before," she said, grazing his eyes quickly with her own before darting hers away. "I've never discussed with a man what I want, before we... you know... spent some time together... *intimately*."

Mr. Dean sighed. That statement alone had just told him much about the woman: she had a hard time even *talking* about sex. She was obviously not very comfortable with her own sexuality. Maybe she was not a submissive, maybe she was just woefully ignorant, Mr. Dean thought.

"So let's talk about what you *have* done before," he said, trying to put her on comfortable ground. "I take it you are not a virgin?"

"Oh, no, I'm not that," she laughed again, a nervous titter. "I've had sex."

"Many partners?"

She twisted her hands in her lap. "I don't know what you call many," she said. "I mean, in your line of work...."

"I understand," Mr. Dean said quickly, trying to stop her floundering. "So tell me, are there certain positions you prefer? Certain styles?"

Michelle looked down at the floor. "Oh, I like many positions," she said vaguely, her face turning red. Mr. Dean knew immediately she was lying. She was being vague on purpose, but there was a secret looming behind her eyes, something specific she wanted, something she would not share with him. Why would she lie, especially about something like this? Why would she not just tell him? Did she expect him to read her mind? Thoroughly vexed now, he scowled. Michelle failed to notice his rising anger.

"Okay," he said, trying to keep his voice even. He would try to use a more direct approach, keep the questions specific. "Is there anything in particular you had in mind to try this weekend with *me*? A position, or a toy you need a partner to use on you? A fantasy perhaps, or a scene you would like to play out--"

"No, nothing like that," Michelle interrupted. "I just...I just...want to have a good time."

Mr. Dean could feel his frustration grow. The woman was giving him nothing to go on, nothing to start with--and she was lying to him. There was obviously something she wanted: it was why she had come to the Hotel Bentmoore in the first place.

She had her own secret agenda for her visit, it seemed. But guests were not afforded the luxury of secrets at the Hotel Bentmoore, a fact she had yet to learn.

He decided to take a risk.

"May I ask, Michelle, what it was Monique told you that made you decide to visit the Hotel Bentmoore in the first place, and request me personally as your host?"

"Monique told me that you are, um, very strong-willed, and don't have a problem with, um, how did she put it? 'Pushing boundaries' a little."

That was certainly true. Mr. Dean enjoyed testing Monique's boundaries, as he did with most of his guests. Sometimes it went well; sometimes it did not, and Mr. Dean would have to pull back. For instance, he had only tried to insert his finger into Monique's ass once, and her protests had been loud and immediate. Mr. Dean had never tried again. Knowing when to press an issue, and when to stop, was a skill every host at the Hotel Bentmoore had to learn.

"And is this what you are looking for at the Hotel Bentmoore? Someone strong-willed to 'push your boundaries' a little?"

"No, not exactly, I, um...." Her voice trailed away, and Mr. Dean's expression grew stern.

"You what, Michelle? What is it you want?"

"I...." She would not look at him.

"Michelle, look at me." Slowly, she looked up at him. "I cannot help you if you don't give me some idea what you want. So what do you want, Michelle?"

Michelle stared at him, her eyes flooded with hidden knowledge, but said nothing. Mr. Dean tamped down the growl in his throat, then gave it a moment of thought.

Maybe this was exactly the boundary she refused to talk about? Maybe she just needed someone to overcome her shyness, get over her reluctance, and take the upper hand? Maybe she wanted to be dominated after all, and was waiting for him to make the first move?

He took her by the arm and pulled her up roughly from the chair. Michelle gasped.

"Tell me what you want, Michelle," he said, peering into her face. Mr. Dean's voice was coarse and stern. Michelle looked away; Mr. Dean pulled her gaze back with a steady hand on her chin.

"Look at me. Tell me what you want."

"Don't do that, I--"

Mr. Dean began to back her up against the wall, locking her arm behind her back.

Michelle's face paled. "What are you doing?"

"Tell me what you want."

"Let go of me, I told you--"

"You heard I am strong-willed, and you asked for me anyway. Is this what you're looking for?" He turned her around in his arms and slapped her ass, hard. Even through the slacks she was wearing, his hand stung from the impact.

"No, wait! That's not--"

"Then tell me." Mr. Dean's control snapped. He twisted her back to face him with a jerk of his arm, and cupped her breast through her bra, taking ownership of her body. His other hand pressed brazenly into her ass. "Tell me what you want, Michelle."

Michelle's eyes grew wide with fear. Then, she raised her hand, and slapped Mr. Dean across the face.

Mr. Dean stepped back, putting a hand to his cheek, staring at her in surprise.

"I think there's been a mistake," Michelle said tearfully. "I've changed my mind--I don't want to do this anymore. I would like to go."

Taken aback, Mr. Dean reached a hand out to her. "Wait, Michelle. I must have misunderstood--"

"Yes. Yes, you did. I would like to leave now." She began to pull desperately on the door. It was, of course, locked. Mr. Dean quickly pressed the button to summon the liaison, but continued to try to placate her. He had made a mess of things, and needed to fix it fast.

"Michelle, I didn't mean to scare you, I just assumed--"

"I want to go," Michelle choked out. The door opened, and she stumbled out, bumping into the surprised liaison before pushing past him. The liaison retreated against the wall to give her space to pass, then looked at Mr. Dean in surprised shock.

Mr. Dean watched Michelle sprint down the hallway, calling out in desperation.

"Michelle, please, come back inside--"

"No." She only took a second to stop and answer him, then made a mad dash toward the elevator. For a moment, the liaison looked at Mr. Dean, baffled and at a loss what to do; then he, too, ran down the hallway to catch up with their frantic guest.

Mr. Dean leaned his forehead against the door frame and closed his eyes. He had just made a horrible mistake.

***

"What do you *mean*, you ASSUMED?" Mr. Bentmoore roared from behind his desk. "We are not in the business of *assuming*, Dean. You should have made things quite clear between the two of you before you even laid a hand on her! For you to *coral* the woman like that, twist her arm, spank her--she told me exactly what you did, you scared the woman badly--"

"I know, I know, I'm sorry." Mr. Dean put a hand up in a gesture of surrender to stop the tirade, feeling shamed enough. "I thought it was what she wanted. She wasn't giving me *anything* else to go on--"

"In what, the first ten minutes of your meeting? You should have spent more time talking to her! Figured out what she wanted, what would please her! You don't pin her against the wall and start spanking her ass after a brief conversation that isn't going to your liking!" Mr. Bentmoore's face was flushed with anger. He glared at Mr. Dean from across the desk. "Really, Dean, I am shocked at how badly you handled things with this woman. It's not like you at all."

"I know, I'm sorry," Mr. Dean repeated, rubbing his hand across his forehead and sighing loudly. "I don't know what came over me. There is just something about this woman--she didn't just hold back--she *lied* to me."

"Lied to you? About what?"

"There is definitely something she wants, something she's had a taste of before and has a mind to explore further. I don't know if it's a certain position, or a fantasy scene, or what. She won't tell me, and I have no idea why not." He crossed his arms in front of his chest, looking solemn. "It's there, in her eyes, but she won't tell me what it is....I guess I need more time to get it out of her."

"Well, time is precisely the one thing you don't have. She's packing up--she's planning on checking out. She could be on her way to leave the hotel right now."

"Oh, no."

"Oh, yes." Mr. Bentmoore pointed a finger at Mr. Dean. "You are going to make sure she does not. I don't care if you have to get on your hands and knees and give her cunnilingus at the front desk until she agrees, you are not going to let that woman leave this hotel without a smile on her face. We survive on our reputation, Dean. I will not have your stupid mistake blemish it."

"How am I supposed to talk to her? I doubt she will agree to be taken back to the meeting room, even with the liaison as an escort, to meet me again." He remembered her frantic dash down the hallway, and frowned.

Mr. Bentmoore looked grave. "That is why I am giving you permission to go up to her room to talk to her." Mr.

Dean leaned back in surprise. It was strict hotel policy that no host was allowed to visit guests in their private rooms on the upper floors. The fact that Mr. Bentmoore would order Mr. Dean to do so showed him exactly how serious Mr. Bentmoore took the matter.

"Do not leave her room until she agrees to stay," Mr. Bentmoore continued. "Tell her whatever she needs to hear, do whatever you need to do--but get it done." When Mr. Dean didn't move, Mr. Bentmoore motioned him toward the door. "What are you waiting for? Go! Before she's done packing!"

Doing a very good imitation of Michelle from the night before, Mr. Dean got up and sprinted from the room.

***

When Michelle heard the knock on her door, she assumed it was the bellhop coming to take her suitcases. She gasped in surprise when she found Mr. Dean standing there instead. Her first instinct was to shut the door in his face.

"Michelle, I need to talk to you," Mr. Dean said quickly, sensing her initial reaction. Michelle still swung the door closed, but not enough to shut it, only enough to leave a narrow crack open. She peered at Mr. Dean from around the door, using it as a shield between her and the man on the other side.

She looked wary. Mr. Dean felt even more embarrassed. Mr. Bentmoore had told him the truth: he had really scared the woman badly.

"Why do you want to talk to me?" She asked, facing him through the tiny crack. "I'm checking out today, as soon as possible. As a matter of fact, someone should have arrived by now to take my luggage."

"Please don't leave, Michelle, not until I've had a chance to make things right. Look, can I just come in and talk to you? I don't want anyone to see me--I'm not supposed to visit a guest's room." He twisted his head from side to side, as if checking for witnesses in the hallway.

Michelle narrowed her eyes, looking suspicious. "If you're not supposed to be here, then why *are* you here?"

"Because I feel bad about what happened. I want to make it up to you."

Michelle's brows furrowed as she thought for a minute. Then she sighed and opened the door. The man would hardly accost her in her private hotel room, where other guests were sure to hear her scream. And he really did seem sincere. And handsome. And appealing. And there was what Monique had told her....

"Very well, come inside," she said. "But only to talk. Don't--don't touch me."

"I won't, I promise," Mr. Dean said, relieved she had at least agreed to let him in. She motioned him to the chair next to the bed. She remained standing.

"What is it you want?" She asked. Mr. Dean smiled in chagrin. Here she was, asking him the exact same question that was circling inside his own head about her. Fortunately, he, at least, could come clean with an answer.

"I want to make you happy," he said. "I treated you very badly before, and I want to make it up to you." When she sighed and shook her head, he put his hand up to stop her from refusing outright. "Hear me out. Believe it or not, I am quite good at what I do. Monique must have convinced you of that, or you never would have asked for me. I just... started off on the wrong foot with you. I'm sorry. It was my fault--I should have been more careful." Her large almond eyes widened at his generous apology. Her breath quickened a bit, but she said nothing.

Mr. Dean decided to turn on the charm, just a little, just enough to sway her. But he would have to move carefully so as not to scare her. Slowly, he rose from the chair and stood before her, keeping his hands safely inside his pockets. He peered down into her face.

"Please, Michelle, let me make it up to you," he said again, lowering his voice into a husky appeal. "I promise I can make you one hundred percent satisfied, if you just give me the chance." He looked into her eyes, and when she looked down to the floor, nervous, he bent down and caught her stare again, an imploring look on his face. She smiled, then turned away, flustered.

As she turned a step away from him, trying to collect herself, Mr. Dean caught a glimpse of her bathroom. The door was open, the light on, and he couldn't help but get a clear view of the counter by the sink. He raised his eyebrows in surprise. A well-sized, tubular yellow vibrator sat next to the sink, drying after having been clearly used and washed.

Now Mr. Dean felt truly ashamed. Not only had he frightened the poor woman, he had reduced her to returning to her room to pleasure *herself.* She was no prude, she could obviously come--she just couldn't manage to bring herself to tell him how, so he could bring her to greater heights, or at least share in her pleasure.

Mr. Dean straightened his back, ready to meet the challenge. He would bring Michelle back downstairs, lock her in one of his activity rooms, one way or the other--he would heft her over his shoulder and carry her down kicking and screaming if he had to--and then he would make her come so thoroughly and so often she would be walking bow-legged out the door.

He walked silently up behind her and whispered in her ear.

"One night," he said. Her head turned. He could see the goose bumps spring up on her sensitive skin. "Give me just one night, and if I can't please you, I will call in one of the other hosts myself to satisfy your needs."

"And you won't... you won't get rough with me, like you did before?"

"I will not do anything you don't want me to do," he said. It wasn't exactly the same thing as what she had asked of him, but for the moment, it was what she needed to hear.

"Very well," she said, turning around to face him. He was standing so close behind her, she almost bumped into his broad chest. She gasped and stepped back in surprise. "I'll give you one night." She looked up into his eyes, and her breath caught at the heat she saw there.

"Thank you," he said in a soft voice, lowering his head until his cheek was almost touching hers. "You won't regret it," he whispered. She shivered.

Pleased, Mr. Dean strode out of the room, leaving her flustered and, he recognized, highly aroused. But he had work to do. He had to prepare for the night ahead, and to do that, he was going to need some help.

***

Mr. Dean went looking for Mr. Shern. Mr. Shern was a fellow host at the Hotel Bentmoore, but he worked with different types of cases than Mr. Dean.

Shern specialized in the innocent female: women both young and old whose lack of experience kept them from reaching their full sexual power and appeal. He had a flare for taking young rich aristocratic brats, barely out of the school room, and turning them into full-fledged beauties, poised, refined, and fully aware of their sexual prowess. He also sometimes worked with women who had faced a sexual trauma and needed help to overcome. Many women used him almost like a sexual therapist.

Mr. Dean found him in the workout room, doing arm reps. Thankfully, there was no one else in the room, and Mr. Dean shut the door behind him. Mr. Shern turned at the noise, looking at him in surprise.

"I need your advice, Shern," Mr. Dean said.

"That's a new one," Mr. Shern replied, putting the dumbbells down on the bench.

"Yeah, well, I've got a unique case here." He laid out everything that had happened between him and Michelle, leaving out nothing about his impressions, his concerns, or the way he had mistreated her. By the time he was done, Mr. Shern was shaking his head and chuckling.

"An obviously classy lady, not a sub, who's here on her own volition, and you turn her around and spank her--in the *meeting room*? When discipline wasn't specified, or even discussed?" He asked, his expression incredulous. "Well, you took a risk...and it certainly backfired on you."

"Yes, and now I have to make things right. The problem is, this woman is so closed-mouthed, she can barely articulate herself. She couldn't even bring herself to say the word 'sex.'"

"I can see how you would find that frustrating," Mr. Shern said, laughing harder. "You're not one to handle the shy types."

"No, I'm not," Mr. Dean growled in response to his friend's ill-placed humor. "And not only that, she *lied* to me."

"Oh? Now that's interesting. What did she lie about?"

"Just some basic information. I asked her straight out if there's anything specific she enjoys, and she said no, but it was obvious she was lying--she had something on her mind, but just didn't want to tell me. Now why would she do that? Why wouldn't she want to just tell me if there's something she enjoys, so I can help please her?"

"Well, that's an easy one to answer. She's ashamed."

"Ashamed?" Mr. Dean sat down on the bench, surprised. "Why?"

"There are many reasons why women get ashamed of these things. Sometimes they think what they want is wrong, or dirty... sometimes they're ashamed of their own fantasies. It depends on their upbringing and their hang-ups. But in these cases, you really have to delve into the mindset of the woman, figure out what's stopping her from exploring, and enjoying, her sexuality completely." He laughed in the face of Mr. Dean's stricken expression. "You've really never had to deal with a woman like this before, have you? I'm guessing she's probably pretty innocent, unaware of her own sexual appeal, and for whatever reason, feels guilty of her own passion. Maybe even afraid of it. You need to overcome all that."

"And how am I supposed to do that?" Mr. Dean looked overwhelmed. Mr. Shern laughed again; he was not used to seeing his associate and friend in such a predicament. Mr. Dean looked like he was drowning. Mr. Shern smacked him on the back.

"Dean, it's not as hard as it sounds. Here's what you do...."

***

That night, Mr. Trowlege brought Michelle straight to one of Mr. Dean's activity rooms, and as per instruction, closed the door behind her immediately as she walked through. Michelle was startled by the sudden noise of her main escape route being sealed off. She stared at the door for a moment. There was no backing out now, she realized. She turned around and scanned the room.

Four lamps sat in each corner, and where their light did not reach, ceiling bulbs did the job. A wardrobe sat against one wall, large and stately; stained almost black and polished to a high shine, it looked more befitting a King's royal chamber than an activity room of the Hotel Bentmoore. Across from it was the bed, large and inviting, made up in crimson sheets and matching pillows--but there were no blankets.

Next to the bed were side tables that matched the wardrobe, and a strange metal wheeling-tray, which at the moment, lay covered with a small towel. Next to the tray, leaning sideways against the wall with his arms crossed, was Mr. Dean.

She was not ready to acknowledge her host just yet, and so kept looking around the room. It was then she noticed the two poles, stretching from floor to ceiling, set about three or four feet apart from each other. She looked them both up and down. They didn't seem to be support columns, and they weren't there for aesthetics. In fact, they looked like stripper poles.

"They've been screwed in tight," Mr. Dean said, "And can take a lot of weight on them. I've tried them out myself, many times."

Michelle would not look at him as he came forward. She was too nervous.

"Why would someone put them in the middle of the room like this?" She asked. Was he going to conduct some sort of strip show for her? Did he expect *her* to do it for *him*?

"Why indeed?" Mr. Dean replied, a slight smile curving his lips. "I think you'll understand soon enough. Are you ready to begin, Michelle?"

Michelle finally turned to look at him, her expression filled with unmasked trepidation. Mr. Dean was wearing a pair of dark suit pants, creased and belted at the waist. But he wore no shirt, and with his arms crossed in front of his chest the way they were, he looked very wide, and very strong. The heat in his eyes directed her way was potent and overpowering, and made her draw back.

"What are you going to do to me?" She asked in a throaty whisper. Mr. Dean took a calming breath. He was not used to his guests asking such questions; he was used to taking control, letting his guests know only as much as he wanted. But he would have to make allowances for this one. He would go slow and easy--at first. Once he discovered what her secret was, what she was hiding from him, he planned on using that information to his full advantage.

"Nothing that will hurt you," he said. "Here, let me show you." He motioned her over to the two poles. Michelle stood between them, looking at her host curiously; and then, getting the idea, she grabbed onto the poles, one in each hand. The stretch wasn't bad. She could grab both tightly and still bend her elbows.

"There are going to a few very simple rules tonight," Mr. Dean said, moving behind her and talking gently into her ear. She could feel his warm breath against her skin. Her hands tightened around the poles. "All I'm going to ask you to do tonight is one thing: hang on. Don't let go of the poles--don't take your hands off. Just keep grabbing them, and we'll do fine."

"You--you want me to just hold on to the poles? That's it?"

"Yes. I'm not even going to restrain you in any way. If you can't help it, if you have to let go, there will be no repercussions. But I'm asking you to try not to."

"But what will you be *doing*?"

"I am going to touch you." Michelle took a sharp intake of breath, and Mr. Dean moved to face her. "I will be gentle, Michelle, and move slowly. If at any point, I am doing something that makes you feel uncomfortable, tell me, and I'll stop. Do you understand?"

"Yes," she said. Her voice was ragged and afraid. But she had agreed, and Mr. Dean took a breath of relief. He was awarding this guest more control than he ever had to any other woman. But if this is what she needed to remain here, where he could get his hands on her and help her reach satisfaction, than he would oblige her wholeheartedly.

"One more thing," he said. Mr. Dean moved back behind her, taking a long strip of soft black leather out of his pocket. "You will be blindfolded."

"What? Why--" Her question was cut off as she felt the blindfold come over her eyes and tie around her head. She touched the soft leather on her face. It wasn't tight or uncomfortable, but it hadn't been expected, either.

"Hands on the poles, Michelle," Mr. Dean reminded her. Michelle brought her hand away from her face and gripped the poles. "I want you to focus on what I'm doing to you, what you're feeling," Mr. Dean explained. "Remember, if I do anything you don't like, you can tell me, and I'll stop. There's nothing to be afraid of. Do you understand?"

"Yes," Michelle whispered. But it was clear she was afraid, despite the power Mr. Dean was offering her. He would have to tread carefully.

"Good. Let's begin," he said.

He pressed his weight into her back, not a lot, but enough that Michelle had to hold on tight to the poles so she wouldn't stumble forward. She was such a tiny woman, he thought; Mr. Dean shadowed her entire form. He could hear her heavy breathing, feel her back heaving against his chest.

He dipped his head into her hair and took a deep breath: she smelled of lavender, sweet and feminine. Carefully, he unclasped the pin from her hair, and felt her thick tresses fall into his hand. Her hair was long, it turned out. It fell past her waist.

"You should wear your hair down more often," he murmured. Michelle didn't answer.

Spanning out his hands, he spread his fingers over her tightly sealed fists gripping the poles, then began to trace his fingertips up her arms, over her shoulders, and down her midsection. Michelle jumped a bit, tickled; but then she quieted back down. Mr. Dean smiled.

Through her shirt, Mr. Dean ran his hands up and down her wiry arms, around her soft sloping shoulders, and across her lightly muscled back. He massaged her neck a bit, kneading his hands into her flesh. Michelle relaxed and let her head lop to the side.

He moved down her spine, rubbing his thumbs against her skin in deep, circular motions, then pushed his hands back up and stroked her arms again, but harder this time. He could feel Michelle's tension slip away as he massaged her, lulling her into a sense of comfort.

His hands came up to graze her collarbone; and then, slowly, they began to descend into the V of her shirt. Michelle's head snapped back up. She stood up straight, holding her breath in anticipation.

Mr. Dean's warm hands disappeared into her shirt, pushing underneath her bra. They lightly grazed against the soft skin of her breasts, then squeezed them ever so lightly. Michelle gasped. Mr. Dean stopped, but when Michelle didn't immediately protest, he squeezed them again.

To his surprise, her large breasts were real, and just as full as they had looked through her clothes. Michelle didn't wear a padded bra after all. Her tits felt warm and heavenly in his hands, and he kneaded them inside the confines of her bra cups. When he felt her nipples pressing into his palms, he grazed them with his thumbs, then pinched them softly between his fingers.

"Oh!" Michelle cried. Mr. Dean let go a bit, but when it was clear Michelle would say nothing to stop him, he grazed her nipples again, then pinched them harder for a brief second before letting go to knead her soft flesh. Michelle arched her back, pushing her tits into his hands, tensing at the teasing assault on her nipples.

Now Mr. Dean alternated his movements, kneading, stroking, grazing and pinching. Michelle's head swung from side to side as her breath became hoarse and raspy. She had very sensitive nipples, he discovered, and was clearly enjoying all the attention he was paying them.

He gave her a moment to collect herself, then, with nimble fingers, began the process of unbuttoning her shirt. It was obvious Michelle could feel his hands moving against her skin; goose bumps rose across her flesh.

Mr. Dean was afraid he would have to help her remove her bra to get better access to her breasts, which would mean allowing her freedom from the poles, if only for a moment. But he was in luck: the tight stretching material had a front clasp, nestled between her snugly-fitted tits. He undid the clasp now, and had the satisfaction of watching her heavy tits spring free.

He moved in front of her now, and spread the opening of her shirt and bra wide, getting a good look at her sleek torso and orbicular breasts. They sagged a little from their heavy weight, the dark ovoid aureoles crinkling around the brown dusky nipples. Her nipples were hard and swollen now, and he grazed one again with the pad of his thumb. Then, he circled the breast in his hand, testing its considerable weight. He lowered his head and took the nipple in his mouth.

Michelle moaned. Mr. Dean worked the nipple, stabbing it with his tongue, circling and sucking it until it distended prominently, plump and proud. He bit it softly between his teeth, and heard Michelle take a hissing breath. Then he moved onto the other breast, and gave it the same treatment. Michelle made a series of "oooh" sounds, tilting her head back, clutching at the poles.

Mr. Dean knelt down on his knees and found the zipper of her skirt. As he lowered it, he kissed the satiny skin of her stomach, dipping his tongue into the hollow of her belly button. Then, in one single pull, he lowered her skirt down to the floor.

Under her skirt, Michelle was wearing thong panties, coral pink and translucent. The shimmering material was sopping wet at the crotch; it clung to her pussy lips, barely covering the soft skin. Mr. Dean hooked two fingers into the narrow waistband circling both of Michelle's compact hips and traced them down her legs, taking the flimsy thong with them.

Michelle's thighs squeezed together in alarm. She couldn't see, but she knew her host was kneeling at her feet, getting a good look at her exposed pussy lips. But Mr. Dean lifted one of her legs at the knee, pulling off her shoe, and then did the other. He spread her feet wide across the floor, moving them apart until she could feel the cold metal of the poles pressing against the sides of her feet. Michelle was now in an X pose.

"Stay like this," Mr. Dean said. "Don't move."

When Michelle had opened her legs, so had her pussy lips. Mr. Dean reached down now, and, placing his thumbs on the soft flesh of her lips, he opened them wide, drinking in the sight of her wet, swollen inner folds.

"Wait--" Michelle's voice rang out, sharp and alarmed.

"Am I hurting you?" Mr. Dean didn't move further, but he didn't take his thumbs away, either. To her credit, Michelle gave the question a moment of thought.

"N-no, but...."

"Then there is no reason for me to stop. Let me touch you, Michelle." His voice was a soft plea. He lowered his face between her legs as he spoke. Michelle could feel his warm breath against her crotch. A moment later, she felt his lips nuzzling against the swollen folds of her cunt.

Michelle cried out. Mr. Dean widened his tongue and ran it up inside her folds, moving it slowly, grazing her with soft, wet licks. He lapped at her thickening moist flesh, hot inside his mouth; then he rested his tongue right on her throbbing clitoris, pulsing his tongue against it.

Michelle's breath came out in thick gasps. Her hands moved up and down the poles, slick and wet from her sweaty palms. Mr. Dean kept up his wet homage to her cunt, lapping and sucking greedily.

Then he stood up. "Don't move," he ordered again, this time moving away from her. Michelle tilted her head this way and that, trying to listen to the sounds of his movements, resisting the urge to let go of the pole for the second it would take to peel down the blindfold.

A moment later she sensed Mr. Dean return. What she didn't know was that he had wheeled over the small metal tray and was now uncovering a long smooth vibrator, one that strongly resembled the toy he had glimpsed in Michelle's bathroom. It did not match hers exactly, but it was close enough, or so he hoped. In his other hand, he held a tube of water-based lubricant.

Michelle's pussy was sopping wet, glistening from her own inner juices and Mr. Dean's talented mouth. But even so, he lubed up the vibrator and rubbed it in his hand, warming it to the touch. He didn't want to shock Michelle too badly by pressing something dry and cold against her skin.

He turned the vibrator on, and watched Michelle's reaction to the sound of the toy humming merrily in his hand. She jerked her head up, realizing at once what the sound was.

Mr. Dean touched the vibrator to Michelle's inner thigh, and Michelle instinctively jerked her leg away.

"Hold the position, Michelle," Mr. Dean said, his voice stern. She dutifully put her leg down, pressing the outside of her foot against the pole.

Mr. Dean continued to slide the vibrator up the inside of her leg, letting her get a good feel of the quick, steady vibrations, watching the way her muscles tensed and rippled beneath her supple skin. Then he moved the length of the vibrator to the crease separating her pussy lips, slid it back and forth a couple times against the soft, wet slit, and pressed in.

Michelle bent forward, lowering her head all the way down, until the tips of her hair were brushing the floor; but she held the position, keeping her sweaty palms hugging the poles and gripping them hard so she would not fall to her knees. She groaned.

Mr. Dean took note of her tense movements. But he said nothing--so long as her hands and feet kept in contact with the poles, she was free to move all she wanted. The point of this exercise was not to keep her completely immobile. It was to discover what excited her, and what it was she was hiding from him.

She was gyrating her body now, undulating her torso and reedy arms between the poles like a snake dancer. Mr. Dean held the vibrator deep inside the wet crease between her legs, sliding up and down her velvety layers of flesh, watching the way her skin flushed and the reedy muscles of her waist undulated. He kept her hips steady with his other hand, holding her pressed against the persistent vibrator nestled between her pussy lips.

Michelle's face slackened, and her fingers relaxed around the poles. A dreamy smile played across her mouth; she hummed in delight, swaying in time to her own private, sensual rhythm. Mr. Dean took note how she relaxed her body into the vibrator, how she tilted her head back in warm abandon...and furrowed his brows.

It was not enough. Michelle was obviously enjoying what he was doing, true; but there was no tension in her muscles, no sense of urgency to her movements. She was easing herself into the steady humming of the snuggled vibrator, not straining against it.

He wasn't sure if Michelle understood the difference, but he did. She would not come this way. There was something else she needed him to do, and he needed to figure out what, or she would not come at all.

He let go of her hips and reached his hand up to pinch her nipples, one at a time. Michelle gasped, but continued to sway her body, twisting and rocking her tiny frame as before. He flicked her nipples, hard; Michelle cried out and swung her head back, but once he was done, her features slackened again.

Trying a different route, Mr. Dean tilted the tip of the vibrator inward, and lunged it inside Michelle's tight cunt, burying it deep. He waved it around with his hand, making circular motions inside Michelle's clinging pussy. Michelle released a long, plaintive "ahhh," but otherwise, did not react with any rise in tension or need.

Feeling his frustration rise, Mr. Dean stood up and moved around her, sliding the vibrator in and out of her cunt from behind. Michelle danced for him, leaning her weight against his wide chest and then jerking herself forward; but even after a few moments of this blissful pleasure, she did not look any closer to coming.

He rubbed her clit as he pumped the vibrator, but not gently, oh no. His own rising vexation made his fingers press hard against her skin. Michelle leaned her head back against his chest again and sighed in delight, then continued to sway.

With a jerk of his hand, Mr. Dean pulled the blindfold off her face, and dropped it to the floor. He thought maybe having her see him touch her body would arouse her enough to send her over the edge. But Michelle kept her eyes closed, lost in her own carnal pleasure. Mr. Dean lightly pinched her clit, pulsing his fingers against her throbbing button, and got only a series of short squeals in response.

She was aroused, that much was clear. She was skimming across the edge of desire from his ministrations--she was just not showing him a single sign of how to get her up and over.

He wanted to yell in frustration. Michelle *could* come, he knew that. She had obviously used the vibrator in her bathroom to her own satisfaction. He was not dealing with a woman who was completely non-sexual, or physically unable to climax, or maimed in some way. But *how* did she pleasure herself? What did she do with the toy, alone in the dark, when it was only her own hands doing the work? Maybe she had to be lying down? On her back? On her stomach? Maybe he would have to maneuver her to the bed and try something new?

Growling at his own ineptitude, Mr. Dean lowered his eyes and watched the way Michelle's narrow hips and high-set, compact bottom bobbed and danced under his gaze, forming tight figure-eights between the poles. Her butt was smooth and small; beneath the hem of the open shirt, the crease separating the twin domes of her buttocks dipped low, making her ass cheeks look widely sloped and, to Mr. Dean's opinion, absolutely adorable.

Without thinking, he ran his hand down the length of her back, then grabbed a butt cheek and gave it a good squeeze. The entire mound of flesh fit perfectly into his wide, calloused hand. He smiled.

Michelle gasped. For a moment, her dancing halted, and when her hips began to circle again, they seemed to push against Mr. Dean's hand still holding firm against her ass. Mr. Dean noticed, and a tiny kernel of an idea began to take shape in his head.

With an intent look on his face, he turned his wrist, and ran the back of his hand up Michelle's crack, grazing the crinkling ring of her anus.

Michelle stopped her rhythmical dancing and held still.

Inspired, Mr. Dean diddled his middle finger inside Michelle's wet pussy; then, sliding it back against her the skin of her crack, he slowly pressed his finger pad against the small opening of Michelle's asshole.

A shudder ran through her; her eyes squeezed shut, and she let out a short, breathy moan.

But she said nothing in protest. In fact, she held her ass stock-still, as if waiting for him to continue.

"I think...finally...I'm beginning to understand," Mr. Dean said under his breath. Michelle did not respond; she held her body motionless, tense and waiting.

Mr. Dean pressed his finger in, pushing the fingertip past the clenching ring of muscle of Michelle's ass. But he pushed slowly, not wanting to hurt her if he was wrong. To his surprise, Michelle thrust her hips back, pushing his finger all the way in, impaling herself until he could cup her ass-cheek against his palm. The knuckles of her hands turned white around the poles as she gripped them tightly, her body tense and waiting.

And finally, Mr. Dean understood.

Michelle didn't ask for him because of his strict brand of discipline, he realized. She had asked for him because her friend Monique must have mentioned in passing how he had tried to enter her ass. And while Monique was vehemently against the notion of anything entering her rear-gate, her friend Michelle, clearly, was not.

Mr. Dean could have roared in triumph. But he kept quiet, intent on the task at hand. Now, in complete control over the waiting, whimpering woman, he knew what to do.

He began to slide his finger in and out of Michelle's asshole, increasing his tempo as Michelle began to groan. When her hips started to rock back against his palm, he dropped the needless vibrator back onto the metal tray and circled her ribs with his arm, holding her steady and trapping her against his chest as his finger plunged in and out of her needy hole. When that wasn't enough for her, his one finger became two, and then three. Michelle's tight anus stretched under the assault of his fingers; it gripped them like a tight sleeve.

"*Don't move*," he ordered gruffly. Then he let go of her completely and pulled his fingers out.

Shocked by the retreat of his talented fingers, Michelle whined and thrust her butt back, searching for his hand. But Mr. Dean stepped back; he needed to assess the situation. He looked at the tray: the vibrator lay there, motionless.

Instead of reaching for it, he grabbed the tube of lubricant sitting close by, quickly lowered his pants, and greased his stiff cock. Stepping forward once more, he set the bulbous tip of his prick inside the shadowy crease of Michelle's bottom. Grabbing her by the hips with both hands, he pulled her back until she was slightly bent over. Then, finding his target, he fitted his cock against her pulsing, cringing asshole, and pressed in.

"Aah!" Michelle cried out, arching her back in a perfect bow-curve. Mr. Dean continued in with his assault, pushing his hips forward while he pulled Michelle's back, impaling her ass on his cock. In a single, smooth push, he was all the way in. He could feel the smooth skin of Michelle's ass cheeks grinding against his thighs.

"Oh God," Michelle whispered, bending her body down until her torso was parallel to the floor. Mr. Dean could make out the deep crevasse between her shoulder blades under her shirt as she held the pose. Her arms strained back to hold the poles.

Mr. Dean closed his eyes and held himself still. Her asshole was warm, and tight, and pulsed around him in sweet agony. He held her hips against his pelvis, reveling in the feeling of her incredibly tight hole squeezing his cock.

Then, he slowly began to pull his cock out, letting it slide in the hot grip of her rectum. It seemed to try to pull him back in, milking his cock like a hungry mouth. When only the helmeted tip of his prick was still inside, he lunged, slapping the bent-over woman with his thighs and getting a shriek in response.

Then he was fucking her asshole brutally, pounding into her with hard thrusts of his hips and burying himself in as far he could. Michelle grunted and yelped, holding onto the poles for dear life. She spread her feet as far as the poles would allow, bending forward so her rear cheeks would open even more, trying to make it easier for him to ram her from behind.

As he ravaged her asshole, Mr. Dean looked down at the bent, shuddering woman, and felt all of his usual authority return in full force.

"You should have told me," he said between thrusts, his voice grating.

"Yes," she whimpered.

"Yes, *Sir*," he corrected.

"Yes, Sir," she groaned. The highly charged woman was jerking her body back against him, rocking on her heels and thrusting her hips back and forth, grinding her ass against his groin as he held onto her and pulled at her body. Mr. Dean used her asshole like a wet cunt, pumping in and out, feeling the stabbing thrills of her rear-gate pulling on the entire length of his cock.

As he fell into a rhythm, Michelle began matching his thrusts, caught up in the effects of her own heady thrills and trying to bring herself off.

"Oh, yes, please, yes, Sir, please," she entreated.

Mr. Dean kept up his steady rhythm, pounding into her with powerful strokes. He was about to reach around for Michelle's clit to rub it and help her come, when he felt a convulsive shudder run through the tiny woman. Michelle flung her head up in wild abandon, whipping him with her hair, and let out a high-pitched cry.

Mr. Dean widened his eyes in surprise. He realized, to his amazement and delight, that Michelle was already reaching her own climax, without any clitoral stimulation at all.

Little Michelle was, apparently, an anal slut.

"Oh God yes!" She screamed, pushing her ass back and doing a very good job of fucking herself on his cock. Her innards squeezed him almost painfully as she came, her asshole spasming around his thick staff like nothing he had ever felt before. The sudden stabs of ecstasy were too much for him, and Mr. Dean came himself, erupting inside her clenching sleeve, slapping against her butt cheeks until he had collapsed on top of her in shuddering release.

As the breathing of the two sweating, ragged people returned to normal, Mr. Dean pulled his softening cock out of Michelle's shrinking hole and stepped back. Michelle stood up, leaned her weight against one of the poles, and smoothed the hair out of her face.

Standing behind her, Mr. Dean could not see her face. But after a moment, he could hear the unmistakable sounds of her crying. He came around to face her, afraid.

"Why are you crying?" He demanded. "I know I didn't hurt you."

"No, you didn't hurt me," she said, looking down and covering her eyes in shame. "But--what's wrong with me?"

"Wrong with you?" Mr. Dean asked after a moment. "What do you mean, what's wrong with you? There's nothing wrong with you."

"Look at me!" She cried. "I can't have sex--not the *right* way, not the way normal people do it. I've never been able to come with a man the way I'm supposed to."

"The way you're supposed to?"

"You know, with him in my...my...."

"Your pussy?"

"Yes! But it's never worked for me! Never! I can only come with a man's dick in my *ass!*" She stretched her arms up, as if begging the heavens for help. "There must be something wrong with me! I'm a--a sexual deviant! A freak! I was hoping I could come here and learn to enjoy sex the normal way, but I can't, I just can't," she sobbed. "Tell me--what man wants to have sex with a woman who will only enjoy it if he comes in her *ass?*"

For a second, Mr. Dean stared at her, surprised.

"You--you really think there's something wrong with you for liking it up the ass?" He asked incredulously.

"Yes! There must be!" When she caught his look of shock, she stopped and stared at him, confused. "No?"

Mr. Dean smiled; then, in a rare moment of abandon, he tilted his head back and laughed.

"Michelle," he said, "you and I *really* need to talk."

***

The next night, Mr. Trowlege brought Michelle down to Mr. Dean's favorite activity room: the large wardrobe contained much of his standard equipment and toys, primarily anal toys. Even so, he had borrowed some other choice items from the wardrobes of other rooms. He wanted a fully stocked collection at his fingertips by the time Michelle arrived.

He chose the furniture with great care, picking a piece that would not scare her straight off and have her running in the opposite direction. Once he had her immobilized, situated the way he wanted her, it would be easier to work past any lingering resistance; but he had to get her in place first, and locked in the proper positioning.

When Michelle entered the room, she was greeted with the sight of Mr. Dean looking at his furniture masterpiece, smiling in anticipation. He was looking forward to an interesting, and hopefully highly entertaining, night.

"Hello," she said, taking him in. Like yesterday, he wore dress slacks, but no shirt; and while his imposing form still scared her a bit, she now she felt her body react in a purely wanton way. She sucked in her breath as he looked at her, his dark eyes probing. She looked down, uncertain.

"Hello, Sir," he corrected her once again. Michelle's eyes snapped up; for a brief second, she looked at him in defiance. But then the moment passed, and she lowered her eyes to the floor once more.

"Hello, Sir," she repeated with a sigh. Mr. Dean knew it grated her to address him like this, but he would keep insisting until it became second nature to her. She was no submissive, he knew that now, and he would not try to dominate her the way he did most of his other guests. But at the Hotel Bentmoore, there were protocols that had to be followed. And, he had to admit, he derived a certain wicked pleasure in forcing her to bend to his authority, even in this seemingly small way.

Mr. Dean took in the sight of her: she was wearing her hair in a loose ponytail today, gathered in a red stretch-band at the nape of her neck. The long tresses weren't completely free, but the ponytail was a vast improvement to the tight bun she had worn before.

"You look very nice," he said, walking up to her. Michelle was wearing a black cotton sweater, thin and clingy, and a short, snug, matching skirt. Except for her high-heeled shoes, her legs were bare. The skirt was also a great improvement to the pants she worn before. Mr. Dean wondered if anything else was bare under that skirt. Probably not. That, too, would require some training.

"Thank you...Sir," she replied to his compliment. Mr. Dean nodded.

"Are you ready to begin, Michelle?"

"I don't know. I'm a little afraid," she admitted. She shifted her feet nervously.

He took on a look of surprise. "Why?"

"Because you're going to do things to me, and I don't know if...if..."

Mr. Dean held her by her upper arms, looking down into her frightened face. His chest grazed the tips of her breasts through her sweater. He did it casually, making it look like an innocent mistake instead of the calculated move it was.

"Don't be afraid," he said softly, holding her by the arms. "I won't do anything to hurt you. I didn't hurt last night, did I?" His tone was low and soothing, but as he spoke, he began to back her into the bed, forcing her to take tiny steps in time with his as they did a tight dance across the floor.

"No, you didn't hurt me...." Michelle's voice was hesitant and nervous. Her feet continued to step back as her host forced her into retreat.

"And I won't now, either," Mr. Dean continued. "Let me prove to you there is nothing wrong with you, Michelle. You are a very beautiful, very sensual woman, and lots of men would jump at the chance to...make love to you the way you like it," he finished, quickly amending his choice of words. He was about to say, "fuck you in the ass," but he knew Michelle would not appreciate the vulgarity, and it would ruin the moment. She was clearly responding to his gentle, caressing tone; she wasn't putting up any kind of fight. Yet.

Michelle's legs hit the back of the bed. The impact jarred her, bringing her back a little. Her eyes filled with trepidation.

"What do I have to do?" She asked.

"Well, first thing is to get you undressed," Mr. Dean answered, trying to keep his voice casual, as if he were asking her to do nothing more than share a drink with him. "Would you like to do it, or would you like me to....?"

"I can do it," she replied.

She crossed her hands, grabbed the bottom hem of her sweater, and in one fluid movement, lifted it over her head. Then she stood up and stepped out of her shoes. But when she slipped her fingers beneath the waistline of her skirt, ready to shimmy it down her pelvis, Mr. Dean stopped her.

"Slow down," he said, reaching around her waist and covering her small hands with his own. "Relax. We have time. Better yet--lie down on the bed. I'll do it." With both hands on her arms, he lowered her backward onto the bed, slowly so as not to scare her, and grabbed her skirt by the waistband to pull it down her hips. Peeling it down past her thighs, he got his first look of Michelle's white, thin, thong panties.

They barely stretched over the mound of her pussy, cinching between her legs in a straight line and disappearing inside the tight crease of her ass, before rising up her back to the circling waistband.

His eyes suddenly mischievous, Mr. Dean dug his fingers into the thin wisp of material ensconced up Michelle's bottom, and gave it a sharp pull.

"Hey!" Michelle squealed.

"That was rude of me," Mr. Dean said, not at all contrite. Michelle gave him an accusatory look, but Mr. Dean was already pulling down her panties and flinging them aside.

"That's better," he murmured. Her pussy was smooth and shaved, and looked delicious.

At the moment, it was closed up tight, thick lips caressing up against each other; but that would change soon. Mr. Dean would not be ignoring that area completely, despite Michelle's predilections. It would simply not be the area he would be giving his full attention to tonight. The idea of getting his hands on Michelle's choice rump again made his balls tighten and his cock twitch.

The only thing left was Michelle's bra, and Mr. Dean made quick work of it by pulling her up, unhooking the front clasp, and peeling it off her shoulders. He decided: one of the best inventions in the history of modern man was the front-clasping bra.

Michelle's heavy breasts swayed a little as they were freed. Her nipples puckered from exposure to the room air.

"Now, let's get you comfortable," he said, trying to sound matter-of-fact. "Turn onto your belly."

Nervously, Michelle complied. She was wound up tight, tense and stiff. But taking a lesson from what had worked the night before, Mr. Dean began to massage her, running his hands up and down the backs of her legs and thighs with gentle pressure, trying to put her at ease. When Michelle closed her eyes and relaxed, Mr. Dean moved his hands up, and began to massage her butt.

"Mmmm," she hummed, cradling her head in her crossed arms, her eyes closed. Mr. Dean kept up his gentle kneading until Michelle had entered a state of languid contentment, completely at ease. It was time to move on.

"Let's prop you up," he said. Michelle didn't respond; she looked like she was half asleep. "Move your butt up a little," he repeated.

"What?"

"Kneel up on all fours for a minute," he said.

Slowly, Michelle complied, raising her body onto hands and knees. Then she looked behind her to see what her host was up to.

Reaching under the bed, Mr. Dean had pulled out what seemed to be a pillow--only it was unlike any pillow Michelle had ever seen. It was large, well stuffed, and in the solid shape of a mound. "Lie down on this," Mr. Dean instructed. "Put it under your hips."

When Michelle continued to look at him, confused, Mr. Dean took matters into his own hands. He slipped the pillow under her, centered her across it, and pushed her back down. Michelle grunted. With her hips resting over the pillow, her ass was stuck up in the air. She felt very exposed, and tried to shimmy down the pillow a little.

But her host would not let any sense of propriety get the better of her. He held down her ass, but began to massage it again before she could protest. Michelle stopped her wiggling.

"That's better," Mr. Dean said. Michelle quickly decided it *was* good. The angle of her bottom was much better this way for his hands to knead her soft flesh. She folded her arms again and rested her cheek on the soft sheets, her ass fully supported, high in the air.

And then, with one naughty finger, Mr. Dean poked into the crevasse of her bottom and tickled her asshole. Michelle shrieked in surprise and lifted her weight off the pillow.

"Now, now," Mr. Dean said. "I didn't hurt you, did I?"

"No, but you goosed me," Michelle said, lowering herself down slowly, her eyes now cleared and filled with apprehension.

"Well, see, this is a problem," Mr. Dean said. "I'm not going to hurt you, Michelle, but I can't have you wiggling and jumping all over the bed every time I surprise you the slightest bit. Then I really *might* hurt you." He seemed to think for a minute, then walked briskly to the wardrobe and returned with a blindfold. "Let's get this on you," he said.

"Why?"

Mr. Dean sighed.

"Because, Michelle, I want to move you around a little and make sure you're not going to hurt yourself. But I've got to use, some, uh, *things,* to keep you from twisting around too much, and I don't want you to get scared. I don't want your fear to stop us from having some fun," Mr. Dean said, trying to choose his words carefully. He was not used to talking things out and explaining things to his guests, especially once they were inside the activity room; he was used to giving orders. Michelle had no idea she was one of only a few women who could dare ask Mr. Dean for an explanation to his actions and not get a stern spanking in response.

But Michelle was still stalling. "If you're so sure what you're going to do is going to scare me, why do you think I'll like it?"

"Because I've had quite a bit of experience in these matters," Mr. Dean said dryly. "But if you don't like what I'm doing, I'll stop. Same as before. I promise." He didn't move. Now was the time he had to let her think *she* was in control and making all the decisions. She had to agree to do this on her own free-will. Of course, if she continued to balk, he would resort to other methods. But things would go much better later on if she thought she had agreed to this little lesson of his on her own volition.

But Michelle only gave it a moment's thought. She was worried...but she also wanted his hands back on, and in, her ass.

"Okay," she said, burying her face in the cradle of her arms and squeezing her eyes shut. "Go ahead."

Mr. Dean grinned; he had won. He placed the blindfold over Michelle's eyes, brought the two strings together behind her head, and tied it tight.

Working fast while she lay still, he began to pull his supplies from under the bed where he'd hidden them. Hiding his supplies was also a new experience for him: he typically kept his tools out in the open, sometimes scattered around the room, ready to collect when and where he needed them. But he rather enjoyed this game of subterfuge with Michelle. It made the conquest that much more fun and satisfying.

The bed Michelle was resting on looked like a normal, antique, four-poster bed. But wooden slats going across the top connected the posts at both head and feet, and the short headrest had wooden slats going across it, too. What Michelle had failed to notice, resting on the large bed, were the many hooks and eye-bolts screwed into the frame: perfect for attaching lengths of chain, snap-hooks, rope...for all its innocent, elegant look, Michelle was resting on a fully functional dungeon bed.

Careful not to make too many rattling noises, Mr. Dean now set about attaching lengths of chain to different points of the bed.

"I'm going to move you down a bit," he said. "Ready?" Without waiting for an answer, he grabbed Michelle by the ankles and pulled her down the bed, the pillow wedged beneath her pelvis dragging along with her. Michelle squealed.

When the end of the pillow met the edge of the bed, Mr. Dean stopped his tugging and let Michelle's ankles go. Her legs now dangled down to the floor, but with her hips and ass propped up as they were, her feet could not touch bottom. She could not even graze the floor with her toes.

Quickly, Mr. Dean attached cuffs to Michelle's ankles and snapped them into the lengths of chain. Michelle's sharp intake of breath told him she had finally figured out what he was doing. She jerked her feet, and found them well and properly restrained to the bed.

Moving quickly now, Mr. Dean moved up the bed, took her hands, and slipped a pair of cuffs over each wrist--and then he pulled. But he had attached each cuff to a length of chain that was snapped into the opposing edge of the bed. Michelle's arms were crossed into an X; she could not uncross them. The chains were long enough that she could bend her elbows and grip her fore-arms, or cradle her head in the hollow of her arms, but she could not straighten them, and she certainly couldn't raise them.

When Michelle tested her wrist restraints and realized how quickly her host had rendered her harnessed and chained to the bed, bent over and exposed, she began to protest.

"Now wait just a second--"

His work just about done, Mr. Dean folded his arms across his chest and gazed down at her chained body, giving himself a moment to admire the view. A triumphant look covered his face. Michelle couldn't see it, of course; she was stuck looking straight ahead at the bed post. He could take a few moments to alleviate some of her fears, he decided.

"Are you being hurt?"

"No, but--"

"So you're not in any kind of pain?"

"It feels uncomfortable--"

"What does? The cuffs? Is it too tight somewhere?"

"No--" She rattled the chains, testing her bonds-- "But I don't like it."

"Why not?"

"Because I can't move!"

"That's true," Mr. Dean agreed. "But that's where the trust needs to start. You need to trust me, Michelle, if I am to pleasure you. So here's what *I* want: I want you to tell me if something starts to hurt. If I do something that causes you pain, then you say 'hot,' and I'll stop, immediately, no questions asked. But *you* have to promise me you'll only use that safeword if you're in pain, Michelle--not if you're just feeling uncomfortable or scared for a moment."

Michelle opened her mouth to protest, but Mr. Dean stopped her. "I'm not saying you have to stay completely quiet. You can still tell me if you're scared or uncomfortable about something I'm doing. If I'm pushing your boundaries, you tell me, and we'll talk about it. I'll help you get through it. But the safeword--the safeword is for pain only. Do you understand?"

Michelle swallowed hard.

"Yes," she said.

"Yes, what?"

"Yes, *Sir.*"

"Good." His triumph came clear through his voice. "And what's your safeword?"

"Hot."

"*Very* good. But there's still one more thing."

From behind her, Mr. Dean bound thick leather cuffs around Michelle's thighs, then took his last item out from under the bed: a spreader-bar. He fit the bar between Michelle's thighs, and fastened it into place with the help of the special cuffs. Michelle's legs were now locked apart, spread wide and bent over the edge of the bed. She had never felt more vulnerable in her life. She whimpered.

"I know you're new to this, and it feels strange," Mr. Dean said soothingly. He smoothed down her hair across her head. "But you'll enjoy it, I promise." Michelle didn't answer. Her chest was rising and falling fast; she was breathing hard.

"Let's get you a little more at ease," Mr. Dean said, having pity on her now that he had her the way he wanted. He went to the side table next to the bed and reached into the drawer to get a bottle of lube. Coating two fingers with it, he returned to stand behind Michelle's compact and trussed up behind.

Spread as she was, he got a good inside her thin, shadowy crack: the deep division between her twin domes lay slightly open, revealing the puckering ring of her spasming anus. Beneath that was the gently sloping mound of her pussy; her cunt lips were closed and dry, but her asshole winked at him coyly.

With his dry hand, Mr. Dean splayed her ass crack even more, opening it wide. Then, with his lubed up fingers, he began to gently feel her up, running his fingers up and down her crack, tickling her asshole. Michelle groaned.

Mr. Dean set the pad of his index finger against her clenching ring. Applying gentle but steady pressure, he pressed in, testing her resistance, and quickly had his finger in all the way to the knuckle. He was amazed at her control: while the rest of her body seemed tense and stiff, her asshole allowed him easy access. A low, breathy moan escaped from Michelle's lips as he took ownership of her rear-gate.

Mr. Dean pushed his finger in further, watching as it smoothly disappeared up her ass. He was soon cradling one of her small cheeks in his palm. His finger was pressed up tight, and he gave it a tiny wiggle. Michelle jerked. Slowly, he pulled it out; but when he pushed his way back in, it was with two fingers this time, not just one.

Thrusting fast now, Mr. Dean began to finger-fuck her ass, listening as Michelle sighed in delight at the head of the bed. Her asshole hugged his fingers, and her cries of pleasure were like music to his ears. His cock swelled and twitched, jumping for the chance to replace his fingers.

For a second, he debated whether he should slow things down, make Michelle wait to come. But then he thought: Why? It might be fun to see how many times Michelle could come tonight by ass-play alone. And her coming now would certainly do them both good, and set the tone for the rest of the evening.

But in the end, it was his cock that decided for him, straining against his pants.

As his fingers continued to dip in and out of Michelle's asshole, Mr. Dean quickly shimmied out of his pants and flung them away. He pulled out his fingers from her warm, pulling sleeve for the few brief seconds it took to grab the lube and grease up his cock. Michelle whimpered again, this time in need.

Holding his cock in his hand, Mr. Dean opened Michelle's plaint cheeks once more, centered his straining prick against his small target, and pushed in. He wasn't slow, and he wasn't gentle. He thrust fast and deep, ramming into her, all the way up to his balls in one fell swoop. Michelle snapped her head up, and a gurgled cry came from her throat; she tried to raise up her body, as much as the chains would allow. But she did not use her safeword. Her host grunted in approval.

Then Mr. Dean stood still, savoring the feel of Michelle's clenching asshole squeezing around him, her delicate tissues hugging him tight across his long length. He grinded his hips against her butt, rubbing himself within her and pushing himself in that last little bit, pressing into her soft derriere hard with his stomach.

Michelle lowered herself down and hugged the pillow at the head of the bed, squeezing hard--both the pillow, and Mr. Dean's cock.

He pulled out, slowly, until only his helmeted tip was still inside. Then he lunged in again, pounding hard, pushing Michelle up from the impact. She let out a short shriek and grabbed onto the sheet this time.

And then he was fucking her ass furiously, grabbing her by the hips and pulling her to meet his thrusts, closing his eyes in delight and trying desperately to hang on. Michelle's asshole was just as tight and hot as he remembered from yesterday, and it squeezed him like a vise. It swallowed up his rock-hard prick with each push of his hips.

Michelle struggled against the sheets and pulled the chains, trying to prop herself up more and meet his thrusts; but bound as she was, it was up to Mr. Dean to set the pace and force. That was, of course, what he had planned from the beginning.

But even so, Michelle was soon crying out in ecstasy, building up to her own orgasm and straining with the need for release. She whipped her head from side to side, moaning out to her god and her host, as her asshole throbbed and spasmed around Mr. Dean's prick. Then she went up and over, coming in a clenching, locking squeeze of her muscles around his stiff length.

Her tight grip and cries of delight were her host's undoing, and Mr. Dean came himself in blinding eruption, shooting his load up Michelle's warm rectum that seemed to milk him to his last thrust.

As he slowly pulled his withering cock out from her, Michelle shuddered in response, getting tiny aftershocks from his depleted cock caressing her sensitive inner skin.

Mr. Dean recovered first.

"Feel better?" He asked, his voice ragged.

"Oh, God," she answered into the sheet. Mr. Dean smiled.

"Good. I'll give you a few minutes to rest before we continue."

She said nothing to his statement, but rested her head on the bed as her breathing evened out. Her legs lay limp over the edge of the bed; she looked utterly spent. But the pillow and spreader-bar kept her in the wanton pose, a fact Mr. Dean found most endearing.

As she rested, Mr. Dean walked over to the wardrobe and began to pull things out, barely looking them over before loading them up onto the metal tray nearby. They were sex toys, all of them anal toys, but he wasn't being too picky with shape or size. Tonight, strangely enough, he didn't feel the need to pick his tools with his usual care. Tonight, he hoped to try them all, and make thorough use of Michelle's adorable little ass before their evening came to a close.

He wheeled the tray over to the bed, placed the bottle of lube on the edge of the tray, and admired the neat line of toys.

"Let's start with some beads," he said by way of introduction, letting Michelle know he was about to begin.

"Beads?" Her voice was still hoarse, and barely above a whisper.

"Anal beads. Here, let me show you." He took a few steps around the bed, pulled off her blindfold with a yank, and held the beads up in front of Michelle's face. Michelle squinted for a minute to regain her focus before staring at the beads.

They looked like glass balls, hanging from a length of thin thread. It was like a strange bracelet, she thought, only there was no clasp. A short piece of the thread hung down from the last ball. As her eyes traveled down, Michelle realized that each ball grew a little bit fatter than its sister above.

"What are...what are..."

"What am I going to do with them? Why, stuff them in your ass, of course."

"But--"

"Don't worry. You have your safeword if you start to feel any pain. Otherwise, it's just the fear talking, right? I haven't hurt you so far, have I?"

She didn't say anything, but shook her head no.

"You should learn how to enjoy your ass to the fullest, Michelle--there's nothing to be ashamed of. So let's do this. It'll be fun, I promise you."

He returned to his spot behind her and carefully greased up each ball on the string. Then, with a look of happy anticipation on his face, he held apart her ass cheeks.

"Bead number one."

He pressed it against her asshole, still spasming from her orgasm minutes before. The crinkled ring glistened with lube, and puckered in reaction to the sudden poking. But the tiny ball popped in fast, and soon disappeared. Michelle gasped.

"Bead number two."

Mr. Dean had to poke this one in a bit, but like its sister, it, too, went in happily enough.

"Bead number three."

This one needed slightly more effort, as the ring of muscle stretched around the widest rim of the ball. Mr. Dean had to push it in with his finger, sliding it deep inside Michelle's tight rectal sleeve next to the other two. She groaned.

"Bead number four."

He applied steady, unrelenting pressure, mesmerized as Michelle's asshole swallowed up the thick ball. It sat right on the other side of her gate; her anus flared and constricted, as if trying to push the ball out. But it was about to accommodate something even larger.

"Bead number five--last one. Try to relax."

Mr. Dean pushed the ball hard against her tight ring. At first, it would not give. Then, slowly, her hole stretched and dilated, widening around the huge orb. Michelle whimpered and squeezed her eyes shut. Her asshole throbbed around the stubborn ball that was filling her up to the hilt.

Even after the widest part was through, Mr. Dean had to keep pushing it in the rest of the way, making space inside Michelle's stuffed, tight channel. But by the time he was done and had let Michelle's ass cheeks snap shut, the only thing he could see was the bottom length of the string, hanging down from Michelle's bottom like an obscene tail.

Michelle twisted her hips above the pillow, struggling against the chains and spreader bar. Her ass felt stretched wide, pulled taunt, and packed full. It throbbed, and ached a bit from the fullness...but it didn't exactly hurt, she realized. In fact, the fullness was beginning to feel rather good.

"I'm going to pull them out now. Ready?"

Before she had time to respond, Mr. Dean grabbed hold of the bottom string hanging out of her ass, and pulled the balls out of Michelle with a steady yank. The thrilling sensation of the balls being pulled out of her clenching asshole sent a shocking jolt of pleasure up Michelle's spine, hitting all the right nerve endings. She let out a high-pitched, stuttered yell, feeling her asshole pull, stretch, and close...pull, stretch, and close...Five times over. And then it was done.

"How was that?" Mr. Dean asked politely.

"Again, please, Sir," Michelle said.

Smiling broadly now, Mr. Dean did as she asked, stuffing her with an ass full of beads, and then pulling them out in rapid speed. By the time he had pulled out the last bead on the third round, Michelle had felt very close to coming again.

"Let's move on to something else," Mr. Dean said, placing the string of anal beads on the metal tray. He kept it away from the clean toys, so as not to get any cross-contamination. "I'm going to try an anal dildo on you. This one happens to be made out of glass. You should learn this, Michelle--anal dildos are different from regular dildos. Regular dildos are typically tubular in shape. Anal dildos, the good ones, have a wide handle at the top, and a slightly narrowing notch beneath it, where your asshole can close in, to keep you from swallowing the whole thing up inside. If you're with a partner, and your partner is holding onto the toy, you don't have to be so careful about what the end--the flange--looks like, you can just ask him to make sure it doesn't get sucked up your ass. But if you're playing with yourself, you should always have a wide handle to grip. Here, let me show you."

He moved around to show her, but when Michelle caught sight of the huge, obscene-looking dildo, she cringed and closed her eyes.

"Don't turn away from it, Michelle. Look at it. It's nothing to be afraid or ashamed of." She opened her eyes, her face clouded with reluctance, and barely grazed over the naughty dildo.

"It's going to fit?" She asked before she could stop herself.

"Let's find out," Mr. Dean said, his voice merry.

He stepped up behind her. Greasing the monstrous toy quickly, he pointed the tapered tip against her tiny bud, and pushed.

It slid in halfway before meeting any difficulty; but then Michelle grunted and pulled at the sheet, squeezing her ass closed.

"Now, now," Mr. Dean said. "Just relax." He waited until Michelle was in the middle of a deep breath, then pushed the dildo in with his palm against the base, oozing it up her tight channel. Michelle tried to kick her legs up and press herself into the pillow, but it was no use. Mr. Dean caressed her butt with his other hand and made calming noises to soothe her, but kept going.

Soon the toy had reached its widest diameter inside her tight ring, and Michelle's asshole was dilated thin around the anal dildo, hugging it tight. But she could not stretch wide enough. The rim of her anus began to ache and burn, but Mr. Dean kept pushing, forcing the thing into her like a battering ram from behind. Michelle opened her mouth to cry out her safeword.

"Ho--"

"It's in."

As he spoke, the toy slipped the last way through. Her anus sucked the rest of it in all the way to the handle and clutched it around the base with a tight squeeze. The wide handle rested against Michelle's soft buttocks, but the large toy had disappeared inside.

If Michelle had felt stuffed by the anal beads, it was nothing compared to what she felt now. She could feel her rectum throbbing around the glass dildo. The sensation was overwhelming. She took a few deep breaths.

"What now?" She asked.

"Now, just get used to it." Mr. Dean stepped away from her a bit, watching her reactions as she got used to her packed ass. She was breathing hard again, squeezing her eyes shut and clenching her hands into tight fists.

If Michelle had been able to turn her head around and see the way her host was watching her, she would have been left with the sneaky suspicion he was waiting for something.

He was. He was waiting for Michelle's natural sensuality and highly charged rectal nerve endings to take over, sending her to a place where the pain and fullness would turn into full-blown arousal, an aching need to come again.

After a few moments, when the discomfort had dissipated somewhat and the throbbing had turned into a maddening sort of wanton itch, Mr. Dean began to notice different kinds of movements coming from Michelle's bottom. She began to shift her thighs a little inside the restraints. The cuffs and spreader bar kept her from moving too much, but it was enough for her to feel the thrilling jolts titillating her ass every time the dildo pressed or shifted a certain way inside her. Her legs trembled, and her hips began to wriggle against the pillow.

She began to make some tiny but obvious thrusting movements with her pelvis. But bound and trussed up as she was, could not move the way she wanted. The maddening tickle from the anal dildo filled her with an agitating need to *do* something.

"Mr. Dean, um, Sir...."

"Yes?"

"Could you, um...."

"Could I what, Michelle?"

"Um...Jesus. Could you....?"

"What? You'll have to do a better job than that, telling me what you want."

Michelle turned her head over her shoulder as much as she could to try and find her host with her eyes, but he was standing too far behind her. If she *had* been able to see him, she would have noticed his obvious look of smug satisfaction.

From the beginning, Mr. Dean had wanted her in a position where she would have to tell him exactly what she wanted him to do. He would make no more assumptions. She would have to learn how to ask to be fucked in the ass, loud and proud. No: he would get her to *beg* for it. Only then could she begin to get over her obvious, and misplaced, feelings of shame surrounding her sexual needs.

"Please, Sir, I...." She halted.

"Come on, Michelle. I know you have the necessary vocabulary. Finish the sentence. What would you like me to do?"

"I want you to, um...oh god...I want you to move the dildo?"

"You want me to take it out?"

"No, no. I want you to just move it around a bit."

Reaching a hand out, Mr. Dean took hold of the flange pressing against her smooth buttocks, and screwed it in even further against Michelle's quaking twin domes, twisting it hard as he pushed. Michelle twitched and moaned.

"Like that?" He asked, taking his hand away. He would not give her any more relief than what she explicitly asked for.

"No... yes...could you um...." Taking a ragged breath, she said in a rush, "could you pull it in and out?"

Feeling truly wicked now, Mr. Dean pulled the dildo out just enough to get the widest part through the squeezing circle of muscle, then poked it back in. He did this a couple times. Her asshole was looser now, but even so, the wide toy popped in and out through the circular gate.

"Like that?" He asked, his voice light. Michelle's eyes flared. She twisted her head around again, trying desperately to find her host. There could be no doubt now he was toying with her, and enjoying it, too. She groaned.

"Sir, please," she implored. *Why* had she agreed to this? She was an idiot, she decided.

"You will just have to pick your words better, Mi-chelle. Remember, I'm here to help you, but I think you need a lesson in how to say what you need. Just tell me exactly what you want--and how much you want it. There's nothing embarrassing about telling a man exactly how to please you."

She pushed her face into the mattress and groaned again. But he would do nothing to alleviate her suffering unless she asked, and now she needed his help, badly.

"I want you to thrust the dildo in and out of me," she said in a muffled voice.

"What was that?"

"I want you to thrust the dildo in an out of me!"

"So...you want me to fuck you with the dildo?"

"Yes."

"In the ass?"

"Yes," she said, her voice cracking.

"So say so--or better yet, ask. Ask to be fucked in the ass with the anal dildo."

"Sir, please fuck me in the ass with the anal dildo," she whispered.

"Much better," Mr. Dean said in approval.

He began to pull the large toy in and out of her, all the way, watching as her asshole stretched and closed around the tapered toy. He thrusted fast, pushing hard, ramming the toy through her clenching hole...and very quickly, Michelle's whole body began to tremble. She jerked inside her restraints. She thrusted her pelvis be-tween the pillow beneath her hips and the dildo impaling her from behind, moving her body back and forth as much as she could and trying to set her own pace. But very quickly, Mr. Dean realized what she was trying to do, and wouldn't let her get away with it. When she pushed back, trying to stuff herself with more of the toy, he pulled away.

He would not let her come so easily, she realized. His "lesson" was not over yet. She would have to give him even clearer instructions on how she wanted him to violate her ass, however humiliated she felt about it.

"Slower, please," she said. Mr. Dean slowed down, but also made his thrusts more shallow.

"Deeper." Her voice was soft and throaty. Mr. Dean pushed harder with each poke, the way he had before.

"God, yes," Michelle whispered. "Now...circle it a bit?"

With the dildo still up her hole, Mr. Dean circled it wide around her rectal rim, watching as her muscles relaxed even further.

"Oh god, that feels so good...now pound me, hard."

Mr. Dean stopped his hand. "Ask nicely, Michelle."

"Please Sir...please pound my ass." She flung her head up, ready to submit completely and say whatever he needed her to, so long as in the end, he would finally let her come. "Please, fuck my ass with the anal dildo, hard, pound my asshole hard and fast until I come, Sir!"

"Very nice," Mr. Dean said, impressed. In reward, he did as she asked, moving his hand and the dildo with blurring speed, jerking the huge toy in and out of her.

Michelle could feel the orgasm building, the sensations spreading across her pelvis, until they came to a crescendo...and, with a strangled cry, Michelle came. For one second, her whole body became rigid and frozen, pulling tight against her bonds; then she relaxed completely, letting out a breathy moan.

Mr. Dean continued to ream her ass until he was sure she was done with any aftershocks, and then smoothly pulled the dildo out of her. Her asshole closed shut as the well-used toy exited her body. Michelle barely responded; she was too depleted.

"I think you're finally beginning to get it, Michelle," Mr. Dean said, gazing down at her heaving back and flushed face. "You're doing great, by the way. But I think there's more we can accomplish tonight."

As Michelle recovered from her second orgasm of the night, Mr. Dean looked to the metal tray, and picked his next toy.

"Let's move on to something that vibrates," he said. "You're used to having a vibrating toy in your ass, no?" He didn't mention he'd seen her vibrator that day he'd come into her room and spied into in her bathroom. Michelle's eyes narrowed, wondering how he'd known. "I'm guessing, though, you didn't know about *anal* vibrators," he continued. "Again, they are made differently from vibrators that go inside your pussy."

He rubbed his hand lightly inside the gaping lips of her cunt; Michelle gasped. Her pussy felt swollen, wet, and very, very sensitive. She was not used to feeling like this after she came. Then again, she was not used to coming twice in one night, either.

"The anal vibrators have the wide handles, same as the non-vibrating kind. But they come in all lengths, shapes, and sizes...even textures. Here, I'll show you one."

He came around again to show her, and this time, Michelle looked at the toy with some interest. It wasn't tapered like the last one. It had a round, smooth head, and kept its basic tubular shape until the narrowing orbit around the base. But it was studded with tiny bumps down its long length, hard knobs that would rub against her inner skin.

"Let's get this in you, see what happens," Mr. Dean said.

Michelle's eyes furrowed. She was not afraid of any pain; she was beyond that. But she felt drained. She wasn't sure she would be able to come again.

Mr. Dean took his place behind her, coated the novel vibrator with lube, and pressed it against Michelle's slick asshole. Her anus squeezed in protest. She had tightened up considerably after her last orgasm. She would need some inducement.

So he used his fingers first, pushing them in and spreading her open from the inside. Michelle groaned softly.

"Relax," Michelle," Mr. Dean instructed. "You're all tight back here."

"I'm not sure I can come again, Sir," she said, voicing her fear.

"It's okay if you can't. Just learn what feels good. Relax and enjoy what I'm doing to you," he replied, dilating her asshole with his fingers as he spoke. Michelle took some deep breaths and relaxed, enjoying the manual stretching.

When he felt she was stretched enough, Mr. Dean set the head of the toy against her hole and pressed in. He had to go slow; every time a bump went through the ring of muscle, Michelle's sphincter would contract around the vibrator. But at last it was in, and Mr. Dean twisted the knob at the base to turn it on.

Vibrations shot up her back, making Michelle stiffen and squeal. But Mr. Dean let the toy be, watching as his guest started to accustom herself to the strange sensations.

"I'll be right back," he said. Then, mischievously: "Don't go anywhere."

"Wait, where are you going?" Michelle asked in alarm.

"Just to wash off a bit," Mr. Dean replied. "I'll be back in a minute."

"But what about the vibrator?"

"It's not going anywhere, either," he chuckled. Then he walked across the room and disappeared through a door that had been well hidden by both the wood paneling and the angle of the large wardrobe. Michelle realized there must be an adjoining bathroom back there, and he was going in. To wash, he had said. Why did he need to wash? What the hell did her host have planned now?

In Mr. Dean's absence, Michelle could do nothing but try to relax and get comfortable with the deep-rooted rumbling in her ass. She was accustomed to having a vibrating toy inside her, but not one this large, and certainly not one textured. And she was used to having control over its use.

After a couple moments, the feel of the sharp bumps churning inside her narrow channel became a maddening tickle, a titillating buzz, and she felt herself grow wet between her legs. Sweat, and a heavy dose of her own inner cunt juices, coated her thighs; she knew she was slick with it. Her pussy felt flushed and swollen. She would have scissored her legs if she could have, but the spreader-bar prevented her from even that small relief. She could nothing to help herself and alleviate this rising, aching need.

Where the hell was her host?

After a maddening amount of time, Mr. Dean finally appeared from around the wardrobe. He looked slightly damp, relaxed, and completely at ease in his nudity. Michelle's eyes immediately went to his prick, and noticed it was soft, but thick. He was looking down at her plugged, humming bottom, but when he caught her looking at him, he met her stare head on. Then he gave her a smug smile.

He knew exactly what she was going through, she realized. He had been in control of everything that had happened between them since the moment she had entered this room. He knew what he was doing when he had left her alone with the toy ensconced up her ass; he knew that, without even working for it, he could reduced her to a state of mindless need. She was being primed to submit to whatever he instructed, and she didn't even have the will to protest. She was certainly in no position to fight back. All she could do was capitulate. The only question was when.

Dignity and principles were done with. All she wanted now was to come again, without having to torture herself for it. But if she asked for his help nicely enough, asked quickly and got it over with, he would have to help her, right? Wasn't that the deal?

"Sir, could you please play with the toy in my ass, could you please--"

"Not yet."

"What?"

"I have a few questions for you first. Answer them for me, and then I'll play."

"But--"

"It should only take a minute." He knelt down on one knee by her face, resting an arm on the bed as he looked into her eyes. The toy hummed in the background.

"So you play with yourself with a toy in your ass, yes?"

Michelle turned her head away and buried her reddening face in the cradle of her arms. She wanted to ignore the question. No, what she wanted to do was get the hell away from this man who had no mercy. But her growing need could not be denied, he would not release her, and he would not help her unless she answered his questions. Were all the hosts of the Hotel Bentmoore this evil? Or just this one? How could someone so merciless know how to make her come so thoroughly and so often?

"Yes, I use a toy in my ass."

"Do you touch yourself in any other way?"

"Yes," she admitted, her voice hoarse. "Well, sometimes, when I need to." It was hard to think when the vibrator was pushing all thoughts away except the need to come.

"How do you touch yourself?"

"What do you want me to do, show you?" She snapped. She flailed her hips and flung up her feet as much as the chains would allow, struggling hard within the restraints.

"I want you to tell me," Mr. Dean said patiently, ignoring her vain attempt to lash out her frustration. "Describe to me what you do."

"Oh, God." Her mortification complete, Michelle covered her head with her arms. Her host would not stop until he had broken through her last shred of modesty, decency, and defiance. He would bring all her secrets to light, play with her as he wanted, and in the end, break her completely.

So be it. She was done trying to fight him. All she wanted now was to come.

"I...I tap myself."

"You tap your clit?"

"Yes."

"Say it."

Michelle's voice quivered. "I tap my clit, Sir."

"Okay. How hard?" He walked around her and stood behind her spread legs. With his hand, he reached under, spread her pussy lips wide, and with one finger, lightly began to tap her clit. Michelle groaned.

"Like this, Michelle?"

"No, ah, a little harder, Sir."

Mr. Dean tapped harder. "Like this?"

"Oh. Oh god. Yes, but harder. Sir."

With his entire hand, Mr. Dean began to lightly slap her clit.

"Like this?"

"Yes, like that, oh god, yes, that's good, don't stop."

"That's not a tap, Michelle. That's a slap. Now say, "I like to have my clit slapped while I have an anal toy vibrating in my ass.""

When she didn't answer fast enough, Mr. Dean stopped his hand and waited. Michelle could have shrieked in frustration.

"I like to have my clit slapped while I have an anal toy vibrating in my ass. Sir!"

From the tone of his voice, she knew her host was smiling. "There you go. It's not so hard to say what you want--you just needed some training. But let's try something else with it."

As he slapped her clit, Mr. Dean positioned his erect cock at the entrance to her pussy and began to push in. With the toy being stuffed up her asshole as it was, Mr. Dean had to ease in slowly; but once he was all the way in, having made a place for himself inside her snug and wet cunt, he began to pump in and out, thrusting his hips with even strokes. He could feel the reverberations of the novel toy coming through her thin membranes. He pumped harder.

"How is this, Michelle?" He asked her between thrusts.

"It's, oh, it's good, it's very good, Sir," she said breathlessly. Michelle felt utterly packed, stuffed both fore and aft, and could focus on nothing but the pleasurable thrills coming from her entire pelvic area: the toy humming in her ass, her host's thrusting prick inside her sopping pussy, and his hand slapping against her clit.

"Oh, oh, oh!" The shocking jolts of pure erotic pleasure grew in intensity until she couldn't hold back any longer. She came in blinding light, craning her head back and screaming like a wild animal.

A minute later, her host joined her over the edge, pumping into her pussy with hard thrusts, and groaning loudly as he came.

This time, it took Mr. Dean a couple minutes to recover. After he pulled out, he sat on the edge of the bed, breathing hard. Then he turned off the droning toy still going in Michelle's shuddering ass and carefully pulled it out of her.

As she felt him pull the toy out, she groaned. "I'm done," she declared. The toy rubbed against her sensitive inner flesh as it left her, each bump jolting her ragged senses.

"Are you sure?" Mr. Dean asked, disappointed. "We have time, you know. I can give you a break. I have more toys I think you should try."

Michelle gave it a moment of thought, then smiled at Mr. Dean. After the amazing orgasm he had just given her, she felt much more generous toward her host. "Well, maybe just one or two," she agreed. "But I really don't think I can come again."

"That's what you thought last time," Mr. Dean said with a smile.

In the end, Michelle did come again, twice more that night, and Mr. Dean had her yell "I AM AN ANAL SLUT" each time she came. He also released her from her bonds at some point, sure now she would not try to struggle or fight him. This first lesson was done, and he considered it a resounding success.

Mr. Dean tried to get yet another orgasm out of her, but by that time, Michelle was practically unconscious, and no longer responding to any stimuli on either ass or pussy. But Mr. Dean felt far from defeated. He felt invigorated, and immensely proud of the work they had done together.

As he helped Michelle get dressed, he smiled at her languid movements. She was half asleep on her feet. The liaison would have to physically help her get back to her room.

And now he would have to utter the words he had been dreading to say all night. But it had to be done. Hosts of the Hotel Bentmoore had their own rules and regulations to follow.

"I would love to be your host again on your next visit," he said. "But there are other hosts here, all very qualified to help you and each with their own strengths. If you want to try someone else, I can give you names and suggestions--"

"No, that's okay," she answered in a dreamy voice. "Maybe at some point I'll want to try one of the others, but for now, I want to stay with you. You...you give me what I need, even when I don't know I need it."

Mr. Dean gave a sigh of relief. "Thank you, Michelle," he said. "You'll be visiting the hotel again soon?"

"Oh, yes. Very soon. As soon as I can get away." She smiled. "I am so happy I didn't leave before."

"Me, too," Mr. Dean replied.

Mr. Trowlege arrived. He had to hook an arm around Michelle's waist and support her over his shoulder to help her out the door--nothing he wasn't used to. Michelle made her way drunkenly down the hallway, hanging on tight to her escort, who was trying very hard to make sure she didn't fall.

Mr. Dean watched them go until the elevator closed. The grin never left his face.

***

The next morning, Mr. Dean made his way back to Mr. Bentmoore's office and knocked on the door softly. He was not expected, but Mr. Bentmoore allowed him entrance anyway.

Once seated, Mr. Dean gave his boss an accusatory look across the desk. Mr. Bentmoore was grinning, and obviously trying not to laugh outright. Mr. Dean sighed, then shook his head.

"You knew, didn't you?" he asked, chagrined.

"I have no idea what you're talking about," Mr. Bentmoore replied.

"You knew Michelle is an anal slut." The label came out like a term of endearment.

"I didn't know, no. But I had a suspicion, based on some of the things she said over the phone. She mentioned how you'd tried to make use of her friend Monique's ass, you see. I thought it was a strange thing to mention--unless she was looking for some of the same."

"Why didn't you tell me?"

"Because you deserved a bit of a challenge. You've become too used to having it easy, Dean. Women telling you exactly what they want, and tripping over their feet to please you--that's not how you keep your skills up as a host of the Hotel Bentmoore. You need to get into a woman's head once in a while. And you see? You clearly did need a brush up on your skills. You almost lost her."

Mr. Dean breathed in heavily, moving his eyes away and focusing somewhere on the far wall. He thought about Mr. Bentmoore's words.

Mr. Bentmoore was right, he had almost blown it with Michelle. But in the end, it had worked out. Better than worked out: he was already looking forward to Michelle's next visit, when he could introduce her to more types of anal stimulation. There were enemas, probes, speculums, ginger...different positions, different tools, hell, they could try different furniture: chairs, tables, desks...the possibilities were *endless*. And he planned on being the first one to try them all out on Michelle's delectable ass.

"Thanks for giving her to me," Mr. Dean said. For him, a moment of rare sincerity.

"No problem," Mr. Bentmoore replied. He looked down at his papers. "Now, I have another new guest visiting us next week, and it sounds like someone right up your alley...."

Khloe

KHLOE WAS A BORN and raised small town Nevada girl. At twenty-three, she had set out on her own and moved to Las Vegas for some adventure. Now twenty-five, she held a prestigious job at an upscale world renown casino, watching as fortunes were made, and lost, overnight.

She was generally happy with her life. She had a wide circle of friends, a great apartment, looks most women her age would kill for, and a fantastic career. She even had a boyfriend, one that made all her friends drool with longing and mad with jealously…or had, until last week.

The breakup had not been that much of a surprise. Tom and Khloe had been having problems for a while, at least in Khloe's mind. The surprise had been the method of the breakup.

Khloe had discovered Tom having an affair with her best friend. She had found this out in the worst possible way, too: by walking in on the two of them fucking…in Khloe's apartment. On Khloe's bed.

The shock had sent her zooming down into a deep depression, the likes of which she had not felt in years. She was frozen, stuck in that moment, the instant she had walked into her bedroom and found her boyfriend happily rutting her so-called best friend. The deep betrayal had cut her to the quick. Khloe's mind had pulled back and shut down from everything going on around her.

For Khloe, this reaction was all too typical. When confronted by something she couldn't handle, Khloe would often lock herself somewhere deep inside her own mind, somewhere cold and dark. It was like she became a puppet of herself: she would go through the motions, seem to be living life, and look fine from the outside...but inside, she would be completely numb. She wouldn't let herself feel anything at all.

A therapist had once told her this type of reaction was a coping mechanism, a way to protect herself from emotions too powerful for her to work through.

Khloe was also a cutter.

She cut throughout high school. She would escape into the girls' bathroom, lock the stall closed, pull the razor from her pocket, and sigh in pleasure as she felt the sharp glide of the blade slicing across her own skin. She would watch in fascination as the blood dripped into the toilet, swirling and floating down into the water. But she was always careful to cut far from exposed places, like arms or ankles. Her favorite places were under her breasts and along her inner thighs.

Then, the summer of her junior year, she'd begun to get more daring: she started cutting her stomach, hips, and along her upper arms.

At first, her parents had thought nothing of her reclusive behavior. They thought she was just acting like a normal, moody teenager. And if she didn't want to put on a bathing suit or wear the short shorts all the other girls were wearing, well, it was because she was becoming self-conscious about her looks, just like all women grew to be sooner or later.

It wasn't Khloe's mother who discovered her daughter's secret, but a cousin visiting from out of town, who had walked in on Khloe dressing one day, saw the nasty-looking scabs and bloody lines all over her body, and told Khloe's parents immediately.

Khloe found herself in therapy the next day.

Her parents had tried to support her. But they could never understand why she did it, and Khloe didn't know how to explain it to them: Sometimes, it was the only way for her to crack open the frozen shell she would build around her soul and *feel* again. The therapy had helped, it had kept her alive…but she still continued to cut.

Then, in college, Khloe was passed up for an internship she had desperately wanted. The disappointment had sent her running to the bathroom, blade in hand. A fellow student had walked in on her by the sink, knife at the ready, poised to cut open an artery.

The student did not called Khloe's parents. He did not tell the school. He drove Khloe to the Hotel Bentmoore, and personally delivered her into the safe hands of Mr. Shern, a host and Master of the hotel.

Khloe had not cut herself since.

She never saw that student again. The only thing she knew of him was his first name: Adam. She never got the chance to thank him for saving her life.

Khloe had remained at the hotel for a good long while. Then she went back to school, but continued to see Mr. Shern regularly. Then her visits grew shorter and farther between, until it was months before she realized how long it had been since she had seen Mr. Shern.

She had not gone back to the hotel at all since meeting Tom. She'd only spoken to Mr. Shern by phone, giving him an update on her life and letting him know she was okay.

But now she needed him more than ever.

The drive to the hotel seemed to take an eternity. When she finally saw the grand building of the Hotel Bentmoore come into view, she wanted to weep in relief.

Khloe pulled into the circular entrance, threw her keys to the valet, and ran inside. The guests in the lobby watched in curiosity as she ran to the front desk, sharing hushed words with the desk clerk.

Khloe didn't care what the other guests were thinking. All she wanted to know was how long she would have to wait to see Mr. Shern. To her relief, she learned she wouldn't have to wait long at all.

"Your host left strict instructions: once you arrive, you are not to be left alone, not even for a moment," the receptionist said gravely. "If you need to go up to your room to prepare for your visit with him, I will have to send someone up with you. But, if you prefer, I can have the bellhop take your suitcase up to your room, and have your liaison take you down to the activity room to see your host right now."

"I would like the liaison to take me down now," Khloe said quietly.

"Very good." The receptionist picked up the phone, pressed some buttons, and started muttering quietly into the receiver. Meanwhile, she pointed to a chair in the lobby right across from the desk, motioning for Khloe to have a seat. Khloe watched as the bellhop disappeared into the elevator with her suitcase.

A few minutes later Mr. Phillips, her liaison, arrived. "Please follow me, miss," he said softly, motioning Khloe towards the elevator. "Your host is expecting you."

Khloe almost smiled in relief--almost. She knew she was in for a hard time. Mr. Shern would not go easy on her, not after he saw....

She followed Mr. Phillips quietly, feeling her heartbeat speed up as she walked. But finally, she broke into a smile: she was feeling nervous, she realized. It was the first time in days she had felt anything at all except icy desperation.

Inside the activity room, Khloe closed her eyes and took a deep breath, feeling some of the numbness that had been enveloping her begin to melt away. The next hour or two would not be pleasant, but just feeling anything again, excitement, fear, trepidation, *anything*, was a welcome change from feeling nothing.

"Khloe," Mr. Shern greeted her from the center of the room. "What's happened?"

"Tom broke up with me." Her voice was flat. Indifferent. Like she didn't even care, even though her very soul was shattering into pieces.

"I'm sorry, Khloe. But you mentioned to me on the phone last time we talked, you thought things with Tom might not last. What happened?"

"He cheated on me with my best friend. I found them together, fucking on my bed. *On my bed.*" Her voice cracked. "They've already moved in together, into her place. I'm not talking to either one of them. I wish they were dead. I wish...I wish *I* were dead." The admission seemed to surprise even her, and she looked down in shame.

"Khloe, what have you done?"

"I...I...." She couldn't finish. Mr. Shern studied her with furrowed brows.

"Get undressed," he ordered.

"Sir, I--"

"Undressed, now, all the way," he repeated. "I will see the damage for myself."

Khloe began to peel off her clothes, lifting away her shirt and bra before moving down to her shoes and socks.

She did her pants and underwear last, stripping them off her legs and stepping away from them slowly. As she did, she could hear Mr. Shern's sharp intake of breath.

"Under the light," he said. Khloe moved to stand under the ceiling light, her head bowed. "Spread your legs."

Khloe spread her legs until they were about shoulder length apart. She kept her eyes closed; she did not see Mr. Shern's expression of deep concern. He knelt down and traced the fresh lines of cuts along her inner thighs, grazing them lightly with his finger.

He got up and circled her slowly, checking every inch of her skin for new cuts. When he was sure he had found them all, he stopped and faced her.

"Look at me, Khloe," he said. When she didn't obey immediately, he picked up her chin. Khloe opened her eyes. Her host was standing mere inches away from her face. "How old are these? How recently did you cut yourself?"

"On the way over to the hotel, in the car," she whispered. "I thought I could wait until I got here, but I just couldn't, so I pulled over...."

"The razor you used. You brought it with you? Or did you dispose of it before you got to the hotel?"

"I brought it with me, Sir."

"It's in with your luggage?"

"No, Sir. I left it in my car."

"When you leave this room, I will have someone take your car keys from you, and they will search your car for the razor, and dispose of it. You will not be touching it again."

"Yes, Sir." They both knew how significant it was, keeping the razor she used to cut herself. Once Khloe designated a certain razor as her "cutting razor," it was as if the blade would take on a life of its own. It would call to her, begging her to use it again, to let it slice into her soft flesh and make her bleed.

"You will have to be punished for this, Khloe."

"Yes."

"But not tonight. Tonight, you need help."

"Yes, Sir." Her words were choked off as something in her chest suddenly squeezed and released. A cry? A sob? Was some emotion finally injecting itself into her shell of a body?

Mr. Shern walked over to the wide wardrobe and returned holding two leather suspension cuffs.

"Hands."

Khloe dutifully presented her hands, and Mr. Shern attached the cuffs. They were made of thick leather, wide and strong, and each had two buckles: one to go around the wrist, and one to go around the palm. Snap-hooks were already attached to the D-rings on the outside of each cuff.

Once the cuffs were on, Mr. Shern took her by the arm and brought her beneath the suspension bar. It was long, made of iron, and had rings on each end for the snap-hooks. A length of chain ran from end to end, and welded to the center was an O-ring. Another piece of chain looped through the O-ring and went straight up to the ceiling, disappearing through a tight hole.

Working silently, Mr. Shern lifted Khloe's hands and, one at a time, snapped the hooks of her cuffs into the rings of the suspension bar. Then, he walked to a switch on the far wall, and turned on the mechanism to lift Khloe into the air. Khloe went up, and up, until her body was stretched taut and her toes were a good two feet off the ground.

Satisfied, Mr. Shern turned off the switch and went back to the wardrobe to retrieve the tool he would be using on Khloe's pale and vulnerable body.

"I'm not going to start slow, Khloe," he said. "I don't think there would be any point. You need the pain. Now let's get this good and done."

Khloe looked down. Mr. Shern was holding a long, thick, coiled whip. Khloe knew that whip well. She had hoped never to see it again.

No, please, don't. She could hear the words in her head, but they were an echo, like hallow sounds coming from down a dark tunnel. They were soft and weak. They would not rise up.

Mr. Shern took his place behind her. "You know what has to happen for you to make this stop," he said. "How long it takes is completely up to you."

With that, he let the whip fly. A hiss crackled through the air, and then a snap. The end of the whip bit into Khloe's trim and smooth rump.

The first impact hit her right across her buttocks, snapping into her soft flesh with a resounding crack. Khloe flinched, but said nothing. She barely felt it: it was like nothing more than a gentle graze.

Hiss SNAP

The second crack of the whip hurt a bit more, but nothing too bad; more like the shocking stab of a quick needle, barely felt, and only after it had left the skin. Khloe closed her eyes and held her breath.

Hiss SNAP

The pain was worse this time, but Khloe only felt it in slow degrees.

Hiss SNAP

The tail of the whip came down again, and again, and again, welting lines into her thighs, hips, and buttocks. Each one felt a little worse.

The whip was chipping pieces off her icy shell, but slowly. Too slowly.

Finally, Khloe could feel the pain through the safe buffer of her numbing cocoon, and she began to gasp with each one.

The whip was starting to feel ugly now: Khloe was squeezing her eyes shut and whimpering with each hiss of the whip. But still, she said nothing. She was not completely free of her cold inner prison just yet.

The next flick was particularly vicious, cutting across two previous lines of welts, and Khloe finally cried out.

"Oh, that hurt--"

Mr. Shern let fly another one, cutting into the deep muscles of her thighs.

"Oh God, it hurts, stop--"

He circled around to her other side, hitting her from a different angle, working methodically down her body.

"Oh Jesus, please, stop, it hurts, it hurts--"

Mr. Shern kept his aim lower now, working her upper legs. Khloe began to bellow with each slice of the whip, struggling against her bonds.

"Please, please, PLEASE!"

Mr. Shern didn't let up. In fact, his blows became more brutal, hitting her harder and faster. Khloe began to scream, her voice rising to a shrieking trill every time she heard the hiss of the whip.

"Please, please!" her voice broke down into a bray of sobs. But it still wasn't enough. Mr. Shern knew it, and Khloe knew it, too. She had not been broken yet, not completely.

Only when the tail of the whip came down in a perfect line right beneath her ass-cheeks for a third time, making her feel like her body was being severed in two, did Khloe finally break. She screamed loud and long, breaking through her protective numbing field.

"BALLOONS, BALLOONS," she cried, her voice hysterical. It was her safeword, the word Mr. Shern needed to hear to know Khloe was broken, shattered, her frozen shell dissolved. From the beginning of Khloe's ordeal, they had both known he would not stop until Khloe could bring herself to scream out her safeword.

Mr. Shern dropped the whip and ran over to the wall to flip the switch that would lower Khloe to the floor.

Khloe came down to the ground, but her feet could not support her. She crumpled. Mr. Shern kept lowering the bar until Khloe had sunk into a heap on the floor, her cheek resting on cold stone. Her arms remained high, locked in the restraints.

Working quickly, Mr. Shern unbuckled her cuffs, lowered her arms gently to her sides, and took her in his arms. Khloe was sobbing, and swaying a bit from the force of her wails.

Her ass hurt, her back hurt, her legs hurt, but most of all, her heart hurt.

"It's okay now, Khloe, it's okay, I've got you." Mr. Shern wrapped his arms around her, holding her close. Khloe clung to him, crying into his chest.

"It hurts. It hurts so bad. It hurts so bad," she said over and over. She didn't mean the welts from the whip.

"I know. I know." Mr. Shern's voice was soft and soothing. He smoothed her hair away from her face as he rocked her and held her tight, right there on the activity room floor, comforting her as best he could.

This was Khloe's aftercare, and it was just as important as the breaking. Mr. Shern would hold her as she cried out her heartache and misery; he would keep her safe as she took these first crucial steps to putting herself back together, and he would not let her go until he knew she was safe to be on her own again.

As Khloe's sobs died down, her body racked now and then by a reflexive heave of her breath, Mr. Shern continued to hold her close, rubbing her back and arms with gentle hands. Finally, Khloe calmed down, and lifted her head away to look at him.

"I'm feeling better now," she said, her voice high like a child's.

"Good. I'm glad. It took quite a bit--your ass and thighs will be covered in welts for a while. But at least they will heal."

"Yes, Sir," she sighed with a small catch in her voice. She understood the underlying message: the welts would hurt like hell, but eventually, they would fade. The cuts she had given herself, on the other hand...those cuts might end up giving her scars she would have for the rest of her life. She hoped not. She had enough scars.

"I think you can get dressed now," he said, helping her up. He found her clothes and handed them to her one piece at a time as Khloe dressed herself. They both said nothing.

Khloe moved slowly, feeling the fabric rubbing against her skin as she donned them, marveling at how scratchy and encompassing they felt. She breathed in the room air, and felt slightly sickened by the smell of her own sweat.

It was always like this after Mr. Shern broke her: her senses would go into overdrive, and she would become hyper-aware of every touch, ever sound, every smell. It was as if her numbness had been a scab encasing her whole body, mind and soul, and now that Mr. Shern had ripped it off, her senses could work again.

"There's one more thing, Khloe," Mr. Shern said. "Your punishment."

He walked over to the wardrobe, and when he came back, he was holding thick pieces of pliant leather that hung down from his hand. Khloe recognized them very well. She began to cry.

"No," she said. "Please, Sir, no."

"You broke the trust. You lost control. I now assume it. You will wear these until I can trust you again. Hands," he repeated.

Weeping quietly, Khloe held out her hands, and felt Mr. Shern encircle her wrists with the wide leather bands that looked almost like bracelets--almost. They were soft and pliable, and could have passed for kinky jewelry, but Khloe new better.

Each band had a small buckle, fitted with a tiny miniature padlock.

They symbolized the fact that her body was no longer her own: it now belonged to her host, Mr. Shern, until he decided he could trust her again. They were a sign of ownership.

Mr. Shern locked the padlocks now, listening for the click, ensuring that Khloe would not be able to take the bands off until he released her at his own discretion.

The cuffs could be hidden under long sleeves, if she chose to hide them. Not that anyone at the Hotel Bentmoore would look at them twice--marks and symbols of possession could be found everywhere at the Hotel Bentmoore. Guests, especially those who lived the lifestyle, grew accustomed to them quickly. Slave collars, chastity belts, henna marks, tattoos...they were all par for the course.

But Khloe hated what they represented. She was a woman with an independent nature, always had been. She hated the idea of someone else having any kind of control over her.

Her body now belonged to Mr. Shern. The bands would be a constant reminder of his control. He would always be watching, always checking to make sure she wasn't abusing his property. The point was simple: make Khloe understand her body was no longer hers to cut. She knew their purpose, recognized their benefit, but hated them just the same.

This time, she couldn't refuse. Mr. Shern was right, she had broken the trust, and this was more than just a punishment--it was his way of letting her know she would have to prove herself to him again before he'd be willing to take the bands off.

So she held her hands out, and felt the buckles tighten, and heard the tiny padlocks click, and cried in shame. But some of her tears were of relief, too: relief that someone *was* watching over her, and making sure she didn't try to hurt herself again. She didn't feel safe anywhere else in the world as much as she did at the Hotel Bentmoore.

"I will call the liaison now," Mr. Shern said, letting her arms drop. Khloe continued to silently cry. "I will not order you to eat dinner. I doubt you could stomach it right now. But I will have you woken early tomorrow, and you will join the other guests in the dining room. You will eat what I have ordered for you, and nothing else. Do you understand?"

"Yes, Sir."

"After breakfast, you will return to your room and have one hour to rest and prepare yourself before your liaison returns you here, to me. When you come to me, you will be dressed in loose clothes, no underwear, and no bra. Is that understood?"

Khloe took a deep breath. She hated being ordered around like this. Hated it, hated it, hated it. "Yes, Sir."

"Good." Mr. Shern went to press the button by the door that would summon the liaison. "Rub some of that ointment we keep in the guests' bathrooms on your welts before you go to sleep."

"Yes, Sir."

"Don't forget, Khloe," he said in a threatening voice. Khloe understood: if she forgot, she'd be getting a punishment far worse than the wristbands.

"No, Sir."

The liaison arrived and opened the door.

Mr. Shern grabbed Khloe by the arm. Turning her around, he wiped the tears off her cheeks with a gentle thumb. "You're going to be okay, Khloe," he said, his voice soft. "I give you my word. I will not let you leave the hotel until I know you'll be safe on your own. And I keep my promises, don't I?"

Khloe looked at him with longing, gratitude, and complete submission. "Yes, Sir. Thank you, Sir."

"Have a good night's sleep. We're going to have a lot of work tomorrow, putting you back together."

"Yes, Sir."

Khloe joined her liaison in the hallway, and followed him down to the elevator.

***

The next morning, Khloe awoke to the sound of the phone ringing: the polite wake-up call from the front desk.

It was seven o'clock in the morning, and time for Khloe to get dressed and head to the dining room. She sat up and rubbed the sleep from her eyes. She wanted desperately to go back to sleep, but knew better. They would no doubt call Mr. Shern if she didn't show up in the dining room soon.

She washed and dressed quickly, putting on a long-sleeved sweater to hide the leather bands around her wrists, and pair of comfortable jeans. She might look a little odd, wearing such a warm top, but Khloe didn't care. Better to look a little too warm than have people staring at her bands, wondering at her status.

But as she carefully tugged the long sleeves over the bands, Khloe remembered how she'd thrown the heavy sweater into her bag without even thinking about it. Had she known, even then, that her host might make her wear the cuffs again? Is that why she'd packed the sweater in the first place?

Had she been *hoping* Mr. Shern would make her wear the bands again? Hoping for the forced submission they would grant her?

The dining room, thank goodness, was relatively empty. There was one couple sitting in the far corner, and another sitting at the opposite end, but that was all.

Khloe looked over to the couple closest to her, a man and a woman. A shiny metal slave collar adorned the man's neck. The woman was feeding him bits of French toast off her plate. Khloe watched in fascination as the man carefully bit the food off her fork with his teeth, staring at her reverently as he chewed. They sat in silence, the man giving his companion his full adoration, the woman only granting him passing glances.

At the opposite corner sat the other couple, two women who looked for all the world like they were just two friends enjoying each other's company over a tasty meal. But Khloe noticed one of the women sat very strangely, leaning all the way to the side of her seat. Every time the woman shifted her weight, her eyes would grow wide in shock, and her face would contort with pain. The other woman would stop talking for a brief second, grinning wickedly. Then they would both continue with their conversation as if nothing had happened.

Khloe's server arrived. The first thing he did was ask for her room number. Khloe gave it to him quietly. His eyes filled with secret knowledge, then he turned and glided away. He didn't even bother to ask if she wanted some coffee.

A few minutes later, her food arrived, and Khloe looked down at her tray in disappointment. They had given her toast, one scrambled egg, a fruit cup, and a glass of cranberry juice. That was it. Before the server walked away, he made sure to take all the condiments and spices *off* the table. Khloe would not even be allowed to put salt on her egg.

Khloe knew why Mr. Shern had picked these foods: they would feed her and keep her energy up, but not upset her stomach for what was to come. Which told her something *was* coming, something unpleasant, and Mr. Shern knew whatever it was, it was bad enough to make Khloe feel physically sick from it.

The realization scared her so much, Khloe lost her appetite. But she ate the food anyway, knowing if she didn't, her host would probably be told about that, too.

She finished quickly, then went back to her room to change and wait to be summoned. The hour went by slowly, and Khloe wondered if this was Mr. Shern's way of torturing her a little bit, making her wait and wonder what he had in store for her. But the liaison arrived on time, and Khloe followed dutifully.

He brought her back to the same activity room she had been in the night before. It looked basically the same: empty, except for the bed and the large wardrobe. Mr. Shern stood right in front of the door, waiting to greet her as soon as she walked in, and Khloe's eyes locked onto him as she heard the door close.

"Khloe." Mr. Shern's voice was deep and soothing, and immediately set her at ease. Whatever it was he had planned for her, it would be to help her, not hurt her. Well, it would hurt, she could be sure of that...but that wouldn't be the main objective. The main objective was to see Khloe healthy and safe, and Mr. Shern would do what was needed to see that happen. It was like going to the doctor, Khloe thought: sometimes they had to stick you with needles, but it was only to help you get better.

I hope he's not going to stick with me needles, she thought, and shuddered. She looked around the room to see what evidence she could find of what lay in store for her.

Only then did she notice the other man in the room. He was facing away from the door, handling something on the bed, working quietly. The man was bent over, but Khloe could guess he would be about average height, maybe even a couple inches shorter than Mr. Shern. He

103

looked exceptionally wide, with a linebacker's body: muscles bulged from everywhere and stretched across his white linen shirt.

Like all the hosts at the Hotel Bentmoore, he was wearing tailored slacks, pressed and belted, but while Mr. Shern's were a dark gray, his were a light crème. His hair was a rich, chocolate brown, cut impeccably. Khloe had a sudden deep need for the man to turn around so she could see his face.

"Khloe," Mr. Shern said, "I've asked my associate, Mr. Cox, to join us today. Mr. Cox has certain unique talents, and I thought we might utilize them." Mr. Shern twisted around to peer at the other man. "Mr. Cox?"

Hearing the prompt, Mr. Cox looked over his shoulder, and Khloe got a view of the side of his face. His eyes, like his hair, were a rich creamy brown, and slanted in the most seductive way. But Mr. Cox had not put down what he was holding in his hands when he had turned, and Khloe got a glimpse of what it was: rope.

Her eyes cut over to the bed, and she saw with a start that it was covered with lengths of rope. The rope seemed to be organized by length and thickness, with the smaller pieces on one side and the longer, thicker pieces on the other. There were other pieces of equipment on the bed, too: hooks, snaps, and rings, all made of heavy metal, all with holes for the rope to snake through. One particularly large and curved hook had a thick ball welded to the end, and Khloe's eyes widened in fear.

"Khloe, look at me," Mr. Shern ordered, bringing Khloe's attention back to him. "Mr. Cox is a Shibari artist. Do you know what Shibari is?"

Khloe shook her head no.

"It is the art of rope bondage," Mr. Shern explained. "Mr. Cox is going to tie you up. Have you ever seen pictures of someone tied up in rope before?"

This time, Khloe could slowly nod her head yes. She *had* come across pictures of women tied up in intricate designs and knots before. Khloe had always thought the pictures were beautiful, with the women laced in twining patterns of rope. Sometimes, the women in the pictures were suspended in midair. Was that what they were going to do to her?

"It will take some time for Mr. Cox to get you tied and positioned the way he wants. You will have to pose for him. You will follow his instructions to the letter, and do everything he says. He is your host now, too, and you will show him all the respect and obedience you show me. Is that understood?"

"Yes, Sir." Khloe cast her eyes down in servitude.

"Good. Now take off your clothes."

Khloe glanced at Mr. Cox: he had put the rope down, and was looking at her with open curiosity. It was clear he was waiting to see if she would follow orders. Khloe looked down at the floor and took a deep, nervous breath.

"Khloe, get undressed," Mr. Shern repeated.

"Yes, Sir," she replied this time. She did not look at either man as she began to strip.

Her dress was long and billowy, and zippered up the back. All Khloe had to do was lower the zipper and let the dress fall. The dress pooled around her feet like feathery gauze, and Khloe pressed her legs together, feeling the room air against her skin. As instructed, she had worn nothing underneath.

Mustering her courage, she stood up straight and tall, resisting the urge to cover herself. It would serve no point. These men would ultimately see every part of her, any they desired, whether she liked it or not. Mr. Shern certainly knew her body inside and out better than she did. Probably better than her doctor did.

Khloe stood as proudly as she could, but kept her eyes downcast, unable to look either man in the eyes.

Mr. Cox began to circle her, studying her shapely, feminine body. Khloe's nipples puckered, dimpling the flesh of her petite, cupped breasts. Her mouth went dry under his close scrutiny.

"What about the nipples?" Mr. Cox asked. Khloe jumped. Mr. Cox's voice was deep, and had a slight accent Khloe couldn't place. But he was not speaking to her, he was speaking to Mr. Shern.

Khloe looked up: Mr. Cox had come to stand right in front of her to watch the way her nipples hardened and distended. A look of in mild interest covered his features. "How sensitive are her nipples?"

"Not overly so," Mr. Shern replied. "But I've never tested their limits before." Mr. Cox nodded in response. Khloe straightened her back, feeling a bit of irritation.

She did not like being spoken about as if she wasn't in the room, and she certainly didn't like listening to two men have a conversation about her nipples, even if they were two hosts of the Hotel Bentmoore.

"The thighs will be a problem," Mr. Cox continued, looking at the scabbed, healing cuts lining Khloe's legs. "I will have to avoid that area..." Khloe looked down in shame. "But it will be fine," Mr. Cox said, noticing her reaction. Khloe raised her head: Mr. Cox was giving her a gentle smile. "The ankles will hold, and I can bend the knees...." He continued to circle her. "The hair...I can use the hair...."

"Remember what I said, Cox. It should not hurt beyond a mild ache. The pain is not the point. At least, not that of the ropes."

"I remember. I assure you, the ropes won't hurt her. But it'll help keep her in place--which I think will be necessary."

"Yes, that's true."

Mr. Cox gave her one more cursory glance, then rubbed his hands together, looking eager.

"Let's get started," he said. "Khloe, I want you to come over here by the bed. Stand straight, with your hands in front of you."

Khloe did as told, stepping out of the pool of her dress and walking towards him with silent, careful steps. She put her arms out in front of her, ready for what was to come.

Mr. Cox began to manipulate her stance, turning and twisting her arms and hands. He had her place her palms together, then her forearms together, and raised her arms by the shoulders. Then, he grabbed some rope from the bed, and began to bind Khloe with it.

The rope was only a little coarse, and didn't itch or chafe her skin too much. It was only when Mr. Cox looped or tightened it that it felt a bit irritating.

Her arms took a long time: Mr. Cox was sheathing them in rope, lining and knitting them together like a pair of sleeves. By the time he was done, Khloe couldn't pull her arms away from each other even the smallest bit.

But looking down at them, she quickly decided the rope looked beautiful. She felt sensual and erotic, like one of the women she'd seen in the pictures. Her pelvis tightened and her nipples puckered as a jolt of pure arousal shot from her clit all the way up her spine.

"I see you like the way it looks," Mr. Cox said, giving her a knowing smile. "I hope you like the rest. Now put your feet together, I'm going to do your legs."

He knotted her ankles and calves the same way he had her arms, with tight, binding knots, working steadily. At one point, Mr. Shern had to come and stand next to her to ensure she wouldn't fall: her legs were pressed so tightly together, the slightest movement threatened to send her crashing to the floor. She thought he would keep going up her thighs, but Mr. Cox only worked the rope up to slightly past her knees, leaving clear her cuts.

Next came her torso, and Khloe could see from Mr. Cox's expression this was the hardest part. He was being very careful now, deciding how many times to loop the rope and what kinds of knots to use. He began to use the metal rings now, too, pressing them against Khloe's body and weaving the rope around and through, until Khloe's torso was neatly lined with rings. One ring was even snuggled between her soft tits.

"Take a breath," Mr. Cox ordered. Khloe sucked in her breath and held it, and Mr. Cox began to circle the rope around her breasts, crossing and weaving it like stitch work, until her breasts were laced and tied down snug. The rope ran on either side of her nipples, rubbing every time she moved. It didn't hurt, but it felt strange, and she couldn't do anything about it to move the rope away.

As Mr. Cox continued to bind Khloe's body, she could feel her mind going blank. Her breath slowed, her eyes closed, and her thoughts drifted away, as if she were in a daze.

She was completely immobilized, trussed up tight, and yet, she wasn't panicking. She was scared, yes, worried about what was to come. But she was letting the fear in, letting it lap against her thoughts like a gentle tide. She was entering a new level of subspace, submitting to her body's reactions to being tied and controlled, and it felt good.

"Almost done," Mr. Cox's voice rang out, waking her from her trance. "But she needs to lean over the bed for this."

"Khloe, I'm going to help you lean you over the bed," Mr. Shern instructed, grabbing her gently over the elbow to steady her. With her host's help, Khloe hopped over to the bed, leaning on his support. The bed was now almost empty of rope, and most of the rings were gone. But the wicked hook still remained, and Mr. Cox now picked it up and walked with it behind her.

"What--"

"Lean forward. Elbows on the bed," Mr. Shern ordered. Khloe bent her body forward and rested her weight on her elbows. Her forearms were wrapped up tight, and the pose wasn't very comfortable.

"Lower," Mr. Shern said. "Head down." Khloe bent lower, folding her body as much as she could with her arms and legs tied the way they were. She could hear Mr. Cox's footsteps stopping, and sensed him right behind her.

"What are--"

"Mr. Cox is going to put the hook up your ass," Mr. Shern said, speaking in a straightforward manner. "I will help him. You will not move."

"Please, Sir, I--"

"We will go slow. I know it's going to feel uncomfortable at first, but it needs to be done. Stay down, make as much noise as you need to, but don't move."

"Sir, please!"

"She can't be struggling so much. Shall I cuff her down?" Mr. Cox offered.

"Yes, do that," Mr. Shern agreed. Khloe could hear the wardrobe opening, and clanging chains being dragged across the floor. A second later, Mr. Cox was standing in front of her from the other side of the bed, attaching one large, leather cuff around both her bound hands. He pulled at the chain snaking away from the cuff and stretched her forward until Khloe's stomach was pressed hard into the edge of the bed.

When the chain was taut, Mr. Cox looped it into a bolt on the side of the bed frame. Khloe was now chained down to the bed, bent over, and about to take a hook up the ass.

"Spread her cheeks, please," Mr. Cox said to Mr. Shern.

"Please, please--" Khloe began to panic.

"Has she never had anything anal before?" Mr. Cox asked, his voice only mildly curious.

"She has, many times, but it's not exactly her favorite activity," Mr. Shern replied. Stepping to her side, he grabbed her ass cheeks in both hands and pulled them apart, gripping hard. Khloe could feel the room air hitting her most private, delicate parts. She would have run if she could have.

Something slick and wide touched her spasming anus, and Khloe jumped.

"It's just his finger," Mr. Shern said. "He's preparing you."

Khloe whimpered and buried her face into the mattress. The finger was coating her asshole with lube, poking impertinently into her sphincter a few times with shallow thrusts.

"This will feel cold," Mr. Shern said, letting her know to prepare herself for the ball. Khloe whimpered louder.

Mr. Shern had spoken the truth, Khloe had taken his cock up her ass before. But it was nothing like this: impersonal, calculated, a mere setup for what was to come.

The cold, slippery edge of the ball touched her asshole, and Khloe could feel her entire body tense up.

"Try to relax, Khloe," Mr. Shern said. Khloe said nothing, but closed her eyes and took in a deep, shuddering breath, trying to relax. The metal had obviously been lubed, too, and felt slick against her warm flesh.

The ball was pressed in, pushing against her sensitive sphincter that clenched and tightened in protest. But with gentle, steady pressure, the ball began to slide in, dilating her anus with an aching force.

"Oh, ohhh--" Khloe let out a long, plaintive moan, feeling her asshole being stretched wide. The ball was not overly large, but it was hard and completely unforgiving, and Khloe tried to press her stomach further into the bed to get away from the relentless pressure. This didn't feel sexual at all. This felt like an invasion.

"Easy now, easy," Mr. Shern said. Khloe had no idea if he was speaking to her or Mr. Cox. For a brief second, the ball stopped its forward motion, and Khloe had a chance to breathe. Then it was moving in again, pressing home, sliding up her narrow channel and past the tight ring of muscle.

Khloe let out a high-pitched yell as the ball stretched her insides until she felt like she was about to rip apart. But it kept going.

"You're doing great, Khloe," Mr. Cox said soothingly. "The widest part is almost in." He didn't stop his relentless pressing, and when Khloe tried to move her body away, he moved with her, letting her body's attempts to push the ball out help him press it in even further.

Khloe's yells grew into a series of howls as she felt the ball stretching her past all endurance. She was at Mr. Cox's mercy, and Mr. Cox seemed to be an expert at following the gyrations of Khloe's hips.

Finally, Khloe could feel the hook slide the rest of the way through. Her ass seemed to naturally swallow it up, until she could feel the curve of the cold metal resting against her back and ass crease. Inside, she felt stuffed, but her asshole was no longer aching quite so badly.

"There we go," Mr. Shern said, satisfied. He released her ass cheeks, and they snapped closed around the hook. "You can stand up now."

Mr. Cox moved to uncuff her hands from the bed, and Khloe gingerly stood up. She could feel the ball making its presence known inside her body, hitting different nerve points as she moved.

"Let's get her under the suspension bar," Mr. Cox said. Khloe's eyes widened in alarm. They *did* mean to hang her in midair.

Both men stood on either side and grabbed her by the arms. Using slow, tiny hops, they moved Khloe to the space of floor right beneath the suspension bar.

Mr. Shern went to the wall to flip the switch, and the suspension bar came down. Khloe realized the thing had been improvised: instead of one bar going across, there were now two bars that crisscrossed each other, forming an X, and what looked like pulleys on two sides.

"Time to fly, Khloe," Mr. Cox said. Getting the long, heavy pieces of rope off the bed, he began to loop them around the bars, securing them inside the metal rings going down Khloe's body and between her arms and legs.

It took time, and the use of the pulleys, and more rope. Khloe began to faze out again. She was completely powerless, tied up like a pig being put on a spit, and privy to whatever it was they wanted to do. She could hear her two hosts talking on either side of her, but she wasn't listening anymore. The hard ball ensconced up her ass didn't even bother her like it had. She was swimming in and out of subspace.

A few minutes later, Khloe was jolted back to reality when she felt her feet leave the ground. She made a tiny sound of surprise. She was being lifted up in a cradle pose, arms up, legs up, head bent slightly back.

"Let's anchor your head," Mr. Cox said, coming around to her side. He looped some rope under Khloe's shoulders, secured the pieces through a couple rings down her torso, and then attached another ring through Khloe's hair, resting it at the base of her scalp. Khloe's head was now supported.

"Almost done," Mr. Cox announced. Using the same ring at the back of her head, he looped more rope through, but trailed it down her back this time, and then, to Khloe's dismay, stretched it through the metal ring at the base of the anal hook resting against the crack of her ass.

"Done," Mr. Cox pronounced, stepping away from her. Khloe glanced down to look at him: his eyes were bright and shiny, filled with proud accomplishment, and a heady dose of lust.

"Can I lift her up more?" Mr. Shern asked.

"Sure, she's good."

"Khloe, are you in pain anywhere?"

"No Sir, I'm not," Khloe said, surprised by her own answer. The ball still felt hard and huge stuffed up inside her, and her nipples were tingling, rubbing against the rope, but she didn't hurt anywhere. In fact, she felt good. She felt...light. Carefree. The weight of the world had not been lifted off her shoulders, but she had certainly been lifted off the weight of the world.

Mr. Shern rose the suspension bars until Khloe was high in the air, her ass a good three feet off the ground.

"Relax, Khloe," Mr. Shern said in his gentle voice. "Just relax. Close your eyes."

The two men made no noise. The room was quiet. Khloe could feel herself relax into the ropes, her thoughts dissipating. For all she knew, she could have been three miles off the ground instead of three feet. Gravity had no hold on her. Her body, and mind, felt free.

She was flying.

"Khloe, can you hear me?" Mr. Shern's voice came to her as if from the other side of the moon.

"Yes."

"Do you feel okay? Relaxed?"

"Oh, yes."

"Good."

He let her sway for another minute. Khloe closed her eyes and sighed in delight.

"Khloe, I want you tell me about Tom."

Khloe's eyes snapped open.

"What?"

"Tell me about Tom."

"What about Tom?"

"Tell me what you liked about him."

"What, now? Please, Sir, I--"

Smack!

Mr. Shern had retrieved a long, plexiglass cane from the wardrobe, and had smacked it against Khloe's up-turned ass. Khloe shrieked in surprise and pain.

"Tell me about Tom," he repeated.

Khloe could barely put two thoughts together. The last thing she wanted to be thinking about was Tom.

"I can't remember, Sir," she said.

Smack!

Mr. Shern's voice was cold. "He was your boyfriend. I know you were with him for a reason. Now tell me what you liked about him."

Khloe closed her eyes and swallowed. Tears gathered in her eyes. Whether it was from the physical pain from the cane, or the emotional pain from her memories, she didn't know.

"He was patient," she whispered. "He always took the time to explain things to me, even if I felt stupid for not getting it right away. He asked me my opinion on stuff. And he was fun to be around. He was always thinking up new places to go, new things to see. He was good with my friends. In fact, they loved him. They thought he was the perfect guy."

The tears were flowing hard now, dripping from her face to the floor.

Mr. Shern circled her head.

"Did you love him?"

"Yes."

"Are you sure?"

Khloe was silent.

"Did you think the two of you would last forever? Did you see yourself spending the rest of your life with him?"

Khloe closed her eyes. Mr. Shern didn't smack her again with the cane: he knew she was taking the time to articulate the words stuck in her head.

"No, I didn't," she finally muttered, her voice flat. "I knew Tom and I wouldn't last."

"Why not?"

Khloe pressed her lips together, this time in an act of defiance, and Mr. Shern snapped the cane against her ass once more. Khloe squeezed her face in agony. She tried to lift her butt away from him, but found she couldn't, not with the ball lodged up her asshole.

"Why didn't you think you and Tom be together forever, Khloe?" Mr. Shern's voice grew sharp.

"Because he never really understood me," Khloe cried. "He was always trying to explain things to me, like I was some kind of dumb kid he needed to teach things to, but he never really got what I was thinking. He acted like he appreciated my opinion on stuff, but I knew..." her voice cracked.

"What did you know?"

"I knew most of the time, he was just patronizing me. He would nod his head and look at me like he cared what I was saying, but really, I don't think he did. I think he was trying not to hurt my feelings. I don't think he ever really got me. And how can you love someone you don't understand? Someone you think is stupid?"

"You think he thought you were stupid?"

"Yes."

"Do you think you're stupid?"

"No." This had been an issue they'd had to deal with in the past, for Mr. Shern to get Khloe to realize how smart and clever she really was. "I'm not stupid, but maybe I should have been able to see my boyfriend was cheating on me."

"Were there any signs?"

"No," Khloe sighed. "The two of them hid the affair well."

"So you realize it's not your fault you didn't know he was cheating on you with your best friend."

"Yes. But…."

"But?"

"How could he do that to me? How could anyone do that to someone they're supposed to love? I thought he loved me. But he didn't, not really. I don't know if he ever loved me at all."

Khloe began to sob. She wished she could hide her face in her hands, or at least wipe away her tears. She struggled a bit in the ropes, but all that did was make her sway.

Mr. Shern had pity on her and got her a tissue, holding it to her nose and telling her to blow. He let her cry for a while, wiping her face every now and then, and letting her emotions run out. Finally, the tears slowed.

"How do you feel right now?"

"Right now? Right now I feel tied up and horrible," Khloe spat.

Mr. Shern grinned. "Good," he said. He walked away, out of her line of vision. Khloe was left alone to deal with her surprise, and to think.

She did feel angry, and hurt, and betrayed…but she realized: those were *normal* things to feel. That's what she was *supposed* to be feeling: anger and pain. That was how other people dealt with a bad breakup, by letting themselves feel the hurt, not by shutting themselves down so they couldn't feel anything at all. She needed to let the pain in if she was going to heal.

Up here, suspended off the earth, Khloe had let her emotions in without realizing it. Now she let them ride over the terrain of her heart, pounding it raw. But she wasn't getting trampled and destroyed. The pain was there, but it wasn't overwhelming her. She wasn't afraid.

Khloe didn't try to hold it back anymore. She let go, purging herself of her misery, cleansing her soul with her screams of betrayal. By the time her voice gave out and her breath slowed, she felt much better. The ropes cradled her in comfort, and the gentle swaying soothed her as she quieted down.

She breathed easy, thinking she was done.

But Mr. Shern was not yet satisfied. As he came back into her line of vision, Khloe saw his lips were frowning in a thin line.

"You were hurt so badly because you found Tom fucking your best friend?"

"Yes." Her voice was slow, almost drunk.

"I don't think so, Khloe. Yes, it must have been a shock for you to find them like that. But you admitted a moment ago you never felt like he loved you. Your first reaction when you saw them together should have been one of righteous fury, maybe even vindication, having an excuse to break up with him, at least one that your friends would understand. But you were so hurt, you shut down completely."

"What, I should have been *happy* I saw the two of them together?"

Smack! Mr. Shern slapped the cane against her fiery bottom.

"Don't get lippy. And no, you shouldn't have been happy. But if you really had already decided you and Tom were doomed to fail, this shouldn't have made you go back to cutting. Which makes me think there's something you're not telling me."

"Like what?"

"You tell me. Why did you cut yourself?"

"Because I was hurt."

"You've been hurt worse than this, and you've gotten through it. I know you well enough to know by now you should have been strong enough to handle this without cutting."

"I thought he loved me."

"No, you didn't. You told me yourself, you didn't even think he respected you. You should have been happy to be free of him, not shouldering all the blame of what he did to you. But you're internalizing the pain, taking his betrayal personally...which makes me think he did something, or said something, that makes you think what he did is somehow your fault. What was it, Khloe? What is it you're not telling me?"

Khloe remained silent. Mr. Shern sighed, and swung the cane at Khloe's thighs.

Smack! Smack! Smack! Smack!

Khloe twisted and screamed. Every time she moved her hips, the ball in her ass stretched and ached.

"What do you want from me!" She screeched.

Mr. Shern continued to rain the blows down on her ass and thighs. "Tell me what was really going on," he said, his voice loud over the blows. "Tell me why you felt the need to cut yourself."

"Because I saw my boyfriend fucking my best friend!"

"That's not the real reason."

"I don't know what to tell you!"

"I think you do, Khloe." The swipes of the cane kept coming, and Khloe screamed with each one.

"Tell me," Mr. Shern said again, and Khloe knew the cane would keep swiping into her vulnerable flesh until she revealed her deepest, dirtiest secret.

"I WASN"T GOOD ENOUGH!"

The cane stopped.

"Explain."

"I wasn't good enough for him, sexually," Khloe said. Her most humiliating secret, the one she hoped she would take to her grave, was out. "I tried to keep him happy in bed. I did everything I knew how to please him.

I thought he was satisfied with me...but I was wrong. I wasn't enough for him. He wouldn't have fucked some other girl if I had been enough for him. I must have been a horrible girlfriend who couldn't keep her man satisfied."

Khloe's limbs began to shake. Her thoughts froze, then broke down like shattered glass. She couldn't think. She couldn't feel. Fear gripped her heart.

"Easy, easy." Mr. Shern's voice was slow and smooth. His warm murmurs against her ear broke through her hardening shell, forcing it back, and Khloe took a deep, shuddering breath. Then he pinched one of her nipples and twisted it between his fingers until Khloe shrieked.

As soon as Mr. Shern saw her eyes refocus, saw her limbs stop their involuntary shaking, he let go. "You're safe, Khloe," he said, caressing her wounded nipple. "You're okay." He squeezed and fondled her breasts inside the rope.

Khloe let her body go limp.

Mr. Cox, who had been standing off to the side this whole time, now stepped forward. He came around Khloe's other side and began to caress every inch of skin he could feel between the thick strands of rope. Khloe moaned and tried to arch her body, curling back up only when she felt the pull of the anal hook.

"You think you didn't know how to satisfy Tom? You weren't woman enough to please him?" Mr. Shern's voice was as gentle as his grazing hands.

"Yes." Khloe could barely talk. The two men were fondling her, squeezing her, bringing her to a new and unexpected rise of arousal.

"You are wrong, Khloe. You're enough woman for any man. You are sensual and beautiful, and any man would be lucky to have you, including Mr. Cox and I."

Khloe didn't answer. Mr. Shern tugged at her nipples, extending them beyond the ropes. Khloe's eyes furrowed as she made a tiny whimper of pain.

He held her nipples out as he addressed the other man. "Mr. Cox, shall we show Khloe how desirable she is?"

"I was afraid you'd never ask," Mr. Cox replied.

He stepped in front of her lifted legs and slid his hand up and down her exposed pussy. Khloe cried out, a sound of rising need. Her cunt was slick and wet, but her vaginal lips were pressed tightly together because of her binds.

"We need to get her down. I want to do this right." Mr. Cox's voice was urgent.

"Yes," Mr. Shern agreed. "Khloe, we're going to take you down now. Just relax, and we'll have you on the bed in a few minutes."

As the two men worked fast to free her from her bonds, they seemed to take every opportunity to fondle, grope, and stroke her body. Khloe could do nothing but moan and pant, restrained by the rope and the hands of the two men working as quickly as they could to free her.

At last, her feet touched floor, and Khloe let out a deep, slow sigh. The rope was pulled away, and Khloe fell into the strong arms and chest of Mr. Cox. She looked down: her whole body showed the intricate impressions of the rope.

She felt weak and drained. Mr. Cox picked her up, cradling her like a sleepy child, and carried her over to the bed, resting her on top of it gently.

With half-hooded lids, Khloe watched as the two men undressed, stripping off their clothes and throwing them haphazardly onto a nearby shelf. They finished at almost the same time, and climbed into bed with her, one on each side. Immediately, they began to stroke and caress her body, using their wide hands to touch every inch of her.

Khloe began to twist and jerk in the sheets, feeling her skin flush from the thorough and worshipping attention of her body. She moaned as Mr. Cox took one of her puffy nipples in his mouth, sucking hard. Then he flicked it with his tongue and bit it gently. Khloe's torso came off the mattress: she grabbed his head with both hands, digging into his hair and pulling. Mr. Cox pushed her back down and moved on to her other nipple.

As Mr. Cox paid homage to her breasts, Mr. Shern was working her legs, starting with her ankles. He was massaging and kissing them, slowly working his way up her knees and thighs, until he was kneeling between her legs, lathing each inner thigh with broad licks of his tongue. When Khloe moved to bring her legs together, shutting him out, Mr. Shern pushed her knees apart, giving him ample room.

With Mr. Shern working her upper half, and Mr. Cox working her lower, the stimulation became too much for Khloe. She began to struggle and push the men off, trying to regain a measure of control.

Mr. Shern's head popped up from between Khloe's legs. "Mr. Cox, go get some restraints, please."

"Of course." Mr. Cox padded to the wardrobe and retrieved some cuffs, snaps, chain, and a stiff metal spreader bar. He handed the pair of ankle cuffs and the spreader bar to Mr. Shern. Then he took control of Khloe's wrists, cuffing them together and snapping the cuffs to a bolt screwed into the headboard. Khloe's arms were now stretched taut above her head, useless.

Mr. Shern placed the ankle cuffs on her quickly, then put the spreader bar between them and locked everything in place. He raised the spreader bar, taking Khloe's legs with it, and chained it to a well-placed hook in the slat that went across the corner posts of the bed. Khloe's hips were still resting comfortably on the mattress, but her legs were spread and elevated.

Once the two men decided she was properly stretched and restrained, they got back to work, exploring and tasting Khloe's body. Mr. Cox straddled her lean torso, playing with her breasts, as Mr. Shern reclaimed his place between her legs, spreading her wet folds open for his mouth and teeth and tongue.

Khloe twisted this way and that, trying to get away from brazen hands and tongues that were sending her to the edge and making her lose all control, but couldn't.

Mr. Shern's devilish tongue lapped her wet pussy as Mr. Cox worked expertly on her swollen extended nipples. Both men were bringing her to the edge of orgasm, but when they saw she was almost there, ready to come, they would pull back, forcing her to wait for release. Her orgasm was up to them to let loose, and as Masters of the Hotel Bentmoore, they knew how to control her body well.

Khloe was soon lying in a pool of sweat and cunt juices, begging to be allowed to come.

"Please, please...."

Mr. Shern had been running his tongue around her labia and stabbing it into her pussy. He was careful not to hit her clit. He knew, at this point, the slightest stimulation would make her come.

"You look so beautiful, Khloe: flushed hot, and begging to come. No man would have the strength to resist you like this. Do you know that?"

Khloe didn't answer, but moaned again as Mr. Cox pushed her breasts together so he could rake his tongue over both her nipples. Mr. Shern raised his head up, and Mr. Cox moved to the side, continuing her nipple torture by flicking them with his fingernails.

"Say you're a good fuck, Khloe. Say it." Mr. Shern knew the coarse words would pull her out of her aroused daze and get her attention, and he was right.

Khloe lifted her head to peer at her host between her legs.

"But I'm not a good fuck."

"Yes, you are. There's nothing wrong with admitting it."

"But--"

Mr. Shern pressed his lips against her labia, giving her folds the barest of kisses, then raised himself up to look her in the face.

"Say it, Khloe."

"I'm...I'm a good fuck." Her voice was barely a whisper.

"Louder." Mr. Shern's lowered his head back to her cunt. Khloe sucked in her breath, watching as her host's face disappeared between her spread legs. His cool breath blew over her wet, warm skin, making her shiver.

Mr. Shern pressed the tip of his tongue right onto Khloe's throbbing clit, but didn't move it further.

Khloe groaned in frustration. "I'm a good fuck," she repeated. Her voice was a fraction stronger, and heavy with desire.

"Louder." Mr. Shern moved his tongue over her clit slowly, grazing the tip, and Khloe shuddered.

Her voice was deep with conviction as she said again, "I'm a good fuck."

"Much better. Keep saying it. I want to hear you scream it as you come." Mr. Shern started to lap her clit, using wide strokes of his tongue, and Khloe's body arched off the bed.

"I'm a good fuck! I'm a good fuck! I'm a good fuck! Oh! Oh God--"

Mr. Shern took Khloe's clit between his lips and pulled, and Khloe came with blinding speed, shooting her hips off the bed and screaming at the top of her lungs.

Mr. Shern didn't stop until Khloe had finished convulsing with her last aftershock. The power of her orgasm made her breath come out in short wheezes.

As Khloe lay limp on the bed, her breath returning to normal, the two men went about uncuffing her wrists and ankles from the restraints. They handled her limbs carefully, knowing she had no strength left in them. As soon as she was completely free, Khloe turned her side, snuggled her face into the pillow, and closed her eyes.

The two men got comfortable next to her, sandwiching her narrow body between them, and let her rest. Khloe felt safe and warm, nestled between the two hard and hot bodies.

But after a while, they began to caress her once more, sliding their hands over and around her warm satiny flesh. Behind her, Mr. Cox began to rub and squeeze her ass, while in front of her, Mr. Shern started to fondle and pinch her nipples.

Khloe began to respond to the gentle stimulation with twists, jerks, and moans. She rubbed her hands up and down the arms and back of Mr. Shern while grinding her ass into the hard body of Mr. Cox.

Very quickly, the three people maneuvered themselves around so that this time, the two men could claim access to her holes. Khloe soon found herself in the corner of the bed, on her back, her legs spread wide.

Mr. Shern was thrusting inside her hot clenching pussy while Mr. Cox stood by her face, his cock taking possession of her mouth. As Mr. Cox began to pump his hips, plunging his cock between Khloe's jaws, Mr. Shern shoved and grinded his hard prick deep inside her tight cunt.

Mr. Cox rammed brutally, breaching her throat. Khloe grabbed his cock by the base, trying to gain some control over his rhythm and thrusts. But Mr. Cox grabbed her hand away and held it, squeezing it gently with his fingers. With his other hand, he pulled her head further in, bringing his cock all the way down her gullet, and continued to pump hard.

Mr. Shern was using strong thrusts, too, grabbing her by the knees and pounding in. He put her legs over his shoulders so she wouldn't be shoved up the bed and break his associate's hold on her mouth.

Khloe began to make a few high-pitched and plaintive yelps around Mr. Cox's prick. Neither man slowed down, but Mr. Cox sighed in ecstasy at the feel of the vibrations coming from her throat.

Mr. Shern began to rub Khloe's clit, using a tight circular motion of his hand. Khloe moaned deeper around Mr. Cox's prick and pressed her legs into Mr. Shern's back.

Soon, all three of them were coming loudly, Mr. Cox into her stuffed and dripping mouth, Mr. Shern into her spasming pussy, and Khloe around both of them. She shrieked as she came, or would have if her mouth hadn't been muffled with cock. Mr. Cox let his cum explode down her throat, and Khloe swallowed it all in big gulps. Then Mr. Shern was coming too, spraying his cum into her welcoming pussy that held him like a tight fist.

They rested again, then the two hosts helped Khloe to dress. She felt all warm and gooey inside, like melted honey.

Mr. Shern took both her hands in his own as he stood before her, taking in her clouded eyes and languid stance. He smiled.

"Do you understand now how wonderful you are? How any man should feel lucky to have you?"

"I know I feel very lucky right now, after what you and Mr. Cox just did to me."

Mr. Shern frowned. "What we just did to you?"

"I'm sorry Sir. I didn't mean that the way it sounded. It came out wrong." She put a hand to her chest, closed her eyes, and smiled weakly. "I meant, I'm grateful for what the two of you did for me."

"Mmm." Mr. Shern did not look pleased. Khloe was too dazed to notice. "I don't think I'll take your wrist cuffs off you just yet. I want to see you again tomorrow morning."

"You do?"

"Yes. I think we have some unfinished business." He pressed the call-button on the wall to summon the liaison. "But until then, you are free to enjoy yourself however you wish. I don't think I have to worry about you hurting yourself inside the hotel."

"No Sir." Khloe's eyes became bright and glassy. "Thank you for your help, Sir. And also to you, Mr. Cox."

"You're welcome." Mr. Cox grinned.

"Don't say goodbye to him just yet, Khloe. You'll be seeing him again tomorrow."

"I will?"

"Yes, you will. But don't worry, no more ropes or hooks."

The door opened, and the liaison moved aside to give Khloe room to pass. There was no time to ask any further questions. She would have to wait until tomorrow to see what else her host had in store.

***

The next day, Khloe woke up bright and early, opening her eyes to warm sunlight pouring into her room from the window. She had forgotten to close the shades yesterday.

A smile spread across her mouth. It was a beautiful summer day, and she felt wonderful.

She dressed quickly, went down to the dining room, and had the pleasure of ordering whatever she wanted. As she ate, she passed some nods and quick smiles to the guests around her. They all smiled and nodded back, feeling the effects of her good mood, and reciprocating gladly.

Her liaison found her in the lobby. He let her know she had two hours before she was expected in the activity room, and could spend them however she wished. Khloe was grateful for the news: it gave her time to relax in the hot tub before she would need to get ready to see Mr. Shern.

As Khloe sank into the hot tub, letting the heat permeate her muscles, she admired all the sleek and toned bodies surrounding the pool. Many of the women wore skirt-type bottoms, long ones that covered their asses and thighs, probably to shroud the marks covering them. Others wore skimpy bikini bottoms to show off welts and bruises, either because they chose to, or because they were ordered to by their Tops and Doms. Even some of the men had marks going across their skin, evidence of their recent submission.

As Khloe dressed in her room for her time ahead with Mr. Shern, she wondered what he would have in store for her. He had promised her no more rope or anal hooks, and while she was relieved she didn't have to fear anything metal going up her ass, she was rather sad to know there was no suspension planned for her. Maybe Mr. Shern could arrange another suspension for her on her next visit, Khloe thought. She smiled.

Mr. Phillips arrived, and Khloe gave herself a mental shrug. Whatever it was Mr. Shern had planned, Khloe knew she could trust him implicitly.

But when she entered the activity room and looked around, she realized Mr. Shern was not the only man waiting for her, and it wasn't just Mr. Cox with him, either.

No less than six men were in her activity room, milling about and talking amongst themselves. The room had an aura of maleness to it: Khloe could smell their unique manly scents, and sense the mingling levels of testosterone.

She immediately reacted to it. Goosebumps rose on the back of her neck. It was a heady feeling for her: she was the only woman in a room full of hot, raunchy men, all self-assured and good-looking Masters of the Hotel Bentmoore, who all seemed to be there waiting for her.

As Khloe scanned the room, her eyes immediately fell on her host, Mr. Shern. He was talking to a tall, blond fellow, a man Khloe knew to be another host of the Hotel Bentmoore, Mr. Sinclaire.

A few feet away them, she saw Mr. Cox deep in conversation with a man Khloe had been introduced to, but only once. What was his name? Mr. Lamont? The name felt right. Like all the hosts of the Hotel Bentmoore, Mr. Lamont looked exceptionally handsome, although in a different way: his looks were decidedly graceful, almost boyish. With narrow shoulders, tight hips, and a slim torso, he looked like the perfect model for a New York runway.

Mr. Lamont made some kind of joke, and Mr. Cox tipped his head back and laughed. Khloe turned her eyes to the last pair of men standing on the other side of the room.

These two Khloe had never met, but she thought she recognized one of them by reputation alone: Mr. Dean. He was the shorter, younger, and darker of the two. The older, lighter gentleman, Khloe knew not at all.

Mr. Shern caught a view of her out of the corner of his eye, stopped talking to his associate mid sentence, and turned to walk her way. The other men, sensing his shift in focus, turned to face her, too.

"Good morning, Khloe," Mr. Shern said. "How are you today?"

"Fine, Sir," she replied. "I'm feeling much better." Her voice was light, but she continued to look around the room as she spoke, not bothering to hide her confusion as to what the men were all doing there.

Mr. Shern put his hands on her shoulders to focus her. "Khloe, it occurred to me yesterday maybe I hadn't handled your situation as well as I should have. I don't think I let you leave with the right impression."

"What do you mean, Sir?"

"You said you didn't think you were able to satisfy Tom sexually. That you weren't 'woman' enough for him."

"Yes, that's true Sir." A blush rose up her cheeks.

"I hope I made you understand yesterday you are a very desirable young woman, with the power to arouse any man you put your mind to."

"Yes, Sir." She smiled and looked down demurely. Mr. Shern raised her chin with his finger, bringing her eyes back.

"But that was not what really concerned you, was it? Being able to grab the attention of a man is not the same thing as holding it, as well you know. Lots of beautiful women are disasters when it comes to the arts of satiating a man's sexual hunger. They have all the right looks, but don't know how to deliver the goods. I don't want you leaving the hotel thinking you are one of those women, Khloe."

Khloe's brows furrowed as she began to fear she knew what all the other men were doing there. "You're right, that still scares me," she admitted. "But I don't see how--"

"I'm not letting you leave this hotel until you realize, beyond a doubt, you know how to satisfy a man. So I've asked some of my associates to join us, and help you get the message." He put his hand out and circled the room. "You are going to fuck all of us."

"What?"

"If you can satisfy six Masters of the Hotel Bentmoore, there's no way you can doubt yourself again."

"I have to satisfy all *six* of you?" Khloe's eyes widened in fear. "I don't know if I can do that, Sir. Please, Mr. Shern, there's no way--"

"You can do it, Khloe. We'll help you complete your task. But know this: you are not leaving this room until all of us are done." His voice took on a tone that brokered no argument, and Khloe paled.

Mr. Shern grabbed her by the arm and pulled her around the room. "Before you get undressed, let me introduced you to everyone here. You already know Mr. Cox." From across the room, Mr. Cox gave her a tiny dip of his head in acknowledgement. "I think you may already know Mr. Lamont?" Khloe nodded, and Mr. Lamont offered her a wide, lecherous smile. "The other men are Mr. Sinclaire, Mr. Dean, and Mr. Harden."

"It's nice to meet all of you," Khloe said with a shaking voice, trying to keep to the social necessities. These men were all about to fuck her ferociously, and probably simultaneously. It was only polite she should know their names, was it not? A nervous giggle tried to escape her throat, and she swallowed it back down.

"Now let's get started," Mr. Shern said. "I think we should all get undressed. Gentlemen, if you would please?"

All six men began to unbutton their shirts, including Mr. Shern. As they stripped naked, Khloe stood there, watching.

"Why aren't you doing what I asked you to do, Khloe?" Mr. Shern asked as he stepped out of his trousers.

"Because I don't know if I can do this, Sir. Please, can we talk about this? I...I...."

"You can do this, Khloe. That's exactly what I want you to understand. You're woman enough for anyone, even us, even all six of us at once. But you'll never believe me unless we prove it to you. So get undressed."

"But what if I can't? What if...." Doubt contorted her features.

"Please get undressed on your own, Khloe. I don't want to have to ask the other men to help me strip you. It would only embarrass us both."

Realizing she had no choice, Khloe quickly took off her clothes. Fear made goosebumps rise along her arms. Her legs began to quake.

Her thoughts sifted and fell from her mind like drifting snowflakes until she had no thoughts left. Her mind was going blank.

"Oh, no," Mr. Shern said sternly, looking her in the eyes. "You are not going to shut down now. I need you focused on right here, right now."

He slapped her hard across the face. Khloe's head snapped to the side; she cried out. But when she brought her face back around, her eyes were clear and sharply focused on her host.

"That's better," Mr. Shern said. "Stay with us, Khloe. You're safe, you're fine. Everything will be okay."

Khloe took a long, shuddering breath. "Yes Sir. Thank you Sir. What would you like me to do?"

"How about we start with you on your knees. That's it, just kneel on the floor there. Straighten your back. Sit up tall." Mr. Shern gestured around the room. "Gentlemen, I believe Khloe is ready to start. Would any of you care to let her get a taste?"

None of the randy men in the room needed to be asked twice. They joined Mr. Shern in making a circle around Khloe, cocks in hand, pushing their lengthening members towards her head.

Khloe took Mr. Shern's in her mouth first, letting it slide all the way down her tongue until it hit the back of her throat. She pumped her face up and down his stiffening prick a few times until it was good and hard, and then felt Mr. Shern put his large hand on her face as he pushed her over to take the next man.

The one standing next to Mr. Shern, waiting his turn, was Mr. Harden. Mr. Harden's cock was thick and wide, and Khloe had to stretch her lips open to accommodate it. But she managed, and soon Mr. Harden was thrusting into her mouth with little grunts. He did this a few times before shoving her off to the next man over, Mr. Dean.

Mr. Dean's cock was already rigid, with thick veins pulsing right underneath the skin. Khloe let her lips slide down his length until she felt his short pubic hairs tickling her upper lip, then stopped. Mr. Dean gasped, then sighed when he felt her tongue circle his broad base. Khloe flicked and licked, and Mr. Dean began to lunge in and out of her playful mouth, holding her head still as he did so.

"Share, Mr. Dean," Khloe heard. She was grasped by the arm and pulled over to the owner of the voice,

Mr. Lamont. Mr. Lamont gave Khloe no time to study his cock, but shoved it between her teeth as soon as he was in range of her mouth, making Khloe gag. Like Mr. Dean, he grabbed her by the back of the head and held her still, thrusting hard. Spit began to dribble from Khloe's mouth as she struggled to maintain control, taking choking breaths whenever she could.

"My turn." Khloe was pulled again, this time by Mr. Sinclaire. Khloe caught herself before falling between his legs. As she lifted her face, her eyes widened when she saw his cock: Mr. Sinclaire's prick was enormous, much more than she could possibly fit in her mouth. But she had only a split second to gasp in fear before he was pressing it in, forcing her to open wide and take it all.

Khloe let out a series of high-pitched cries around his cock: it was stabbing the back of her throat, forcing its way farther down, and Khloe couldn't get a handle on it. Thick tears pooled her eyes as they watered from the exertion. Her forehead beaded with sweat.

"Don't suffocate the poor girl." Khloe was grabbed by the hair and pulled off Mr. Sinclaire's suffocating cock. For a couple seconds, she gasped for air, taking huge gulps like a fish. Then she was situated in front of the next cock and forced to open her mouth once more.

This cock happened to belong to Mr. Cox. Mr. Cox held her chin and pulled it down gently, opening her mouth wide as Khloe continued to catch her breath. He tickled her tongue with his prick.

"Whenever you're ready, Khloe," he said, his voice light with humor. Some of the other men chuckled. Khloe gave him a grateful smile before tightening her grip around his cock with her lips and hallowing out her cheeks. She sucked hard, sliding her mouth up and down his velvety skin. Her way of saying thank you for all his help, including rescuing her from Mr. Sinclaire's demanding cock. Mr. Cox closed his eyes and sighed.

Khloe took pains to pleasure Mr. Cox for the few minutes she was granted, using all her tricks with her mouth and tongue to bring him to the height of arousal, until she felt his cock jump in her mouth, and she thought he might come right then. Then she was suddenly pushed away. His cock made a popping noise out of her mouth as it jumped free.

"I don't want to come like this, Khloe," Mr. Cox admonished her. "At least, not yet."

Khloe smiled up at him, a wicked, knowing grin, and Mr. Cox gave her a playful look of reproach. She smiled wider. She felt very smug, drunk with her own power over the group of men. She was doing it, she was pleasing them all.

"I think we should move her," Mr. Cox said to Mr. Shern. "Time to liven things up."

"Agreed. Let's get her on the bed."

They lifted Khloe off the floor and half walked, half dragged her to the bed, lowering her down on it and surrounding her quickly. Mr. Lamont crawled over the mattress to her head and pointed his cock at her face. Khloe opened her mouth, and he claimed it swiftly with a triumphant growl.

Two other men planted themselves at her sides, and Khloe extended her hands to grasp and stroke their cocks. But that still left three men unattended, a fact they noted with consternation.

"She needs to be put on top of one of us," Mr. Dean said. "Which one will it be? Mr. Shern, you are her host. What say you?"

"You may have the honor of taking her pussy first, Mr. Dean. Mr. Lamont, since you are already making use of her mouth, I see no reason for you to change positions now, but let Mr. Cox share. Harden and Sinclaire, you will be putting her hands to work."

"And what about you?" Mr. Sinclaire asked.

"I am going to be making good use of her ass."

At that, Khloe turned and looked at her host in fear. All the confidence she had been reveling in a minute ago was gone.

"I have to take two of you inside me *at once*?" Her voice was a high-pitched squeak.

"Get her up so Mr. Dean can lie down," Mr. Shern said, ignoring her. "We need to get her positioned right."

They pulled her aside, and Mr. Dean lay down on the bed close to the bottom, with his knees bent over the edge. His veined cock lay thick across his stomach, reaching up to his belly button.

Mr. Lamont and Mr. Cox each grabbed one of her arms and helped her straddle Mr. Dean. Then, slowly, they let her ease down on his prick, holding her pussy open to smooth the way. Khloe's whole face scrunched up as she felt herself go slack against Mr. Dean's groin. She already felt very stuffed inside, and instinctively tightened out of fear of what was about to happen.

The men gave her no time be consumed by worry. They put her hands on their cocks, covered them with their own, and pumped them up and down, letting her know what she should be focusing on. Khloe soon got back into the task, and began to give Mr. Sinclaire and Mr. Harden the best hand jobs she ever had. Meanwhile, she opened her mouth and immediately received Mr. Lamont's prick, which he happily stuffed into her face.

Vaguely, she heard Mr. Shern shuffling behind her.

Then she felt a finger probing her ass.

Khloe yelped around the cock in her mouth. Mr. Lamont grabbed her head to keep her attached to his prick, thrusting even harder into her face.

Mr. Sinclaire gripped her hand that had stopped moving around his prick. She had been shocked still by Mr. Shern's probing.

"Don't stop, Khloe," he ordered. Khloe resumed her gentle yanking, but her eyes grew wide with fear as she felt Mr. Shern's thick digit shove up her bottom. He had coated it with lubricant, and was now using it to grease her back passage so it would be ready for something much larger.

Mr. Cox grabbed her by the back of the head and pulled her by the hair to twist her face around to his cock. Khloe cried out, and continued to cry out as his cock slid down her throat. Her muffled plaintive cries became louder as she felt the helmeted tip of Mr. Shern's cock press through her sphincter.

Khloe tried to focus on the four other cocks in front of her and the one buried up her pussy, not on the one pushing itself deep up her rear channel. She pumped the pricks in her small fists and worked hard to tease and tantalize the two pricks sharing her mouth. She sucked and licked and flicked and groped each cock presented to her, listening in satisfaction as the four men groaned in delight.

But Mr. Dean was still filling up her pussy, and Mr. Shern continued to cram himself in from behind, stretching her asshole painfully. Finally, when she thought she could stretch no more, she felt Mr. Shern stop. He was all the way in. She could feel his groin press against her buttocks, shoving her forward up Mr. Dean's cock.

As she continued to suck and pull at the four cocks she was working on, out of the corner of her eye, she caught Mr. Dean give a nod to the man behind her. Then, he lifted her by the hips and pulled his prick back, sliding it out of her hot pussy until only the tip remained inside her. Then, just as slowly, he eased her back down.

As Mr. Dean let gravity pull Khloe back onto his cock, Mr. Shern pulled out of her ass, giving Mr. Dean more space. The feel of both pricks sliding across her sensitive inner flesh made Khloe gasp. She had never felt anything like it. It still hurt, a little, but the pain was quickly subsiding. What she felt now was rising pleasure.

Again, Mr. Dean eased out of her pussy as Mr. Shern eased into her ass, and Khloe groaned around Mr. Lamont's cock. What they were doing to her felt wicked and perverted. She was being used like a shameless slut, servicing them like a raunchy whore. Khloe had never been so aroused in her life.

Very soon, all six men were gyrating, rocking, thrusting and pumping against her, making use of all of her holes. Khloe had little control over how she moved: she was being pulled and pawed, with each man demanding her complete focus.

Mr. Lamont and Mr. Cox took quick turns grabbing at her face, using her mouth like an open wet cunt waiting to be filled. Mr. Dean drove into her pussy as Mr. Shern fucked her ass, neither one of them caring anymore about timing their thrusts. They moved instinctively now, pounding her body, and Khloe yelled and hollered like a bawdy slut.

They came within minutes of each other, coating Khloe in cum. Mr. Harden and Mr. Sinclaire exploded over her shoulders and breasts, while Mr. Cox blasted all over her face. Mr. Dean came in her pussy, but Mr. Shern, in the last minute, pulled out of her ass and let his prick hose her across her back in ropy strands.

As Khloe felt Mr. Shern's hot cum coat her back, she came herself, screaming around Mr. Lamont's cock as it continued to erupt in her throat. His thick juices dripped down her chin, mixing with the sticky gobs already drying on her breasts.

They all collapsed across the bed, breathing hard.

Mr. Shern recovered first. For a few moments, he disappeared into the adjoining bathroom to wash off his cock. When he returned, he stood across the bed with crossed arms and spread legs, studying the sweaty and heaving bodies splayed across the bed.

"I got her ass last time, so I suppose I should get her hand next," Mr. Shern announced. Khloe raised her head to look at him in surprise. She had thought they were done!

"I want her pussy this time," Mr. Sinclaire said.

"I get her mouth," Mr. Harden replied.

"And I get her ass," Mr. Dean said.

Khloe balanced on her elbows and looked around the group of men. They were all looking back at her, lascivious grins spread wide across their faces. They reminded her of a pack of wolves, closing in on their prey.

She was about to protest, try to claim she didn't have the strength to bring them all to orgasm again. But then Mr. Dean stroked and pinched one of her nipples, Mr. Harden plumped up and licked the other, and Mr. Sinclaire spread her legs wide to send his tongue gliding along her clit, and Khloe knew she did have the strength after all.

By the time they were done, each man had taken a turn with her hand, mouth, pussy, and ass. All except Mr. Sinclaire, who didn't dare try to breach her back passage. He was simply too big.

As they helped her get dressed, caressing and petting her as they did so, the men thanked Khloe for all her hard work and obvious care. Khloe drank in their praises, proud of what she had accomplished.

"You still think you weren't good enough for Tom?" Mr. Shern teased her as he removed her bands. They would no longer be needed. Khloe could be trusted now on her own to leave the hotel.

Khloe smiled with dazed eyes: it was the smile of a woman who had recently been well and thoroughly fucked, and knew the power of her own feminine wiles.

"Oh no, Sir. I'm thinking now, maybe Tom wasn't really good enough for me. I deserve someone much better."

"That's what I like to hear. And I don't have to worry anymore about you cutting, right?"

"Right, Sir." Her eyes focused on her host, and became conspicuously moist. "Thank you again, Mr. Shern, for everything. You always know exactly what I need. I don't know what I'd do without you."

Mr. Shern pressed the button to summon the liaison, the door opened, and Mr. Phillips stood outside, waiting for her to walk through the threshold.

"You don't have to thank me, Khloe. That's why we're here. Take care of yourself."

Khloe raised herself on tiptoes and kissed Mr. Shern on the cheek.

Then she left the room quickly before the tears started to fall. Mr. Shern put his hand to his cheek and held it as he watched her disappear from the door.

Once he knew she was down the hall and out of earshot, he turned around to look at the other men. They were all sprawled about, looking only semi-conscious.

"Who has another guest they have to be ready for in the next hour?"

Two of the men groaned. The others laughed.

Postscript

Khloe stepped out of the elevator and walked toward the front desk, bag in hand. She was ready to go home. All she had to do was check out.

A man leaning on the front counter and talking softly with the desk clerk blocked her path. Khloe couldn't see his face, but there was something familiar about him. Something....

"Adam?"

The man turned around, and Khloe's hand rose to her mouth in surprise.

"Do I know you?" He asked, narrowing his eyes.

"Yes. Kind of." Khloe waved her hand away, suddenly embarrassed. "You're the one who drove me here, years ago, after you found me in the bathroom...."

"Yes, I remember," he cut in, saving her from further embarrassment. "Your name is Khloe, right?"

"Yes." Khloe's face flushed with pleasure. He remembered her name.

"I'm sorry I didn't recognize you, but you look so… different. Better."

Khloe felt her face grow even hotter. "Thank you. I am better. This place has really helped me."

"That's good." Adam continued to stare at her, raking his eyes across her face, down her body, resting for a moment on her swelling breasts, then finally coming back to her eyes. Khloe felt her chest tighten and her cunt tingle in response.

"Are you here visiting the hotel? Oh my god, I'm so sorry, that was totally inappropriate."

"No, it's okay," Adam laughed, a rich, deep chuckle. "In fact, I'm not. I'm visiting my brother. He works here."

A sinking feeling fell through Khloe's belly. "Oh really? Who is he?"

Understanding came into Adam's eyes. "Mr. Pierce. Do you…know him?"

"No, I don't, sorry." Her voice sounded anything but disappointed.

"Oh, that's okay." Relief was clear in his voice. "There are so many hosts here, there's no way a woman could know them all. So, are you just arriving, or…?"

"Actually, I'm checking out."

"That's too bad." The look in his eyes matched the sincerity in his voice.

"Time to start the drive home," Khloe sighed, sorry there was no more time.

But Adam's face suddenly looked excited. "Drive? You live close by then?"

"I guess so, relatively. I live about an hour west of here."

"Really? Me too."

They stared at each for another moment. Khloe waited for him to say something, anything, that would keep their mild flirtatious banter going, but when it was clear he wouldn't, the fingers of hope that had been tapping down her spine soon stopped.

"Well, it was nice seeing you again," Khloe said. "I never got a chance to say thank you for helping me that day. You really saved me."

"You're welcome."

He moved aside to give her room at the counter, and Khloe signed the paperwork to formally check out. She said goodbye to the desk clerk, gave a last smile to Adam, and turned to exit the lobby.

"Khloe," Adam called after her. She turned to find him running toward her. "You really want to thank me?"

"Yes...."

"Let me take you out for dinner sometime. That would be a good way to thank me."

The grip of hope returned full force to squeeze her heart so hard she could barely breathe. "I can do that," she said. "Let me, um, let me give you my number." She fished inside her bag for a pen. Cellphones were not allowed in the hotel lobby: nothing with a camera was permitted out in the open.

"Let me." Adam ran to the front desk, came back holding a pen and a piece of paper, and quickly scribbled something down.

"This is mine," he said, ripping off the piece and giving it to her. "Don't lose it, Okay?"

"Okay." Khloe couldn't hold back the laughter bubbling over. She put the paper carefully into her purse. "Here's mine…" She gave him the numbers, and Adam repeated each one back to her to make sure he got it right as he wrote them down. Then he ripped the number off the paper, folded it gingerly, put it in his pocket, and started writing her number down again on a clean edge of the paper.

"Why are you writing it again?" Khloe asked.

"In case I lose the first copy. This way I have a backup." He ripped the second copy off, too, but this time, put it in his wallet. "I know it looks silly--"

"No no, I do that, too. But I thought I was the only one."

"Nope. Sometimes I write things down right on my hand, just so I'll remember. But ink washes off."

"I do that, too!" Khloe felt like her heart was melting inside her chest. Adam gave her a wide, beautiful smile.

"Here." He took her hand, opened her fingers, and started writing his number down on her palm. Khloe

stared at him in wonder. His hand was warm and strong around hers, and felt perfect. The pen tickled, sending gentle shivers up her arm.

"It was nice to see you again, Khloe. I'll call you soon."

"Thank you Adam. I'll be waiting."

"Not too long." He let her hand go, gave her one last look of longing, and disappeared inside the elevator.

Khloe left the hotel feeling better than she had in a very long time.

Evie

THE TWO MEN GREETED each like old friends, smiling, back slapping, and yelling their salutations the way men do in lieu of hugs. It was obvious they were well acquainted, but hadn't reconnected for quite some time, the reason for the loud and joyful reunion. In their reconciliation, neither of them paid any attention to the woman in the room, who was watching them both silently with wide eyes.

"Cox! It's good to see you," the older and taller of the two said, continuing to shake the other man's hand.

"Altman," the other replied in the same tone of joy. "It's been too long. How have you been?"

"Good, good. Business is going well."

"Yes, I know. I keep track of those letters letting me know my shares are going up."

"It's good to know someone reads those letters," the older man said with a laugh.

The man named Cox motioned his friend into a nearby chair. Both took seats opposite each other in the tiny room.

The woman remained standing. No one had offered her a chair, despite there being two more available around

153

the small table. In fact, since entering the room, no one had given her so much as a passing glance. She stood by the door, her arms crossed in front of her, watching as the two men settled down and got reacquainted.

"So, Altman," Mr. Cox said. "What brings you to the Hotel Bentmoore?"

"It's my girl here, Evie." Mr. Cox turned around, and for the first time, acknowledged the woman he had entered with by motioning her over with his finger. "Come here, Evie, and say hello to Mr. Cox."

Evie stepped forward and offered the other man a polite smile, but did not put out her hand in greeting. "Hello, Mr. Cox."

"Give him your hand, Evie," the older man snapped. "Don't be rude. He won't bite."

The young woman put her hand out. Rather than shaking it, Mr. Cox put it between his own and gave it a gentle squeeze. For a brief second, he took in her liquid brown eyes and soft chestnut hair. Then his eyes raked over her young, firm body in open appreciation.

"There, see?" Mr. Altman said from his chair, watching the byplay. "I know you're frightened, Babygirl, but you mustn't forget your manners."

"Yes, Daddy." The young woman looked down, contrite. "I'm sorry, Daddy."

"There's a good girl." He reached his hand up and caressed the woman's ass, letting his palm glide, then gave her firm flesh a gentle squeeze. The woman made no reaction to his touch.

Mr. Cox watched his friend petting and fondling the woman's bottom, studied Evie's passive face for a brief second, then turned back to his friend.

"So Evie is your Babygirl?"

"Yes," Mr. Altman said with pride. "She's been mine for a while now. Generally she's a good girl, but lately she's been a bit clingy." His jaw clenched for a brief second. He sighed. "I have to go on a business trip for a few days, Cox, and I'll be working non-stop, what with meetings and dinners and all that. I don't want to leave Evie alone, I don't want her to get bored. So I thought I'd drop her off here, with you. I know there's no way she'll get bored at the Hotel Bentmoore," he said.

"I see." Mr. Cox's expression turned contemplative. "Did you mean for us to simply keep her out of trouble while you're away? Or did you mean for me to work with her, a little one-on-one?"

"Ah, Cox, I knew you would see it immediately," Mr. Altman laughed. "The truth is, I think Evie would benefit from some of your tutelage. It feels lately like some of Evie's fire has gone out. She's lost her verve. She's too, how do I want to put it…she's too quiet. You know how I like my women, Cox."

"Yes," Mr. Cox grinned. "You do like them lively."

"Exactly. I was hoping you could spend some time with her, show her some fresh tricks. I'm sure after a few days with you, my Evie will go back to being her old usual spitfire self. Think you can do that for me?"

"Oh, yes." Mr. Cox's grin turned wolfish. "I can do that."

"Good. I'm sure a few days with you is just what my Babygirl needs." He passed Mr. Cox a laden look, and Mr. Cox nodded.

Evie looked from one man to the other. She knew some silent message had just been communicated, but she had no idea what it could be. Goosebumps rose on her arms.

"Any hard limits I should know about?" Mr. Cox asked.

"Not really, nothing beyond the lines I know you won't cross. Piercing, branding, burning, things like that."

"But punishment marks are okay? Welts and the like?"

Mr. Altman waved the comment away with his hand. "Oh, you'll need to mark her," he said. "Evie needs a heavy stick applied to her rump now and then to keep her in line. But basically, she's a good girl. Aren't you, Evie?"

"Yes, Daddy." Her voice was slow and toneless.

Mr. Cox studied her bland expression and raised his eyebrows, but said nothing.

Mr. Altman patted his leg. "Come sit on Daddy's lap for a minute, Evie," he said. Evie dutifully came over and sat, snuggling into Mr. Altman's wide chest. She wrapped her arms around his neck and kissed him on the cheek. Mr. Altman smiled.

"Daddy's going to go now--"

"Please, Daddy, don't leave me here. Take me with you." A crack in her shell of indifference finally broke through, and her voice trembled. Mr. Altman smiled in response.

"None of that now, Babygirl. I'm leaving you in very capable hands. Mr. Cox will look after you while you're here at the hotel. You are to follow his instructions and do everything he says like a good Babygirl. Understand, Evie?"

Evie looked at Mr. Cox, somewhat fearful, but said, "Yes, Daddy."

"Good. When I come back, I want to hear how you were a good Babygirl and listened well. I want you to be the best Babygirl you can be. Make your Daddy proud. Understand, my sweet?"

"Yes, Daddy." She hugged him tight. "I'll miss you."

"I'll miss you too, Babygirl. You be good, and I'll bring you back a treat."

"Thank you Daddy. I love you."

"I love you too, Babygirl. Be good." He untangled her arms from around his neck, stood up, shook Mr. Cox's hand one more time, and disappeared into the hallway, where the liaison was waiting to escort him out of the hotel.

Mr. Cox's gaze fell back on Evie, and this time, he did not look away. Evie looked back at him nervously, crossing her arms in front of her again.

"So," he said. "I guess you're mine for the next few days."

Evie said nothing. The statement hung in the air like a threat.

"Well, let's start by putting you through your paces, and see what you can do," Mr. Cox said. "Come, it's time to head over to one of the activity rooms."

"What? Now?"

"Why not? Unless you have a more pressing matter to attend to?" His voice was clipped. He was already displeased with her.

Evie shrugged but kept her mouth closed. She didn't move. Mr. Cox took her by the arm and pulled her from the room.

"The liaison is probably still escorting your Daddy back upstairs," he said. "So this time, I'll take you to the activity room. But usually it will be the liaison who brings you to me. Did your Daddy explain to you how the Hotel Bentmoore works?"

"Yes, he told me about the rules."

"Did he also make clear what I'm going to expect from you?"

"Yes." She blushed. "He said you may be much harder on me than he is--"

"Oh, I have no doubts about that."

"--but I am to obey your every word. He said you'll probably try to teach me a few things."

"Did he now? Well, first I need to see where your weaknesses lie."

They arrived at the designated activity room, and Mr. Cox slid his card through the security lock. The door clicked open, and Evie was pushed through. As soon as Mr. Cox was around the door, he pushed it closed. Evie heard it lock from the inside.

"Now then," Mr. Cox said, "he may have explained some things to you, but I want to make sure everything is clear between us before we start. I will be your host for the remainder of your stay here at the Hotel Bentmoore. What that means, Evie, is that I am not your friend, I am not your confidant, and I am certainly not your lackey. I have complete authority over everything that happens to you while you are a guest here. You will call me 'Sir' at all times."

Evie's eyes grew wide as he spoke. Mr. Cox noted her look of fear, but ignored it.

"All the activity rooms of the Hotel Bentmoore are on this underground floor. Some of us call it the sub-floor. Others call it the dungeon. I'll do my best to make sure we can always meet in the same activity room, so you can feel more comfortable, but I can't promise. Different rooms have different pieces of equipment, and other hosts might need ours. Understand?"

Evie nodded.

"For the remainder of your stay, we will see each other only when we are together in an activity room. Hosts cannot visit guests in the private rooms of the upper floors. It is against hotel rules. If you need to get word to me, or send me a message, you can do it through the liaison. The same goes for me: if I need to give you new instructions, I will send word through the liaison. But

I expect you to follow any instructions I send as if you are hearing them from me. Now matter where you are, while you are at the Hotel Bentmoore, you are under my authority, and you will follow my orders to the letter, day and night, no matter what. Is that clear?"

"Yes, Sir." The words were quiet, but obedient enough, and Mr. Cox nodded.

"Good. Now. Get undressed."

Evie looked up, startled. The order had come from nowhere, and was the last thing she had expected.

But if Mr. Cox thought the order would shock her into noncompliance, he was wrong. Evie began to strip off her clothes, working fast.

But she stared down at the floor as she did it, looking bored.

"Don't look down like that," Mr. Cox snapped. "Look at me. Look me in the face."

Evie pulled her face up and stared into his eyes as she finished undressing. But she didn't look provocative, or even aroused. She looked nervous, and more than a little irritated. By the time she was done, her clothes were a moat around her feet, and Mr. Cox could see her trying hard not to scowl.

"Very good, Evie," he said, trying to encourage her. "Now come here, to me. But don't walk. Get down on all fours. I want you to crawl." He decided he would have a little fun irritating her, see how far he could take it before she blew up in fury.

Evie sank to the floor. Keeping her face bent down, she crawled to her host, sashaying in a rather awkward manner. Her tits swayed beneath her as she moved.

"Very good," Mr. Cox said again despite her ungainliness. "Now sit up."

Evie sat on her heels and looked up at her host.

"Reach up and open my pants."

With nimble fingers, Evie reached for his zipper. The grating noise of the metal pulling down was the only sound in the room.

"Now reach in and pull out my cock."

Evie looked at her host for a minute; their eyes did a battle of wills. Then, carefully, she reached inside and pulled out his swelling, stiffening cock.

"Show me what you can do with that lovely mouth of yours."

For a moment, Evie looked like she might finally protest. But with a small shrug of her shoulders, she held his hardening prick in her hand, then slowly, looking him in the eyes, she lowered her mouth on the bulbous head.

She kept lowering her lips, filling her mouth with stiff prick, until her mouth touched the base of his groin. Mr. Cox inhaled sharply; he could feel the back of her throat.

Carefully, she began sliding her lips back up, keeping her teeth well away from the tight skin of his shaft. Mr. Cox closed his eyes in ecstasy, marveling at her tight grip and the delicious warmth of her mouth.

Evie began to suck him off with long, hard pulls of her jaw, bobbing her head up and down his prick, shoving him down her throat and making swallowing motions all around his staff with her tongue, until Mr. Cox was digging his hands into her hair and throwing his head back in delight.

But after a few moments of this exquisite torture, he noticed her bored disinterest in the task, the lack of pleasure in her face and stance. He shoved her off, pushing hard. She yelped in surprise at being knocked down to the floor.

Mr. Cox scowled down at her. "Evie, why aren't you enjoying this?"

"I am, Sir," she said, surprised.

"You like sucking my cock?"

"Yes, Sir."

"Then why are you looking at me like you're bored out of your fucking mind? You're not giving me any sign you're enjoying yourself at all. If you don't like having my cock in your mouth, tell me. We'll move on to something else."

"But I *am* enjoying this, Sir. I like to suck cock."

"Really," he said dubiously. "Then keep going, and this time, show me how much you like it."

Evie got back to work, licking and sucking Mr. Cox's prick. She soon felt his warm cum shooting down her throat, and sucked him dry, cleaning off his cock with her mouth. Then she sat back on her knees, awaiting further orders.

Once he had recovered from his orgasm, and his breathing returned to normal, Mr. Cox looked down at her with piercing eyes. He did not look pleased.

"Go to the bed and brace yourself against the edge. Ass in the air," he growled. Evie began to stand up, but stopped and gave her host a questioning look. When he nodded, letting her know she could walk and not crawl, she stood up all the way and walked over to the bed, bracing herself with her hands and leaning down into the mattress. She could hear Mr. Cox zipping up his pants and taking his place behind her.

With her body bent over, Mr. Cox took a moment to admire her narrow waist and softly flaring hips. Evie's ass was smooth and compact; her twin mounds were perfectly round, with only a thin dark crease separating them. Her cheeks were blushed crimson.

"Your Daddy recently spanked you," Mr. Cox said. "Were you in need of a punishment?"

"Yes," she said, wincing as Mr. Cox traced a pale welt, almost hidden under the curve of her young bottom, with his finger.

"Yes, *Sir*," he corrected. His finger continued to trail lazily around the soft mountains of her ass, dipping now and then into the valley of her tight crease.

"Yes, Sir," she replied, shivering from the goose-bumps that were rising on her skin. His hand continued to caress her, more aggressively now, and Evie stiffened, but did not move to stop him.

"Let's see if I can get you to lose some of that composure," he said, pulling his hand away from her backside.

He walked to the large, elegant wardrobe by the wall, opened the double doors, retrieved something from inside, and walked back to her tense and bent form. Evie could not see what he had in his hand. He held it slightly behind his back.

"Close your eyes," he said. Evie closed her eyes.

A second later, she felt a slap against her ass, and let out a little shriek. Whatever he had spanked her with, it stung like crazy. Mr. Cox spanked her again, and Evie buried her face into the mattress.

He began to pepper her ass with short, powerful spanks, working fast and hard and keeping her guessing as to where the next smack would land. Evie kept her face down, maintaining the bent position, but was soon hopping from foot to foot, trying to shake away the sting.

The spanking continued, and Evie hoped desperately it would soon come to an end. She didn't know if she would be able to sit down after this.

But she held the pose, and bit her lip to keep from screaming.

Finally, Mr. Cox stopped, and told her to stand up.

"Did you enjoy that, Evie?" His voice was soft.

"No, Sir," she hiccuped, trying her best not to cry. Mr. Cox studied her quivering, unhappy face.

"Does your Daddy put you on noise restriction? Does he tell you not to make any noise as you're being punished?"

"No, Sir," she replied, surprised by the question.

"Then why did you keep so silent while I was spanking you? Why did you bury your face in the bed so you wouldn't scream? I know I was hurting you. Crying should have been the logical reaction."

"I don't know, Sir." She wiped her eyes and looked down, remorseful, like a small child. Mr. Cox sighed.

"I see now what your Daddy was talking about," he said. "It's clear what kind of lessons he wants me to give you."

Mr. Cox threw the slapper on the bed, shaking his head with scorn. "Get dressed," he said. "The liaison will escort you back to your room. Relax for a while, eat in the dining room when you get hungry. I'll give you a few hours, and then the liaison will escort you back here to begin your lessons."

"Lessons? What kind of lessons?"

"The kind of lessons I was entrusted to give you that you obviously need." At her blank stare, he sighed. "What did you think, Evie, that your Daddy was dropping you off here for a nice little vacation? That you'd do nothing but lounge around the pool sunbathing, and visit me at your own convenience? No, he expects you to learn a few things from me, and I see now, you have *much* to learn."

***

He summoned the liaison, and Evie was escorted back to her room above.

For the time being, she was left alone, and she took the time to contemplate her situation.

She had been left at the Hotel Bentmoore for what she *thought* would be a chance to relax and enjoy herself a little bit. Yes, she had been warned she would be spending time with a host of the Hotel Bentmoore, specifically Mr. Cox, her Daddy's old friend. But she had thought the time spent with him would be fun, a way to learn a few new sexual techniques.

Now she realized that was not what her host had in mind. He meant to teach her "lessons," and painful lessons at that. She was filled with foreboding. But her Daddy had entrusted her to Mr. Cox. She had no way to contact her Daddy for some much-needed reassurance.

Evie stayed in her room, watched some television, ordered room service when she got hungry, and cried when her sorrow and loneliness became too much.

She would only have to get through a few days without her Daddy. It was not that much time at all. But the ache in her heart would not go away, and her pillow was soon drenched with her tears. She missed him so much already, and he had only left her a few hours ago! How was she to survive the next few days without him?

Before she knew it, her liaison was knocking on her door, ready to escort her back to the activity room she would share with her host, and Evie barely had enough time to wipe away her tears before she was following him down the darkened hallway.

As she entered the activity room, she remained subdued, still deluged with grief and exhausted from her crying.

"Hello again, Evie," Mr. Cox greeted her. He wore the same suit pants he had worn before, but no shirt this time. Evie noticed the man had thick muscles, a wide chest (but no chest hair), and a very well-defined stomach. "I hope you enjoyed your meal."

"Yes, I did, thank you, Sir." It was a lie, of course. She had barely touched her food. Her worry and trepidation had taken away any appetite she had.

But during her time alone in her room, she had decided: this was where her Daddy had left her, so this is where she would stay, whether she enjoyed herself or not. She would do as told. She would listen to Mr. Cox, even if he acted like a big bully. She would be good.

"You're lying," Mr. Cox said. Evie's head snapped up. "I called up to the dining room. You never arrived. You had room service sent up to your room instead. You were sulking, weren't you?"

"I wasn't sulking," she said, her voice high and defensive. "I was...."

"Sulking."

"*Sad*. I miss my Daddy."

"I know. But that doesn't mean you get to disobey me. My instructions were to eat in the dining room."

Evie blanched. She had thought he had been making a suggestion, not giving her orders.

"I'm sorry, Sir."

"Not good enough. Up against the bed."

Evie walked over to the now familiar mattress and leaned over it for the second time that day, pressing her elbows and head down as before. She knew she would be punished for her disobedience, and cursed her host in her head. The man had no leniency. But she would take his punishment like a good girl.

Mr. Cox came up behind her and began to lift her skirt, bunching up the thin material as it rose. When it was over her waist, he pressed the roll of gauzy cotton against her back and left it there. Under the skirt, Evie wore a pair of translucent cream panties that hugged her hips and ass cheeks like second skin.

Mr. Cox peeled her panties down until they were around her knees, stretched taut by her spread legs.

Evie heard the unmistakable sound of Mr. Cox pulling off his belt.

"You'll get ten this time, since it's only your first offense," he said.

"Ten?"

"Next time it will be twenty, miss," he said sternly. He took position by her side, aiming the looped belt right across her cheeks. "Now count."

Evie squeezed her eyes shut and braced herself. "One--"

The belt came down across her butt, leaving a brand new stripe of burning sting in its wake. Evie inhaled sharply but didn't move.

"Two--"

Again the belt came down, this time low across her thighs. Evie hissed through her teeth.

"Three--"

The end of the belt snapped against her right buttock. Evie almost shrieked, but held herself back.

"Four--"

Her left buttock got the same treatment. This time Evie did let out a tiny yell, but caught it before it got too loud.

"Five--"

Another vicious streak hit her right on the curve of her ass mounds, and this time Evie almost shot upright. Mr. Cox impatiently pushed her back down.

"Six!" She shouted. Another brutal cut. The tears began to flow. Evie wanted to bury her face into the bed to keep from screaming, but she could not. She had to count.

"Seven!"

Mr. Cox added a extra hard flick to his wrist, and the belt pressed into her skin her like a hot branding iron. Evie screamed.

"Eight!" Another stinging smack, and Evie screamed again.

"Nine!" She didn't know how she did it, but she held the pose. Instead of struggling, she cried out in pain. Her ass was smarting, and she wanted desperately to rub the sting away, but there was one more left.

"Ten," she said with some relief, thankful that it was almost over. But Mr. Cox made the last one the worst, raising the belt high and putting all his force behind the blow. Evie's bellow was high and long.

She stood up, rubbed her ass, and looked at Mr. Cox mutinously.

Mr. Cox threw his belt onto the bed next to her and stared into her insolent face, putting his hands on his hips. "You think you'll ignore my instructions again?"

"No, Sir," she snivelled, looking down in defeat.

"Good. Now let's get down to work. That belting you just got served another purpose: It gave me some idea of your tolerance for pain. You can't handle very much pain, can you, Evie?"

"No Sir," Evie said, downcast. "I can't." It was true. Her Daddy was always telling her that.

"That's good," Mr. Cox said, surprising her. "It means your punishments are that much more effective from the get-go, and can be over with faster, as long as you give some sign they're working. I know your Daddy doesn't like to give drawn-out punishments."

"No, Sir," she said, surprised her host would know something like that.

"Which isn't to say he isn't capable of meting out a deserved punishment now and then," Mr. Cox continued.

"Very true, Sir," Evie agreed.

"But he needs to know the punishments he's giving are working, so he knows when to stop. Your Daddy is the kind of man who likes to see immediate results. So tell me something, Evie: How can your Daddy tell his punishments are working on you, if you're trying so hard not to react or cry out?"

The question startled her.

"I don't know, Sir," she said. "I never really thought about it."

"Well, do. And while you're at it, tell me *why* you try so hard to keep quiet."

"I guess I just assumed if he's punishing me, I deserve it, and the right thing to do is to take it like a good girl and not make too much noise about it."

Mr. Cox furrowed his brows. "Is Mr. Altman the first man you've had this type of relationship with?"

Evie shifted her feet in nervousness. He was starting to get a little too personal, and she wasn't sure how much information to give him.

"Yes, Sir," she said, her voice halting. "I've never had before what I have with Daddy. I love him so much. He's...he's my *Daddy*." For her, the word said it all. Thankfully, Mr. Cox understood.

He smiled. "That's lovely, Evie," he said. "But it doesn't explain why you assume silence is the best course of action during a punishment. It also doesn't explain your robotic submission."

Robotic? Robotic! Evie's face flushed with anger. "I am not robotic, Sir," she gritted out. "I obey the way I am supposed to."

"The way you are supposed to. Who says so?"

Evie snapped her mouth shut, looking confused. "Well, everything I've read, everything I see online, tells me I'm supposed to obey immediately and without protest, like a good slave...."

"Ahh, now we're getting somewhere. That's the problem right there. You are not a slave, Evie. So everything you're reading is wrong for you."

"But--"

"You are a Babygirl. Specifically, Mr. Altman's Babygirl. You should be doing what's best for *him*, to make him happy. Not this nonsense you're following from what you're reading online."

"But I--"

"So from here on out, I'm going to make you throw out all these misguided notions in your pretty little head, so you can be the best Babygirl you can be for your Daddy. Understand?"

"Yes, Sir," Evie replied with a sigh.

"And that doesn't mean always keeping your mouth shut, and that doesn't mean taking your punishments so stoically. I need...." He put his hand on his chin, staring at her. Evie shifted her feel nervously. Mr. Cox turned his head and looked across the room, as if contemplating his options.

"Undress," he said, his voice brokering no discussion. "Now. We'll get you on the table."

The table he spoke of sat by the side of the wall on the other side of the room. It reminded Evie very much of examining room tables she saw inside doctors offices. But looking at it closer, Evie realized it was perhaps slightly longer, more narrow, and had thicker padding.

As Evie undressed and put her folded clothes on the bed, Mr. Cox released the brakes on the legs of the table and wheeled it into the middle of the room. When he was satisfied with its positioning, he reset the breaks so it would not move.

"Get on," he ordered. Evie hopped onto the table and lay down on her back, her knees bent but her legs pressed together. She felt nervous, and curious what Mr. Cox would try to "teach" her, but not too afraid. She could take whatever he threw her way. She would be brave for her Daddy.

Mr. Cox went to the wardrobe, pulled out a few things, and returned to her side. In his hand he was holding some thick nylon straps. They had O rings on one end and Velcro strips on the other. He was also holding a bondage bar that had four cuffs already attached.

"First," he said, and began to strap Evie down to the table. He took one long nylon strap, fitted it across her shoulders right above her breasts, and grabbed it from beneath the table on the other side. He slipped the end through the O ring, cinched it closed until Evie grunted from the sudden constriction, and pressed the long length of Velcro down, locking Evie in place.

Then, he positioned another strap across her waist, going through the same procedure he had with the first, and pulling that one tightly down, too. Evie's torso was now strapped down to the table. She could not rise at all.

"Now..." Mr. Cox grabbed the bondage bar, took both of Evie's hands, and fitted them through two of the four cuffs attached to the bar. "Put your feet up," he ordered.

Evie understood what he wanted her to do: He wanted both her hands and feet in the air, locked into the bondage bar. So she rose her legs into the air, brought her feet to her hands, and lay still for Mr. Cox to do his handiwork.

Mr. Cox buckled her ankles into the other two cuffs of the bar, locking them in place. Evie lay restrained to the table, with her arms and legs locked to the bar above her. She felt like a trussed up pig about to be cooked on a spit.

"Is this really necessary?" She asked, looking up at the ceiling. "I won't move if you tell me not to--"

Slap!

Mr. Cox had slapped something thin and stingy against her vulnerable rump.

"You've been working under the mistaken notion you'll only get punished when you deserve it. That may be how your Daddy does things, Evie, but you're in my world now, and in my world, punishments don't always have to be deserved. I'm going to play with this soft little ass of yours for as long as I want. I'm going to warm it up good. Is that understood?"

"Yes, Sir," Evie said through clenched teeth.

"Think you can take it?"

He had made it a challenge, damn the man. "Yes, Sir," Evie said again, sure of herself.

"And what if I play with this tight cunt of yours too while I'm at it?" Mr. Cox slid his hand over Evie's pubic mound and thrust a finger into her hot, but dry, pussy. "Think you can take that, too?"

Evie squeezed her eyes shut, but kept her voice cool. "Yes, Sir," she said.

"We'll see. No need to count the spanks. It's not like I'll be keeping track. I'll stop when I feel like it."

With that, he began to slap her ass again, using quick, measured strokes. "It's a strap," he said between hits, his voice light. "I thought this prim and proper ass of yours deserved a classic punishment piece."

Evie could not reply. She was focusing all her energy on keeping still.

Slap! Slap! Slap!

Mr. Cox continued to pepper her ass with smacks, swinging the strap against her upthrust bottom. Every once in a while, he would switch hands. Evie thought he might be trying to even out the welts between cheeks. But it was obvious he wasn't really keeping track, just like he had warned her.

He was having a merry time of it, too, spanking Evie's exposed and accessible bottom. He was waiting to see how she would react.

Evie bit her lip. She squeezed her eyes shut. She made fists with her small hands, high in the air and locked into the bondage bar. But she did not cry out.

She would not. If this man thought he could break her so easily, make her lose her composure and struggle against his "punishment," he was wrong. She would lay still and not give him the satisfaction of watching her writhe. She would take it if it killed her. And really, how long could he go on? He would have to give up and admit defeat eventually, wouldn't he?

"My arm's getting tired," Mr. Cox said, as if reading her thoughts. "Time to give it a break." Evie took a long, drawn-out breath, then sucked it in when she felt something warm and wet touch her pussy.

"God, you taste good, Evie," she heard her host say. He was standing between her legs. Evie had to close her eyes to keep herself from lifting her head and looking. "Your Daddy must love to eat out this pussy. Does he, Evie? Does he love to eat this delicious pussy of yours?"

"Yes, Sir," she managed to say.

"I thought so," he murmured, touching his tongue to her soft vulva. Evie could feel his hot breath against her moistening skin.

Mr. Cox spread Evie's pussy lips wide, drinking in the sight of her pink folds. Finally, Evie opened her eyes and looked down, and was struck by the sight of Mr.

Cox standing between her lifted legs, admiring her most private parts. It was a highly erotic position, and Evie tightened her pelvic muscles in response.

"Oh, yes, do that," Mr. Cox said, watching her skin, and asshole, constrict. He politely wet two of his fingers in his mouth, then pushed them deep inside Evie's now sopping wet cunt. "God, you're tight," he said. "You're squeezing my fingers." He wiggled them, and watched as Evie's eyes flared. "Squeeze 'em tight, there's good girl. Harder." Evie closed her eyes and squeezed her muscles as tight as she could. "Good girl, Evie. Hold 'em now..." he began to thrust his fingers in and out of her hot cunt, creaming with her inner juices. Evie held back a whimper.

"Squeeze my fingers, Evie," he said, focusing her. "Squeeze 'em tight, don't let them go...harder...."

As Evie worked hard to tighten her pelvic muscles as much as she could, feeling her aching arousal surging to new heights, Mr. Cox brought his thumb up to Evie's swollen clit, and pressed it with the pad of his finger. He began to circle it. The effect on Evie was electric. Her whole body spasmed with exquisite shocks of bliss.

Mr. Cox grinned. "You like that, don't you Babygirl. You like me finger-fucking your cunt and playing with your clit."

Evie would not reply. She refused to give him the satisfaction of hearing her admit how much she liked what he was doing to her. But she whipped her head from side to side as her breathing came in short gasps. She could not quell her body's most natural reactions.

"Your clit's so swollen, Evie. I wonder, if I used my tongue on it now, would you come? I bet you would."

Evie held her breath, waiting for her host to press his tongue against her clit, waiting to come. But Mr. Cox removed his thumb, pulled his fingers out of her dripping, tight pussy, and stepped away from her.

"Break time's over," he announced. "All the color has faded from your ass. I want it nice and red. The spanking I gave you before? That was just a warm up."

He picked up the strap and began to spank Evie's bottom again, only this time putting more force behind the blows. For Evie, after being so close to coming, the shock of the strap biting into her skin was even harder to take. But she gritted her teeth and willed herself to remain still.

Slap! Slap! Slap!

Mr. Cox was no longer confining himself to Evie's buttocks. Instead, he was moving up her thighs, circling the strap around her legs, and sometimes, doing his best to aim the strike between them. Evie began to let out short yelps with each smack when she felt the strap striking into the sensitive flesh of her inner thighs.

"Starting to feel it a bit too much, Evie? Want it to stop?" He continued his relentless spanking, and Evie bit her lip hard enough to draw blood. "I could do this all afternoon, Evie. I'm having fun. Are you?"

Slap! Slap! Slap!

Evie could feel the tears forming under her eyelids. But before the first ones could drip from the corners of her eyes, he stopped.

"Your pussy's gaping. It looks like it's pouting, wanting some attention," Mr. Cox said, his voice jovial. He spread her pussy lips open once more and slipped two fingers inside her drenched cunt with a jerk of his wrist. They made juicy sucking noises inside her sopping pussy. He thrust his fingers straight in a few times, then hooked them so they would rub against her g-spot.

Evie swallowed back a moan. Mr. Cox added another finger into her tight pussy.

"That's it, Evie, that's it," he said as Evie's whole body tensed, her head coming off the table. "Tell me how me how much you like that. Tell me how much you want it. C'mon, Babygirl, tell me..."

"No!" The word ripped out of her throat before she could stop herself. Mr. Cox stared at her in surprise, then stopped his moving fingers, leaving them still inside her cunt.

"No? No is not the word I'm looking for," he said. "No was not the word I wanted you to learn first. But if you want to start with that one, then by all means, let's start with that."

Removing his hand from her well-oiled cunt, he picked up the strap again, and began to slap her with it from thigh to thigh. He moved further away from her this time, letting his arm swing higher with each blow, and reducing the time between spanks.

It stung like a son of a bitch, and Evie didn't know how much more she could take. Her arms and legs trembled above her. She tried to twist her body away from the sting of the strap, but it was useless.

Her host's voice above the stinging sounds of the strap was a vicious hiss. "Tell me, Evie, do you like this?" When she didn't answer, he spanked her faster. Evie began to cry out, her grip of control finally beginning to loosen. "Do you like the way I'm spanking your ass? Does it feel good?"

Slap! Slap! Slap!

"Do you like it, Evie? Do you? *Do you?"*

Slap Slap Slap--

"No," Evie yelled, tears dripping from her eyes.

"Tell me again. Do you like it?" *Slap!*

"No!" *Slap!*

"Do you want me to keep going?" *Slap!*

"No! No!" *Slap!*

"Tell me again." *Slap!*

"*No!*" *Slap!*

"Again!" *Slap!*

"NO! Please, stop!" She screamed. Mr. Cox stopped.

"*That* is how you say no, Evie," he said. "And this is how you want to say *yes*." He pressed four of his fingers together on one hand, twisted them around and inside the opening of her sticky cunt to get them good and wet, and then slowly began to push them into her pussy.

His fingers were blunt, but wide, and quickly felt huge inside her. Evie arched her back, trying to pull away. Mr. Cox put a restraining hand on her hip and kept pushing.

"Please."

"Please, what?"

"Please, I, oh!" Mr. Cox's four fingers had disappeared inside Evie's stretched cunt. His hand had slipped under her pelvic bone, and now rested there, a tight ball of delicious fullness.

Evie had never felt so stuffed in her life. It would not have even occurred to her that a man's entire *hand* could fit inside her pussy. For a moment, she panicked.

"Oh, oh please." She struggled inside her bonds, wriggling around the table, and tightening around Mr. Cox's hand.

"Easy, easy," he said, rubbing her leg with his other hand to soothe her. Evie stopped her writhing and took long, labored breaths. "That's it," he said. "Don't fight it. Let my fingers stretch you. It doesn't hurt, does it?"

"No," she whispered. The exact opposite. It felt wonderful. His hand became a focal point of her growing need, unfurling across her entire body. She was squeezing his hand tightly with her cunt muscles without even realizing it, but it felt like he was the one gripping her, controlling her peaks of arousal from the inside.

And then he began to make a series of push-pull motions with his hand, small ones, and Evie's back arched off the table.

"Yes!" She shrieked. "Oh God, yes, please." Mr. Cox's stuffed hand seemed to be pulling the orgasm right out of her.

He slowed it down.

"Do you like this, Evie?" He asked. "Does it feel good?"

"Oh yes, yes, please don't stop, yes--"

"Would you like to come?"

"Yes, please, yes."

Mr. Cox moved his hand faster, pulling against her pelvic bone with each thrust, and Evie's eyes rolled back in ecstasy.

"Yes! Yes! *Yes!*" She came in wild abandon, bobbing her head up and down and lifting up her hips as high as she could. Mr. Cox didn't stop his hand thrusts until she had crossed the precipice of her orgasm and was well on the other side. He kept his hand still as tiny aftershocks rattled her body, making her muscles spasm all over her racked form.

"Relax your muscles," he ordered as her breath slowed. Slowly, he pulled his glistening, sticky hand out. It made wet oozing sounds as it went.

Once it was out, he held it up to her. It was coated with her juices. Mr. Cox wiped it off on a towel he got from the wardrobe.

As Evie tried to relax her shattered nerves, Mr. Cox released her from her bondage.

"I hope you've learned, Evie, you gain nothing from holding back your body's natural reactions from me," he said as he worked to free her from the table. Her arms and legs came down slowly from the air, trembling and weak. "Your Daddy works the same way. Show your pleasure, and you get a reward. Hide your pain, and you only get more punishment. Do you understand?"

"Yes Sir," she grumbled, pushing herself up into a sitting position, but keeping her head down. She didn't want to look him in the eyes.

Mr. Cox noticed her stubborn posture, but decided not to remark on it. *A little stubbornness can be a good thing*, he thought, *if she can put it to good use*.

"Get dressed," he said. "Go relax. I'll let you have the rest of the evening for yourself, to do whatever you want. But tomorrow morning, Evie, I expect you to rejoin the human population and eat breakfast in the dining room. Understand?"

Evie picked up her head and stared mutinously at her host.

"Yes, Sir," she said, her voice clipped.

Mr. Cox nodded, satisfied. "Good," he said. "I'll be seeing you tomorrow."

"When exactly tomorrow, Sir?"

"Why, when I say so, Evie. When I say so."

***

Evie spent the rest of the night in her hotel room. She fell asleep late, hugging a teddy bear to her chest. It smelled like Daddy.

The next morning, she woke to the sound of the telephone ringing. It was the front desk, waking her on her host's orders, and reminding her she was due downstairs. Evie managed a polite thank-you through clenched teeth.

Mr. Cox was a tyrant, she decided. Trying to control her every minute, trying to get her to bend to his will. Well, he would learn that the only man's will she would bend to was her Daddy's.

Daddy had told her to be good, and being good meant following Mr. Cox's orders. So she would follow them. But only as far as she had to. Evie was expected downstairs in the dining room, so she would head downstairs to the dining room.

But she did not dress nicely for the occasion. She did not even put on a casual t-shirt and jeans. And she certainly didn't adorn the naughty prepschool outfit she had packed.

No, Evie remained in her nightgown, and it was the longest, thickest, most worn-out and ugliest nightgown she owned. Made out of wool, it fell to her ankles and swathed her up to the neck.

Evie had owned it since she had grown to her full height, years ago, and had held onto it only because it was so warm and comfortable. But it was also raggedy, stained, and ripped.

She never wore it when her Daddy summoned her to his bedroom. She wore it only within the confines of her own room, and only when she was sure Daddy would not be making a surprise visit.

As she looked down at the ugly (and somewhat smelly) nightgown, she took on an air of stubborn satisfaction. *If Mr. Cox wants me to act like a Babygirl,* she thought, *I will. And Babygirls don't dress up in fancy clothes for breakfast.*

She got a lot of stares in the dining room. But no one said anything about it, not even the waiter who showed her to her table. Evie studied the wine list and looked around at the other guests until he returned.

He came back holding a tray of food and a cup of juice. Evie frowned.

"I think you've made a mistake," she said. "I haven't even ordered yet."

The waiter looked at her strangely. "You don't want this? You would like to look at the menu instead?"

Evie peeked at the plate. It was filled with fruit, toast, and a bowl of oatmeal. Evie made a face of disgust. She hated oatmeal. "Yes. I don't want that. Take it back."

The waiter shrugged. "Very well, miss," he said. "I will take it back to the kitchen and bring you a menu." He disappeared for only a moment, and returned with a menu in hand.

Evie ended up ordering the loaded omelet, a stack of butter pancakes, and a basket of sliced bread rolls with butter.

When the food arrived, she didn't bother putting her napkin on her lap, and she didn't pick up the fork and knife, either. Evie ate with her hands.

The surrounding diners stared at her in wonder, no doubt because of her barbaric manners, but Evie didn't care. She had no one there to impress. In any case, Baby-girls weren't expected to have good manners, were they? And Mr. Cox expected her to be a good Babygirl.

When she was done, she licked her fingers clean, and wiped her hands on her nightgown.

But by the time she got back to her room, she began to question the wisdom of her heavy meal. She was feeling sick to her stomach, and wanted nothing more than to curl up in a ball on the bed. She was not used to eating such massive amounts of food for breakfast.

As she lay in a fetal position, moaning softly, she heard a knock on her door. It was the liaison, looking stuffy and bored as usual.

"Mr. Cox requires your presence immediately," he said. "Please come with me."

"What, right now? Can I change first?" The idea of appearing in front of her host wearing her frayed and distasteful nightgown made goosebumps rise along her arms in fear. She had known he would get a report of her conduct, but it hadn't occurred to her he might actually *see* her in the ugly thing.

"No," her liaison said. "You are to accompany me immediately."

"It will only take a minute--"

"If you prefer, I can tell Mr. Cox you refused to come."

"No! No. I will follow you down now."

She shut the door behind her and followed the liaison, hugging her arms to her chest and feeling her anxiety rise. Not only was she embarrassed by the prospect of appearing to her host dressed as she was, her stomach was really beginning to bother her. All that heavy food, mixed with the tight knot of fear growing in her belly, was not sitting well.

Maybe once she told Mr. Cox she wasn't feeling well, he would send her back to her room. She could hope.

Her liaison escorted her to a new activity room this time, one Evie had never seen before. This made her feel a bit more hopeful. Maybe Mr. Cox was busy with someone else, and only wanted to tell her something quickly? Maybe he wasn't planning on giving her one of his "lessons" now after all?

But when she entered the room, Mr. Cox wasn't looking all that hurried, and he didn't look very sympathetic to her bent, moaning form. He took one look at her, and his face became a mask of fury.

"What the hell are you walking around wearing *that* for?" He barked, taking a step toward her. He stopped himself from closing the distance, as if afraid to get too close. "I could not *believe* it when they told me you had gone to the dining room looking like--like *this*," he waved his hand at her general direction. "And then you refused the food I had ordered for you--"

"You ordered that food for me?" She exclaimed, surprised. "I didn't know, they didn't tell me--"

"And ate like a pig," Mr. Cox continued, "embarrassing yourself in front of the entire hotel. What were you *thinking*?"

"You told me to behave like a Babygirl," she said, her voice more nervous than smug. She wasn't feeling at all sure of herself anymore. In fact, she was feeling contrite, and more than a little embarrassed. "I ate like a Babygirl. I dressed like a Babygirl."

"No, you are dressed like a street rat, and you ate like a derelict," Mr. Cox said. "Does Mr. Altman know you even *own* this thing?"

He strode toward her until he was peering down at her face, then cringed, getting a whiff of her nightgown. "Oh my god, it even smells awful," he said. "Take it off. Now. I won't have you wearing it in my presence."

Evie hugged her stomach. "Please, Sir, I can't really take it off."

"Why not?" He hissed.

"I'm not feeling very well, Sir. I think I should just go back up to my room and lie down," she finished, trying to look as ill and pathetic as possible, which wasn't difficult. Her stomach was starting to make rumbling noises that were audible to both of them.

"Not feeling well, eh? Your stomach is bothering you?"

Evie nodded.

"Well, we can take care of that right here," he said, giving her a twisted, ominous grin. Evie's skin prickled with dread. "Take that gown off now, before I rip it off you," he sneered.

Evie pulled it over her head in one fluid movement, feeling the cool air of the room hit her body, making her shiver. Before she even had a chance to fling the nightgown to the bed, her host was grabbing her by the arm and pulling her roughly toward a second set of doors that had been hidden in the back of the room by the angle of the deep wardrobe. Mr. Cox now opened the double doors, and dragged Evie inside.

It was a bathroom: a very large, opulent, and stately bathroom. An extra-wide sunken tub took up one corner of the spacious room, while the shower, big enough for four people, stood next to it, lined with multiple water jets. Double sinks took up the other wall, separated by a decadent marble counter top.

A bench, wide and well padded, sat in the middle of the tiled floor, yet the room was so large, there was ample space to walk around it. Beyond the threshold where Evie stood, she could look across the room, down a tiny square hall, and see two more doors, each facing each other. She presumed at least one of them hid a private, secluded toilet. What the other one was, she couldn't fathom a guess.

The room reminded her of the Roman baths she had seen pictures of in books. Well lit, elegant and luxurious, it was obviously built not just for functionality, but for fun.

Evie couldn't appreciate the beauty of the bathroom just then. Her stomach was aching, stretched so tight she thought if she moved the wrong way she might throw up. All she wanted to do was lie down and rest.

The considerate thing for her host to do would have been to let her go back to her room and rest until she felt better. But of course, her host was not a considerate man. He obviously didn't care about her temporary aching fullness.

Mr. Cox pulled her over to the bench, almost as big as a twin size bed, and shoved her down onto it. Evie stumbled, fell with a moan, and curled her legs up to her stomach.

"Lay down on your side," he said. "Bend your knees to your chest."

Relieved that he was finally taking her discomfort into account and trying to help her alleviate it, Evie did as instructed. She felt a tiny bit better. The tension in her stomach muscles eased somewhat, and she took a few deep breaths.

While Evie remained down on the bench, her eyes closed, she could hear her host moving around the large room. At first, she didn't bother looking what he was doing. All her focus was on getting through another stomach spasm. But when she heard him open one of the narrow side doors at the end of the small hallway, she lifted her lids and picked up her head.

Mr. Cox was holding cuffs and straps.

"What are you--"

Before she could even finish the question, Mr. Cox had grabbed Evie's limp and sweaty hands and had cuffed them in front of her. Using a heavy metal carabiner, he pulled them to one side and locked them into an eye bolt fastened to the side of the bench. With both hands cuffed to the same bolt, Evie was now trapped on her side.

"Hey--"

Without pausing, Mr. Cox took a long nylon strap, pushed it underneath Evie's hips (making her jack up her butt in the process), and brought it up to her waist. Evie arched when she felt the nylon riding up her back, but Mr. Cox pushed her back down.

He picked her legs up and flung them over her head, and before Evie had a chance to fight him, he looped the nylon strap behind her knees and cinched it closed, holding down the velcro strip. Evie's knees were now bent up to her stomach, locked in place.

But Mr. Cox wasn't done. He cuffed her ankles together, too, then picked up another carabiner and snapped them into another bolt on the same side of the bench as her hands.

Evie was stuck curled on her side, her ass bent at the hips, her most private parts exposed, and she couldn't move.

"Why are you doing this?" She wailed.

But Mr. Cox was no longer standing next to her. He had gone back to what was obviously a supply closet to gather up more items. Evie had no idea what he could be getting now, or what would be coming next. Angled as she was, she couldn't look down the length of the room to see.

Evie's eyes widened in fear when she heard something being wheeled across the tile floor. Mr. Cox parked whatever it was directly behind her curled body.

Then Evie heard the water faucet turn on behind her.

"What are you doing?" Her voice came out high and loud over the sound of the rushing water.

"You, my dear, are in need of some Babygirl discipline," Mr. Cox replied. "I ordered a meal that I knew you could stomach, food that would be good for you. All that heavy food you ate instead is making you sick. What you need is to be cleaned out."

"What?"

"Come now, you must realize I can't have you getting ill while you're under my care. Your Daddy would be furious with me, and rightly so. Hasn't he ever had to administer medicine to you to help make you feel better? Castor oil, perhaps? Maybe even Ipecac?"

"No, never," Evie whimpered. She could hear the hard echo of the water hitting metal: Mr. Cox was filling a bucket with water. Her heart sped up in fear.

"I'll have to talk to him about that," Mr. Cox said. The water turned off. For a few moments, Evie could hear him rustling about behind her, getting things ready. Then she felt a hand on the smooth hill of her ass.

"You're going to get an enema, Evie," Mr. Cox said almost sadly. "Hopefully this will teach you for next time what happens when you disobey my orders."

"No, please!" She cried. She began to wrestle against her restrains, shaking the bench.

"Don't fight it," her host replied. "It won't do any good."

"You can't do this to me, you can't--"

"Yes, I can."

"My Daddy would never--"

"Your Daddy put you in my care. Listen, Evie: there's more than one way to take an enema. I filled the bucket with some nice warm water, so it won't hurt so much. It might even feel like a gentle massage. If you're good, and relax, I'll let the water go in slowly. But if you fight me, Evie, I'll fill the bucket with cold water, and make it go in faster. And believe me, that's not how you want to get your first enema."

Evie began to cry. "Please, please don't do this to me."

"It's going to happen, whether you like it or not. Now are you going to be good, and get this over with like a brave Babygirl? Or do I have to fill the bucket with cold water?"

Evie stilled her body, trying to get her crying under control. "I'll be good, I promise."

"Good. Now relax your asshole. I'm going to put in the nozzle."

Evie felt something thin and slippery poke against the opening of her ass. Reflexively, she tightened up.

"Relax, Evie," Mr. Cox said again. "Take a deep breath."

Evie took a deep breath, and felt the nozzle shove up her hole. She yelped.

"The nozzle has a balloon at the other end that I have to inflate, so you can't push it out of your ass," he said. "I'm going to inflate it now. You'll feel some pressure inside." As he spoke, Evie could feel something growing bigger just on the other side of her sphincter. Very quickly, it felt huge inside her rectum. She tried to push it out, and found she could not. It was too big.

She began to cry again, her sobs racking her whole body.

"There we go," Mr. Cox said. "Now all we have to do is unclamp the tube, and--"

Evie closed her eyes. A rush of warmth started to flood her rectum and continued into her lower belly. She moaned loudly.

"Just be still, Evie," Mr. Cox said. "I set the water to go very, very slowly. It shouldn't hurt you too much." He came around to her other side and sat on the edge of the bench so she could see him.

"I hate you!" Evie sobbed.

"I get that," Mr. Cox replied. "But your Daddy left me responsible for you, and I'm not going to let you go wild inside this hotel and do whatever you want. You'll be returned to him in the same condition you were in when he left here. Hopefully better."

The water continued to fill Evie's body. She squeezed her eyes shut against the liquid warmth. It didn't hurt, but she had no control over it, and hated how helpless she felt. She was absolutely defenseless against her host's whims and her body's reactions.

Mr. Cox gazed at the bucket. "While we wait for all the water to empty from the bucket, tell me how you met your Daddy."

Evie's eyes opened in shock. For a split second, she forgot about the cuffs binding her wrists and ankles and the water filling her insides.

"What, you want me to tell you the story of how Daddy and I met *now*?"

"Why not? We have time. Unless you want me to make the water go in faster?"

"No!" The pressure in her belly was growing, but slowly. Evie didn't think she could take it going any faster. She was at the mercy of her host, who at that moment, she loathed.

"We met at a restaurant," she gritted out. "He was there alone. I was there with someone else. My date made some kind of rude comment, I don't remember anymore exactly what it was. I threw my glass of water in his face."

"Really?" Mr. Cox chuckled. "Sounds like you really were a spitfire back then."

"Yes," Evie's voice was clipped. "Daddy ran after me as I was walking out of the restaurant, and gave me his number. He told me to call him sometime so he could take me out on a date. I did. That's it." She closed her mouth and took a deep breath. The pressure inside her intestines was growing to new heights, and the nozzle sitting inside of her rectum was starting to strain.

"I understand now what Mr. Altman first saw in you," Mr. Cox said. "An impetuous little brat, looking for someone to take her in hand. So why do you only act the brat when your Daddy's not around to see it, I wonder?"

Evie wasn't really paying attention anymore. She was breathing hard, feeling the bloating in her stomach become an urgent call to action. She began to groan.

"The water's just about done, Evie," Mr. Cox said, watching her frantic expressions flit across her face as the water filled her innards. "I'm going to uncuff you now, then deflate and remove the nozzle. The toilet's right down there, on the left. Ready?"

He uncuffed her ankles first, then her wrists. Evie remained still as he deflated the balloon of the nozzle, then slowly eased it out of her bulging rectum. Evie whimpered. It was all she could do not to embarrass herself right there on the bench.

Once the nozzle was out, she quickly got up, and, holding one hand over her stomach and the other against her straining bottom, ran as fast as she could down the hall. She didn't care anymore about dignity or what her host thought of her. All she wanted to do was make it to the toilet.

Thankfully, Mr. Cox left her alone, and granted her some blessed privacy. Evie still continued to curse her host under her breath.

***

Evie walked back into the activity room naked and shaking. She had been in the bathroom for what felt like a long time, releasing the enema from her body. Now she felt weak and spent.

She looked around the room for her clothes, thinking she would be allowed to dress and return to her room. Not so. Her ordeal was still far from over.

Mr. Cox had put a large bowl on the floor. It was stainless steel, and looked exactly like a dog bowl. It was filled with thick white liquid.

"Drink," he ordered. "You need to get your electrolytes back."

"Where are we going?" Evie yanked her arm away from him, planting her feet in place. She would not follow him blindly to her own demise twice.

"You need a bath," he said. "You stink." When Evie didn't move, her face a mask of resistance, he grinned even wider. "Ah, a glimmer of contention. It's good to see, but I don't think you want to fight me on this right now, Evie. Don't you *want* a bath? The hotel keeps a good stock of bath oils. You can choose one, if you want. And you should brush your teeth."

At the prospect of cleaning herself up and relaxing in a nice hot bath, Evie relented, and let Mr. Cox pull her back to the bathroom. She only hesitated a moment when her eyes clapped on the cursed bench. But all the evidence of her previous experience on it, including the enema supplies, bucket, and tubing, had already been put away. It was as if it had never happened.

Mr. Cox turned on the tub jets, then handed Evie a brand new toothbrush and some toothpaste. As Evie brushed her teeth, the tub began to fill with water. By the time she was done, the tub was already heaping with soapy bubbles, and looked heavenly.

Mr. Cox offered Evie a steadying hand as she stepped inside the tub. She lay down in it and relaxed, closing her eyes as the water rose around her body, making her feel weightless.

A second later, she was opening her eyes in alarm as Mr. Cox entered the tub himself. He had undressed while she had been relaxing in the water, lulled by the soothing warmth.

Evie barely had time to look at his muscular thighs and thick cock before they were disappearing into the opaque water. He sat across from her in the large tub, stretched out his arms on either side, and sighed in contentment.

"What are you doing?" Evie shrieked. She thought she would be able to bathe in peace, and for once, not have to worry about what her dratted host was up to. Now she realized she would have to keep her guard up, even while taking a bath.

"How else am I supposed to wash you?" He laughed. He grabbed a washcloth off a shelf above the tub and began to rub it with some soap.

"I can wash myself, thank you."

"I know."

"Let me rephrase that. I *prefer* to wash myself."

"Ah, more opposition. Very good. But you don't really, you know--want to wash yourself, I mean. You'd much rather have me wash you." He grabbed her foot from underneath the water and raised it, bringing the washcloth around her ankle and rubbing it around her foot. Evie gasped. Mr. Cox smiled.

"Ticklish?"

He continued to rub the washcloth around her foot, getting between the toes, then slid it up her calf, circling her leg. Evie watched him with narrowed eyes, but didn't pull her leg away. What he was doing felt good, like a gentle massage.

Mr. Cox moved up her leg, making deep, kneading circles into her flesh with the washcloth, filling Evie with a sense of warm serenity. When he got to her upper thigh, he stopped, and picked up her other foot, repeating the same process on the other leg. Evie lay back in the tub and moaned in delight.

But this time, when he got to her upper thigh, he didn't stop. He kept going up her leg, kneading deep into her inner thigh, almost all the way up to the crease of her pubic mound. Evie opened her eyes and looked at him through heavy lids, daring him to move higher.

Without saying a word, Mr. Cox moved himself up the tub until he was seated on his knees next to her, then began to slide the slightly coarse washcloth deep into the folds of her pussy. Evie jacked upright.

"Easy, easy," Mr. Cox soothed her. "I'm not going to do anything that hurts you. I promise."

Keeping her eyes focused on her host, Evie slowly sunk back down into the water. She would give him a chance to keep his word, and make up for all his former horrible treatment of her. His skillful massage was too damn good not to give him this chance.

True to his word, Mr. Cox did not become boorish in the task he had taken upon himself. He continued to rub the washcloth in and around Evie's cunt, using slow, gentle strokes, until Evie closed her eyes and relaxed her body all the way into the water, with only her face breaking the surface. It felt marvelous, the way he was washing her inside and out. Evie felt pampered, like a Roman empress being coddled by her slaves, and she never wanted it to end.

But more than that, the washcloth rubbing her clit was making her horny. Every time it glided over her tingling nub and flushing folds, Evie twitched with a jolt of arousal. She couldn't have done a better job of priming her pussy to make her come herself.

Soon, she was moving her hips against the washcloth in her host's strong hand, thrusting and swaying in time to his expert ministrations. She bucked her pelvis, trying to control the pressure hitting her throbbing clit. Mr. Cox let her move as she wanted, pressing in with his expert fingers when she bucked, and holding still as she rubbed her own pussy against the washcloth.

After only a few minutes, Evie was clasping his wide hand inside her two smaller ones, holding it still as she rode it to orgasm. She rocked her body as she came, sloshing the water around them both, moaning loudly.

As she rode the wave back down, she relaxed once more into the water, breathing hard and staring at Mr. Cox with half-hooded eyes.

"That was beautiful, Evie," Mr. Cox said. "You really let yourself go with that one. I love watching you come."

"Thank you, Sir."

"Now turn around. I'm not done washing you."

With languid movements, Evie did as told, turning stomach down into the water. She had to arch her back a bit to keep her face above the water. Her hands reached out in front of her to hold onto the handles on each edge of the tub.

But this was still not the pose Mr. Cox wanted. He put his hands under her hips and raised her until she was crouched on all fours, her ass and cunt high in the air. With most of her body now above the water, Evie felt the temperature difference immediately. Goosebumps rose on her skin. But her tits hung down into the water, and her nipples grew plump and hard.

Mr. Cox began to rub her pussy again from behind, but this time without the washcloth. He fondled and caressed her wet warm folds, dipping into her pussy and making Evie gasp. He poked a finger inside, then another. Evie could hear her wet juices making sucking sounds around his fingers as they wiggled and jabbed.

Mr. Cox took his time playing with her, teasing her with his fingers, until Evie was thrusting back against his probing digits, trying to fuck herself off once more. She was ready to come again, and had no inhibitions about using her body to express that wish to her host.

But that wasn't good enough for Mr. Cox.

"What would you like, Evie?" He asked from behind her.

"I would like to come, Sir," she asked in a light, girly voice. "Please."

"Such an honest request. How would you like me to help?"

She turned her face to look at him and wiggled her hips provocatively. "Please play with my clit, Sir."

"That's one way I could do it. How else?"

Evie stopped moving in the water: she realized Mr. Cox had turned this into another one of his "lessons." She decided to play along. It was only some questions, after all.

"You could put your fingers back in my pussy, Sir. That would make me come."

"Excellent. How else?"

She frowned, thinking hard. Then she smiled.

"You could put your cock in my pussy and fuck me, Sir."

"Yes, and under the circumstances, I think that's exactly what I want to do. But first I want you to ask for it. Go on, Evie. Ask for my cock."

Evie rolled her eyes. "Please, Sir, can I have your cock in my pussy?"

"Not like that, Evie. Ask like you mean it."

Getting frustrated now, Evie made a sound of protest and tried to grind her crotch against her host's erect prick. Mr. Cox slapped her ass and made her yelp.

"If you want to come, you'd better start behaving, Babygirl. Now ask again."

"Please, Sir, will you put your cock in my pussy?"

"Again."

"Sir, will you *please* put your cock in my pussy?"

"Still not buying it, Evie."

"Sir! Please stick me with your cock, *please*, I *need* your cock in my pussy, I need to *come*, please Sir."

Mr. Cox rammed his prick deep inside her wet cavern, making Evie squeal.

His strokes were quick and deep, and Evie had to brace herself against the side of the tub so she wouldn't be pushed face-first into it.

At first, Evie enjoyed the savage fucking quietly, only letting tiny sighs escape her lips. But remembering her lessons, she began to vocalize her passion, letting her host know of her growing arousal.

"Oh yes, yes, Sir, that feels wonderful, please don't stop."

Mr. Cox's thrusts came harder. Evie could feel his prick inside her hit the edge of her womb. It tickled in the most delightful way, and she gasped.

"Oh god, please don't stop, Sir, please don't stop! Oh god! Ohhh."

She cried out as she came again, letting her voice rise and fall with the power of her orgasm. Mr. Cox kept pumping as she came, letting her get the full feel of his hard rod.

Evie was a bit surprised when she came down from her orgasm and realized her host was nowhere near coming yet. But she was content to remain still, and let him finish at his own pace.

Then she realized remaining still would not be good enough. At last, Evie understood what her host was waiting for: he wanted her to help spur him on.

"Oh yes, Sir, ram me with that big prick, it feels so good and my pussy's so tight now." She rocked her body against his probing cock, cramming herself with his rock-hard prick.

But she stopped when she heard splashing in the water. Mr. Cox had removed his hands from her hips to lather them in the soapy water. When Evie felt them return to her body, they were peeling open the crack of her ass.

"No!" She jerked her body forward. After the all-too recent violation of her ass, she was panicked by the mere thought of anything touching her there.

But Mr. Cox circled an arm under her hips, keeping her still. With his other, he teased a finger up and down her crease, tickling her asshole.

"Don't, please don't," she cried.

"Don't what?"

"Don't touch me there, please."

"Why not? Am I hurting you?"

"No, but I don't want you to. Please."

"Does your Daddy always give in to your demands?" He began to circle the pad of his finger around her clenching asshole, targeting in.

"No, but, please, please don't--"

"That's it, Evie. Show me how much you don't want it." He pressed in with his finger, sliding the thick digit up her squeezing sphincter. Then he started thrusting in with his cock again.

Evie exploded with anger and fear. She tried to push her way out of the tub, but Mr. Cox held her under her hips and pulled her back. Evie could feel his finger gain another inch inside her asshole as she struggled.

Screaming loudly, she bucked and fought, trying to dislodge him enough to escape. When that didn't work, she tried to turn around, ready to scratch his eyes out. Mr. Cox only pushed her down into the water, making her splutter and choke. As Evie worked to get her breath back, Mr. Cox worked his finger into her back passage even further. His cock rammed into her pussy, taking up its rhythmic pumping.

"Why are you doing this?" Evie cried. Her tears dripped into the sloshing water.

"Doing what?" The finger inside her jiggled and twisted. Evie yelped.

"Why are you treating me like this? You promised you wouldn't hurt me!"

"And I'm not. I know this isn't hurting you, Evie. You just don't want me to be doing it. Am I right?"

Her voice cracked. "Yes!"

"That's too bad. I like this very much." He pistoned his finger in and out of her asshole in time to his thrusting cock.

"Oh!" Evie struggled again to escape her sadistic host, and found it just as futile as she had before. She began to sob face down into the tub.

"Please stop, please." Her voice became unintelligible through her sobs.

"No, I don't think I will. Reach a hand up and start playing with your nipples."

"What?"

"You heard me. Play with your nipples."

"No!"

"Do it, or it'll be my cock in your ass you'll be feeling next."

Hiccuping on her own tears, Evie reached up and began to lightly squeeze her nipples, twisting them in her fingers. The sensations distracted her a bit from what Mr. Cox was doing behind and inside her. She stopped crying.

"That's it, Babygirl. Pull on them. Twist them. Work 'em good." He continued to glide his finger in and out of her rear gate, but used slow, shallow strokes, never wavering from his rhythm. It felt thick inside her asshole, and Evie's ring of muscle clenched and spasmed around it. But soon, it became a welcome pressure, a stabbing thrill that complemented his pumping cock in a way Evie could never have imagined.

She began to pull at her nipples roughly in the water, gasping at the pangs of pleasure coursing her body.

She forgot about being angry at her host, forgot about her outrage and desperation, and felt only her growing arousal.

"That's it, that's a good Babygirl. Now flick 'em, Evie, flick those nipples hard."

Grimacing with effort, Evie switched hands in the water and began to flick her nipples as instructed. Her tits wobbled and danced above the water. It hurt, but not really...just like his finger in her ass hurt, but not really. Evie began to rock back against his cock just as she had before, only this time she was rocking back against his finger fucking her asshole, too.

Her anger and shame forgotten, Evie began to plead once more, only her pleas were of an entirely different sort.

"Oh God, please Sir, I can't do this."

"Why not?"

"It isn't right." Her voice was breathless with need.

"What's not right?"

"That it feels so good, oh god, so good Sir." She rocked against him, moaning and crying, and behind her, Mr. Cox dug in, making his own little sounds of ecstasy.

"You like it now? You like what I'm doing to you?"

"Yes Sir, oh yes."

"Then fuck yourself off." He stopped thrusting. "Go on, finish us both off. And let me know when you come!"

Evie rocked her body wildly against him now, gyrating her hips with wide circles and thrusts. She was mad to come. She didn't care one whit anymore if her host did or not. But she remembered to show when she came and let her inhibitions go.

"Oh, Sir, wiggle that finger more, harder, yes, like that. Oh my god I'm going to come!"

She rocked her body back so hard, Mr. Cox had to steady himself against the wall. The feel of her round ass slapping his thighs as she cried out her pleasure was his undoing, and Mr. Cox came with a shudder, shooting his hot come deep inside Evie's wet, gripping pussy.

Evie screamed with delight, raising her body and arching against him. In the last second, Mr. Cox grabbed her hair and pulled her head back, keeping her body from dropping back down. Evie continued to come, oblivious to the pain in her scalp and certainly unable to do anything about it.

Feeling only the bolts of pleasure jolting her body, she held her body stiff against his, and Mr. Cox held her head and watched her face contort with the force of her orgasm.

He only let her hair go as her face relaxed, her eyes rolling back and blinking a few times. Her head fell unsupported towards the water, and she almost sank into it before she caught herself.

Evie continued to breathe heavily, quivering on all fours, as Mr. Cox pulled his cock, and his finger, away from her shaking body.

"Time to get out now," he said. He helped her out. Mr. Cox rubbed her skin dry with a thick soft towel, and circled it around her scrubbed and glowing body. Evie stood still and let him dry her, too tired and sated to care if he might still be up to some devious new plan.

But Mr. Cox wasn't up to anything anymore. The plan now was simply to get her back to her room. He retrieved a short thin robe from the wardrobe and tied the belt around her waist in a loose bow.

"This will have to do until you get back upstairs," he said. He went to the wall by the door and pressed the button to summon the liaison.

"I can't walk around the hallways dressed like this," Evie said, her voice slurred. "It's too short, and I'm naked underneath."

"This is much better than what you were wearing earlier, believe me," Mr. Cox replied. When she made a face at him, he said, "it's this or you sleep in the cage tonight. Which is it going to be?"

"I'll go upstairs like this."

"That's what I thought," Mr. Cox said. "Have a good sleep, Evie. I'll see you later."

"When will that be, Sir?"

"Haven't you learned yet, Evie? That's completely up to me."

***

The next morning, Evie woke bright and early, but on her own. No phone call awoke her. She took a few moments to stare out at the sunlit topography beyond her window before rising from the bed. It was then she realized she was still wearing the thin robe in which Mr. Cox had dressed her.

It was eight o'clock in the morning. She had been returned to her room the evening before, had promptly fallen into bed, and had slept the whole night.

Evie stripped off the robe and began to prepare for the day. She felt ravenous, but that was to be expected. She had eaten only one meal the day before, not counting the nourishing drink Mr. Cox had fed her from the dog bowl, and had suffered through an enema besides.

Donning a red cotton t-shirt and a pair of faded blue jeans, Evie made quick time of her hair and makeup. When the elevator took too long to arrive to her floor, she took the stairs down instead, and waited impatiently in the dining room for the waiter to seat her.

But she made sure to tell the waiter her room number, and ask this time if any food had been ordered for her beforehand. Sure enough, the waiter returned not with a menu, but with a tray of food.

Thankfully, the tray was full of dishes she liked. There was even a slice of French toast. Evie ate gladly, and enjoyed a cup of hot coffee when she was done.

But as she rose from the table to return to her room, her waiter scurried over, holding out an envelope and looking nervous.

"This is from your liaison, miss," he said. "You are to open it immediately."

Evie cut the envelope open with her bread knife. The note read:

Your host orders you below. I am waiting for you by the elevators. Come at once.

Evie stuffed the note back in the envelope.

"Please throw this away for me?" She asked the waiter in a feeble voice. Her hand shook as she held out the envelope.

"Of course, miss. Have a good day, miss."

Evie walked briskly out of the dining room, trying to control her breathing. Her liaison saw her walking toward him, and pressed the button to bring the elevator down.

"Did Mr. Cox say what the rush is?" She whispered as the elevator hummed.

"No, miss," the liaison replied without looking at her. "He said only to bring you immediately."

They stepped into the empty elevator, bracing as the doors closed.

Sliding his key-card into the elevator panel, the liaison pressed the button that would deliver them to the lower floor. He did not turn around after he did so, but continued to face the elevator doors, and once they opened, he walked out and down the hallway without bothering to make sure she followed.

Evie did follow, despite her anxiety, but racked her brains to figure out what she could have possibly done now to displease her host. Had she been supposed to wake earlier? Dress nicer? Perhaps she was not supposed to have left her room at all? But there had been no instructions!

One thing was for sure, it didn't matter if she hadn't understood Mr. Cox's requirements for her behavior. If she had displeased him somehow, then she would be punished, whether she thought it was fair or not.

She held her chin up and crossed her arms in front of her. She would *not* go through another punishment like she had yesterday, not without a fight!

But when she entered the activity room and saw the expression on her host's face, she uncrossed her arms. He did not look angry. He looked just as nervous as she was.

"I've just gotten word. Your Daddy's meeting tomorrow has been cancelled. He's not waiting until tomorrow morning to return to the hotel. He's coming to get you tonight," he said.

"But that's wonderful," Evie said, smiling. "I'll see my Daddy tonight!"

"No, that's not wonderful," Mr. Cox scowled. "I thought I would have at least another twenty-four hours to work with you. How am I supposed to teach you everything you need to know by tonight?"

He rubbed his face with his hands, sighing deeply. Then he strode over to the bedside table, picked up a plush brown teddy bear that had been sitting on it, and threw it at her. It looked like a child's stuffed animal.

"Get undressed," Mr. Cox ordered. "I want you to take the bear, and use it to play with yourself."

"What?"

"'What? What?' That's all you ever say when I ask you to do something. Stop acting so shocked by my orders, Evie. Now is the time to get with the program!" He ran a hand through his hair. "I had planned on having you give your Daddy a show when he sees you for the first time after he returns. If we work hard, we can still make it happen."

Looking dubious, Evie quickly slipped out of her jeans and t-shirt, then peeled off her panties and bra.

"What kind of show did you have in mind?" She asked.

"Get on the bed. No, don't lie down. Stay on your knees. Spread your legs open. More. Yes, like that. Open your pussy lips with one hand. Spread them wide. Now," he pointed to the teddy bear. "Take the bear and rub yourself with it."

"Rub myself with it where?"

"Where do you think, Evie? Rub it on your pussy! Make yourself come." He became impatient. "Come on, put on a show with it! Show me what you've got!"

Evie held back her look of uncertainty. Deciding to go along with his idea of a "show" (as long as it didn't involve any kind of tubing being inserted into her ass again), Evie would go along.

Holding her pussy lips open with one hand, she began to slide the teddy bear across her pink folds with the other.

"There you go, yes," Mr. Cox encouraged her. "Use the bear like a sexy play-toy. Come on, Evie, I know you can get creative if you put your mind to it."

Closing her eyes, Evie began to will herself to relax, and feel the soft fur of the teddy bear tickling her folds and clit. After a couple minutes, she did begin to feel stimulated, and started to behave much more at ease using the bear as a plush, snugly sex toy.

She stuffed her fingers into her cunt, squashing and circling the teddy against her swelling clit. She bit her lip and squeezed her eyes shut as she worked, letting her growing need control her movements.

In no time, she had completely forgotten about her host watching her from the other side of the room. Her only focus was on the bear and her need to come.

When her climax rose within her, she came silently, only making weak humping movements with her hips as her orgasm crested and fell. Then she dropped the bear on the bed, sighing heavily.

"That's it?" Mr. Cox yelled. "You already came? I could barely even tell!" He turned around to face the wall, his hands clenched into fists. "Goddamn it, Evie! I'd hoped, after all the progress you showed yesterday, you'd have learned at least *something* by now!"

"But I came. Isn't that what you wanted? What did I do wrong?" Evie wailed. She felt very close to tears.

Mr. Cox sighed and sat on the edge of the bed. "Evie, you still don't understand." When he saw her quivering chin, he shook his head. "I like you, Evie. I really do. I know you think I've behaved very badly toward you in the past couple days, and maybe I have, but it's only because I don't want to see you get hurt."

He tilted his head, as if weighing his words. "I shouldn't be telling you what I'm about to say, Evie. I could get into a lot of trouble by telling you these things. But I like your Daddy, and I like you, and I see how much you care about him. I really want the two of you to have a chance at making it together. So don't ever tell anyone what I'm about to tell you, okay?"

Evie nodded her head, her eyes wide.

"You are not the first Babygirl your Daddy has brought with him to the Hotel Bentmoore," he said. "He had two others before you. At least, two others that I know of. Has he ever mentioned them?"

"He told me about one. Jennifer," she whispered. "He said they broke up when they realized they didn't want the same things anymore."

"That's true. They didn't want the same things anymore," Mr. Cox said. "At first, Jennifer was his Babygirl, just like you are now. But after a while, Jennifer didn't want to be just his Babygirl. She decided she wanted to be his slave. Sounds familiar?"

Evie gasped and put her hand to her mouth.

"When your Daddy realized what was going on, how her needs had changed, he offered to help her find a man who would take good care of her, and treat her like a slave. And your Daddy found her the perfect man, exactly what she wanted: someone who would treat her like a cherished object, like valued property. She and your Daddy parted on amicable terms. I still see Jennifer from time to time. She and her Master visit the Hotel Bentmoore on occasion. She's very happy as his slave. It was a good fit."

Mr. Cox rested his elbows on his knees and steepled his fingers.

"Now, the girl your Daddy had before Jennifer, her name was Clara. She and your Daddy did *not* part on amicable terms. She wanted to be his Babygirl, yes, but only on a part time basis, and only when it met her conditions. She treated their relationship like a business arrangement. I only met her once. I didn't like her at all." He grimaced in memory.

"Soon enough, your Daddy grew tired of her attitude, and told her he was done with her, that they were through. She didn't take it well. She took a baseball bat to his car, and ended up having a restraining order served against her."

Evie shook her head vigorously. "I would never do something like that to Daddy. Never ever."

"I know. You're not like Clara. You're not like Jennifer, either. I really think, if you tried, you could be everything your Daddy wants in a Babygirl. You could be his for as long as you want, maybe even forever. But you're not trying hard enough, Evie."

"So what do I *do*?" Tears began to flood her eyes and drip down her cheeks. "I don't understand what he *wants*."

Mr. Cox sighed. "Do you remember the story you told me of how the two of you met? How your Daddy saw you in the restaurant with your date, throwing water in his face after he'd been rude to you? Mr. Altman ran after you to ask you out, remember?"

"Yes," Evie said, wiping her cheek.

"That's the kind of girl he wants, Evie. He wants a girl who's not afraid to show a man what she's thinking or feeling. The kind of girl who will make her likes and dislikes plain to see. He wants a girl who will *react*."

"But if I do something wrong, and he has to punish me, I still have to listen to him--"

"Yes, you have to listen to your Daddy as much as you can. But you still have to react to his punishments, and show him if you don't like what he's doing. Or if you like it, you should show him that, too. And Evie, even the best Babygirls sometimes don't listen to their Daddies. They have their own opinions. Your Daddy can't appreciate your unique personality anymore if you don't show him you have one."

Evie stared at the bed, thoughtful. "I don't want Daddy to think I don't have my own personality anymore," she said. "I still want to be me. I just want to be a good girl for him."

"I know," Mr. Cox said. "Being a good girl for him means being *you*, Evie. Mr. Altman doesn't want a robot, he wants a girl with fire in her blood. You need to show him you still have it, or you're going to lose him."

Evie was quiet for a moment. Then she raised her chin and met her host's eyes head on, her gaze full of steel.

"Tell me what to do," she said.

***

Late that night, Evie was summoned for the final time to her activity room. She had been given a respite of a few hours to nap and eat, after which she had been ordered to bathe, dress, and prepare for her Daddy's return.

She was ready when the liaison came to take her. At least, she felt ready.

As usual, the liaison made no remark on her attire, or even passed her a cursory glance. But the one other male guest she passed in the hallway stopped to stare at her, giving her a smile of heavy approval as she walked by. Evie smiled back, grateful for the small sign of validation.

Evie had put on a form-fitting white blouse with tight sleeves and a frilled collar. The buttons pulled across her chest, accentuating her softly rounded breasts. She had left the top few buttons open, and while the collar covered up some of her cleavage, by no means did it hide it all. As she walked, the soft frilly fabric swayed, revealing a hint of rising flesh.

Her skirt was brown, A-shaped, and ended just above her smooth, creamy thighs. It hugged her waist and girlish hips, showing off her young, feminine figure most becomingly.

Beneath the skirt, she wore sheer, almost translucent, thigh-high stockings. As she walked, the sashaying skirt would rise above the hem of her stockings, revealing a glimpse of bare flesh and lacy garter. (The male guest in the hallway had obviously caught a peak of the thin satin ribbon, and had stopped to stare.)

Her hair was pulled back behind her ears in a matching brown headband, and fell down her back in a plait. Shiny brown mary-jane shoes with three-inch heels finished her ensemble. Evie looked like a chic, young, haughty school girl.

When she saw Mr. Altman standing in the activity room, facing away from the door and deep in conversation with Mr. Cox, she didn't even try to stop herself. She ran at him, giving him barely enough time to turn around and put his arms out before she was flying into them. She hugged him tight around the neck, then kissed his cheeks over and over.

"Daddy! Daddy, I've missed you so much," she cried.

"I missed you too, Evie," Mr. Altman said with a chuckle, pulling her arms away from his neck a little but still hugging her back. "How is my Babygirl?"

"I'm fine, Daddy," Evie said, lowering her heels and moving her arms around his waist. "But I missed you terribly."

"Did you enjoy the hotel, though, my love? I was hoping you'd have a chance to do some horseback riding, or go on a hike or two while I was gone."

When Evie looked at a loss for an answer, Mr. Cox stepped in. "I'm afraid I kept her too busy for that, Altman," he said. "I didn't want her doing anything too dangerous while she was in my care."

"Oh, well, at least I know you didn't leave her bored," Mr. Altman replied. "You look amazing, Evie."

"Thank you Daddy! Do you like my hair? I'm wearing my new headband--"

"How was your trip, Altman?" Mr. Cox interrupted. "Did it go the way you planned?"

"Not exactly," Mr. Altman replied, peeling Evie's arms away from his waist and turning back to Mr. Cox. "I had to meet with some investors...."

As Mr. Altman resumed his business talk with Mr. Cox, Evie sat down on the bed, waiting for her Daddy's attention to come back around to her. But it was soon clear that, for the time being, Mr. Altman was happy to talk "man to man" with his long-time friend.

Once again, the two were lost in conversation, and had completely forgotten about the woman in the room.

But this time, Evie had no intention of letting the conversation go on without her, while she just sat and waited like a servant to be noticed. She had practiced with Mr.

Cox a little show for her Daddy, and if he was too preoccupied to give her the attention she needed, well then, she would just start the show without him!

As the two men talked, relaxed in their male camaraderie, Evie crawled across the bed and retrieved the teddy bear on the side table that had been so well-used merely hours before. It was about to be used again, and this time, with a new pair of eyes as audience, or so Evie hoped.

Slowly, Evie lay down on the bed and pulled out her hair out from under her head, creating a billowy soft halo across the sheets. Then, she raised her knees and flipped off her shoes, letting them drop with a clatter to the floor. Neither of the men reacted to the sound.

Carefully, she pulled her skirt up her satiny thighs, one inch at a time, until the fabric brushed against the skin of her rounded ass. She wore no panties underneath.

The two men still did not notice her.

Evie spread her legs open wide, feeling the cool room air hit her shaved mound and moistening pussy. She shivered in delight, opening her legs even more.

With her free hand, she traced a trail down her stomach, past her bunched up skirt, until she came to the wet and puffy folds of her pussy. Curving her fingers, she slipped her hand inside.

Out of the corner of his eye, Mr. Altman caught some movement coming from the bed, and turned his head. He stopped his conversation mid-sentence.

"Evie, for the love of God, what are you doing?"

"I missed you, Daddy," Evie breathed. Without stopping her hand from its playful movements, Evie continued to finger-fuck her own cunt. A look of intense concentration flitted over her features.

Now, knowing she had her Daddy's full attention, Evie brought the teddy bear into play. Carefully, she rested the plush doll between her legs, and squeezed her smooth thighs shut. Then she began to scissor them, giving the two men a peak-show of the doll being hugged and rubbed against her mound.

Evie grabbed the head of the bear and began to brush it, ever so gently, against her gaping, wet folds. At first, she moved slowly, but after only a few moments, her tempo began to speed up, the caresses of the ticklish bear rushing her into a frenzy of arousal.

"Evie, stop it! For God's sake, Evie!"

"I want you so badly, Daddy. But you were talking to Mr. Cox. I couldn't wait anymore. I just needed a little..." Her voice trailed off and her eyes squeezed shut. Her hand pressed the stuffed bear against her sopping cunt and rubbed. Evie let out a loud moan.

"Evie, stop this now!"

"I can't Daddy. It feels so good."

The fur of the bear stuck in clumps now, wet and sticky from her juices. Evie began to roll across the bed, the bear held tight between her legs. She squealed with pleasure.

"Evie, stop this right now, or by God I'll punish you right here in front of Mr. Cox!"

Evie came up to her knees in front of Mr. Altman and continued to brush the bear against her open pussy lips with long, hard strokes.

"Are you sure you want me to stop, Daddy? Are you sure?"

When Mr. Altman didn't immediately reply, too frozen to do anything but stare at her, Evie grinned. She continued her quick, steady rhythm with her hand.

She began to buck her pelvis back and forth, moving in time with the coated, prickly bear that had become a squashed ball in her hand, rubbing up against her clit. Evie spread her labia open as much as she could, giving the two men a good view of her inner folds, and circled the bear around it.

"Oh, Daddy, it feels so good...Daddy, I need to come."

"Don't you dare, Evie, don't you fucking dare!"

"Daddy, I can't help myself--"

She began to rub the brown bear roughly inside her folds, gyrating her body around it and making a series of plaintive "oooh" sounds.

"It feels so good Daddy, I can't stop, I can't stop--"

"*Evie!*"

"Ooooh," Evie moaned, rubbing herself fast and hard with the bear and jerking wildly. She arched her back and tilted her head, thrusting her hips and squealing like an animal.

Her orgasm was long and intense, and Mr. Altman seemed to react to it instinctively, reaching a hand to his cock and touching it through his pants without even realizing it.

As Evie rode out her orgasm, her hand began to slow down. The bear lay damp and inert in her limp hand. Evie collapsed on the bed, breathing hard.

For a moment, Mr. Altman stood staring at her, unable to tear his eyes away from her heaving, sweaty body and the lump of stuffed bear that had rolled a bit away from her relaxed grip. Then he turned to look at Mr. Cox.

"My God, Cox, what did you do to her while I was gone?"

Mr. Cox quickly wiped the grin from his face. From behind Mr. Altman, he had been smiling at Evie during the whole show, and giving her looks of encouragement.

"I don't know what you mean, Altman. She's the same girl she was when got here."

"Oh no she's not! The Evie I arrived with would never have behaved in such a way as she just did!"

"Well, do you mind it?"

For a second, Mr. Altman's eyes gleamed, a look of intense pleasure washing over his face. But then he turned back toward Evie, and adopted a stern grimace.

"Get up, young lady," he ordered, pulling her from the bed. "You have behaved like an insolent brat in front of my friend and your host. I will let him watch you being punished, so he knows the matter has been dealt with."

Evie tried to pull her hand away from Mr. Altman's, a fact he noted with some surprise. He squeezed her hand harder so she couldn't pull away.

"Please, Daddy, I--"

"Are you arguing with me, young lady?"

"Please don't punish me! I couldn't help myself!" She twisted her arm, trying to escape his grip. Mr. Altman's lips curled into a devious grin.

"Couldn't help yourself, eh? Well now, neither can I." He forced her to bend over the edge of the bed, kept her down with the palm of his hand, and spread her legs apart with his foot. As her legs separated, her skirt lifted up, revealing the creamy swells of her bottom. Her inner thighs were still glistening from her juices, the aftereffects of her recent orgasm.

With his free hand, Mr. Altman unbuckled his belt and pulled it from around his waist.

"Would you like to administer a few swats, Cox? After all, she did misbehave in front of you, too."

"No, that's okay, Altman. I'll be happy just to watch you handle it."

Evie continued to struggle against the bed, twisting her body this way and that in an attempt to flee her Daddy's hold.

"Please Daddy! Please don't punish me! I promise I'll be better now!"

"Yes, you will, and this will serve as a reminder to you." He raised the belt high in the air and brought it back down against her rump with a resounding *smack!*

Evie hollered and bucked.

Smack!

"Daddy! Please!"

Smack!

"It hurts!"

Smack!

"Ow Daddy please it hurts!"

Smack!

Evie continued to yell and beg, and the smacks kept raining down on her ass, until her skin had taken on a rosy red glow, crisscrossed here and there with pale stripes of welts.

After a few moments, Evie lay motionless on the bed, crying and beaten into submission. But her Daddy wasn't done.

"You will behave yourself--*smack!*--in front of--*smack!*--my friends--*smack!*--like a good girl--*smack!*--should!--*smack!*--Is that--*smack!*--understood--*smack!*--Babygirl?"--*SMACK!*

"Yes, Daddy," Evie sobbed. "I'll be good, I promise."

"Good," Mr. Altman said. Finally, he stood up, and stepped away from Evie's slumped body.

As he looped his belt back around his waist, Evie stood up from the bed and rubbed her bottom, looking like a chastised and petulant child.

"You know I do this for your own good, Evie," Mr. Altman said. "You need to be a good girl for Daddy, okay?"

"Yes, Daddy. I know," she said, staring down at the floor and looking contrite. "I love you," she added. Mr. Altman smiled. The look in his eyes was warm and forgiving, but the bulge in his pants could not be denied.

"Mr. Cox, I think it's time I took my Babygirl back up to our room. I need to give her some Daddy attention," Mr. Altman said, ignoring the tent of his pants. "In case we don't see each other for a while, it was great to see you again."

"You too, Altman," Mr. Cox replied. "If there's anything further I can help you with, just let me know."

"Oh, you've clearly helped a lot, my friend. I have my spitfire Babygirl back. Now I just need to remind her again who's in charge."

"That shouldn't be too hard, Altman. And don't forget what I told you."

"No, of course not."

As Mr. Cox pressed the button to summon the liaison, Evie passed her Daddy a questioning look. Seeing her confusion, Mr. Altman gave her a smug, evil grin.

"Mr. Cox told me how he had to give you your first enema," he said. "He said you didn't much like it. I'll be remembering that, Babygirl."

As he grabbed her arm and pulled her out the door, Evie passed Mr. Cox a look of pure horror. Mr. Cox grinned back, and winked.

He sighed as he heard the elevator hum. Evie had been fun, and he hoped, next time he saw his friend Mr. Altman, she would still be with him. But that was up to her now. He had helped as much as he could.

A scream echoed from somewhere down the hallway. Mr. Cox smiled at the sound.

Samantha

LATER, MR. SINCLAIRE WOULD wonder if he hadn't sensed something was wrong as soon as he saw the couple walk into the meeting room.

For all intent and purposes, they looked liked any other couple visiting the Hotel Bentmoore. In this case he, the Dom, walked ahead with an authoritative gait, while she, the sub, walked behind him, looking submissive and diffident.

Perhaps it was the way the woman glanced nervously around as she walked; perhaps it was the way the man gave no regard to the woman taking a seat beside him, not even to acknowledge her presence. Or perhaps Mr. Sinclaire could see already that the woman only wore her submission like a mask, hiding humbling, quivering fear beneath.

Regardless, as he studied the man and woman sitting before him, he kept his senses on high-alert, looking for any sign of trouble, trying to figure out what was setting off this tingling sense of foreboding.

He reached his arm out to the shake the hands of his guests. They were, both of them, new visitors to the Hotel Bentmoore.

"Welcome to the Hotel Bentmoore," he began in his easy, baritone voice. "I am Mr. Sinclaire. I will be your host." He shook the hand of the man sitting in front of him easily, who gave him a conspiratory smile and a nod, like the two of them were now friends who had just shared a lewd joke. Mr. Sinclaire had to fight off the urge to wipe his hand off on his pant leg, although he had no idea where this aversion to his new guest was coming from.

He shifted his arm over to shake the woman's hand, too. Mr. Sinclaire took note that while the woman wasn't exactly pretty, she was incredibly alluring, two very different things in Mr. Sinclaire's opinion. She had the face any hot-blooded male would turn around to look at twice.

The woman raised her hand to take his, but before Mr. Sinclaire could touch her, the other man stopped them both from completing the social gesture.

"Put your hand down, Samantha," he ordered.

The woman slowly lowered her hand into her lap, looking pained and embarrassed.

"You are not to touch anyone unless I give you per-mission," the man continued. He did not bother to look at her. The woman, Samantha, looked down at the floor.

"These women," the man sighed, giving Mr. Sinclaire a sneering grin. "You gotta keep them in their place, you know what I'm saying? Of course you do," he laughed, leaning back in his chair. Mr. Sinclaire glanced back at the woman, then cut back to the man, this time studying him with shrewd eyes.

The man looked to be in his early thirties, average height, with a wide chest. His arms were like clubs, thick with muscle. His legs, too, looked wide and hard, compressed inside ill-fitting jeans. Mr. Sinclaire thought the man could have passed for attractive, except that his eyes were a little too close together, his brows a little too low, and his face a little too savage.

Right now, the man was giving him a twisted smile, but Mr. Sinclaire realized that in a neutral pose, when he wasn't actively trying to look pleasant, the man would look mean. There was an aura of cruelty about him, like he would have no problem shooting a wounded animal. His smile was malicious, and made Mr. Sinclaire cringe.

Of course, the man's looks weren't his fault, and Mr. Sinclaire could be wrong. It was possible the new guest would end up being a complete gentleman. But given the warning signals Mr. Sinclaire's brain had been sending him since the couple had walked through the door, he wasn't willing to discount his first impressions all too quickly.

The woman, Samantha, didn't seem a match for her companion at all. Dark haired, brown-eyed, with a pert nose and full lips, Samantha looked at Mr. Sinclaire with something akin to wonder. Her eyes were wide, curious, open in their assessment of him and their fascination...and yet, a hint of yearning flitted through them now and then. This one wanted something from him, Mr. Sinclaire was sure of it. He would just have to figure out what. But that was his job as their host of the Hotel Bentmoore: figure out what the guests wanted, then satisfy their every need.

But first he had to get through his instinctive dislike of the man Samantha had arrived with.

"I'm sorry, I didn't catch your name," Mr. Sinclaire said. "You are...?" Of course he knew both their names. He had been given their basic information before walking in the meeting room. But he decided to play ignorant.

"Paul. Paul Derrgy. This is my girlfriend, Samantha." The man pointed back to the woman, who had shifted her seat to sit at an angle, slightly behind him. "We've been together a few months now."

"That's nice," Mr. Sinclaire replied blandly. "What can I do for you, Mr. Derrgy? What, exactly, are you hoping to get out of your stay at the Hotel Bentmoore?"

"Well, like I said, Samantha here is my girlfriend. She's great, a real plum, but she needs to be kept in line. You know, strict rules, strict punishments--she needs to be told what to do, exactly how I want it."

"So she is your submissive? You have a Dominant/ submissive relationship?"

"Yeah, that's right," Paul replied, looking smug. "I tell Samantha what to do, and she does it. She likes it that way." Paul glanced at Samantha, giving her a self-satisfied grin, but Samantha did not grin back. She cast her eyes down, looking fearful. Mr. Sinclaire took note of her reaction and frowned.

"The other thing about Samantha is, she likes pain," Paul continued. "She's a real pain slut, little Samantha is. She can take a beating like a bitch in heat. Can't you, Samantha?" He looked back at her with stern eyes.

Samantha only glimpsed at him before averting her eyes away. "Yes," she said softly, a blush spreading across her cheeks.

"I thought it would be fun to watch someone else work her over, see what she can take, watch her squirm and scream. Might give me pointers on how to handle her better," Paul said, like they were discussing a work horse.

"I see," Mr. Sinclaire said, looking thoughtful. "Is this what you want, Samantha? For me to inflict my own brand of pain on you?"

"Of course that's what she wants," Mr. Derggy snapped. "It's why we're here, isn't it?"

Mr. Sinclaire sighed. During his years working at the Hotel Bentmoore, and being a Master Sadist, he had met many couples adhering to a Dominant/submissive dynamic. Often the sub, typically the woman, was not allowed to answer for herself, at least for the most part. She consented to let her Dom do the talking for her, and went along with whatever her Dom decided.

But before a planned scene, especially one involving humiliation and pain, she was always given the opportunity to make her consent clear and show her willingness to go along with whatever her Dom had in store for her, so there would be no confusion later on that her submission had been of her own free will.

Paul was not giving Samantha this opportunity. Mr. Sinclaire decided his first impression had been right: there *was* something wrong going on here. He would go slowly and figure out what.

"I can help you, if that's what you *both* want," he said. "But we'll have to go through some paperwork first, get some things out of the way so I know what the hard limits are and what I should avoid." He didn't typically do this in the meeting room. Usually he waited until he had brought the guests inside their activity room, where they could get ideas of what they wanted to try as they admired the dungeon furniture, before getting into a discussion of hard and soft limits. But he decided to follow every protocol in the book for this particular couple.

Mr. Sinclaire got up, walked over to a file cabinet nearby, and pulled out a sheet of paper with questions on it.

"Pain implements, for instance," he said, tapping the sheet. "Are there any I should absolutely not use?" When Paul looked at him blankly, Mr. Sinclaire said, "You know, like, needles? Hot wax? Electrical wands?" When Samantha looked at him in horror but remained silent, too afraid to speak, Mr. Sinclaire said gruffly, "Mr. Derggy, please tell your submissive she is allowed to talk. I need answers to these questions if I am to work with both of you, and I need to hear these answers from her."

"Why?" Paul said, surprised. "She is my sub. She will submit to anything I want her to."

Mr. Sinclaire decided at that moment he thoroughly disliked the man. "She may have agreed to that arrangement at home," he said, doubting the words even as he said them, "but here at the Hotel Bentmoore, we hosts have our own rules to follow, and I need to know she consents to everything I will be doing to her once we get started." He stared at Paul. For a second their eyes did a battle of wills; but Paul looked away first, scowling.

"Fine, ask her. She'll just tell you she can take whatever you hit her with."

Mr. Sinclaire's jaw tightened. But when he turned to look at Samantha, he did his best job of making his face look gentle.

"So, Samantha, hard limits...shall we go over them?"

"I don't want needles," Samantha said. "Or electricity." Paul turned around, shock and anger covering his face. Clearly it had not entered his mind she might contradict him, and now his pride was bruised. His brows furrowed and his lips pressed into a thin line, making him look even meaner. Samantha glanced at him, and fear flitted over her face. She closed her mouth.

"Look at me, Samantha." Mr. Sinclaire pulled her eyes in and held her gaze, trying to get her to focus on him, and only him. "Just answer a few questions for me, okay? It'll be over soon. We'll go down the list." He held up the paper again, as if to say, *this is no big deal*. Samantha nodded and looked at him gratefully.

Forcing her to focus on him and ignore her "Dom" as much as possible, Mr. Sinclaire was able to glean what Samantha's hard limitations were: no needles, no electrical play, no fire or hot wax play, no breath asphyxiation, nothing that would require serious medical intervention... some of the questions were mere formality, Mr. Sinclaire wouldn't have tried to inflict those brands of pain on her anyway during her first visit. But some of her answers surprised him.

"So you're willing to be welted and bruised, even if the marks take weeks to fade from your skin?" Mr. Sinclaire clarified. "You can be whipped, spanked, slapped, anywhere on the body?"

"Not on my feet," Samantha said, thinking fast. "And--not on my face. I...I don't like to be slapped across the face." She passed a look to Paul as she said this. Loud, clanging alarm bells went off in Mr. Sinclaire's head again.

But he kept his voice polite and even. "Very well," he said. "That's easy enough to work with. There's just one more thing: your safeword. What's your safeword?" When Samantha simply looked at him, confused, Mr. Sinclaire tried to clarify. "You know, the word you use when you need things to stop? When it's gone too far?"

"I--I--"

"We don't have a safeword," Paul stated. "It's up to me to decide when to stop, not her."

Mr. Sinclaire clenched his teeth. "Here at the Hotel Bentmoore, all guests must have a safeword to use, especially when the activity involves pain," he said, his voice stiff and final. "It's policy."

That wasn't *exactly* true. He had lots of frequent guests who no longer used a safeword with him--but that was because they were familiar patrons of the hotel who visited with Mr. Sinclaire often, if not exclusively. They had requested to do away with the safeword because they trusted Mr. Sinclaire completely, and it excited them to know once they entered the activity room, he could do whatever he wanted to them, and there was nothing they could say or do about it. Of course, Mr. Sinclaire would already know their hard and soft limits, and would always respect their boundaries.

For a new couple who claimed to be in a D/s relationship, who were coming to him to learn new pain techniques to try on the sub, for them to admit they did not have a safeword....in Mr. Sinclaire's opinion, that pushed past the land of suspicious and into the sea of dangerous.

He turned to Samantha and said, "a safeword needs to be a word you would not normally say in the middle of a play or sex scene, because it is used to stop the action from continuing. It is a word you can use to keep things from going too far, so you always have a measure of control. You need to be able to remember it at all times, no matter how cloudy your head gets. Something that will easily come to your mind if you panic. Do you have a word like that?"

Samantha slowly shook her head no.

"I can give you a safeword while you're here at the hotel, but it's better if you can create your own," Mr. Sinclaire said. "Think for a minute."

"What kind of word should I pick?"

"Anything you want." When he saw his answer hadn't helped her, he said, "For some, it's a color--like 'red' for stop, or 'yellow' if you need a rest word, to let me know to slow down. For some, it's a name of a safety object, like a childhood teddy bear or a favorite doll. And sometimes it's whatever the sub sees in her head when her mind starts to rebel against the pain, like balloons, or flowers...."

"Jasmine," Samantha cut in. "When the pain starts to get really bad, I start...." She looked down, embarrassed. "I start to smell jasmine."

"Interesting," Mr. Sinclaire said, tilting his head. Samantha looked up at him, trying to detect any hint of mockery or judgement on his face. She smiled when she saw none. It was the first time Mr. Sinclaire had seen her smile since she had come into the room, and he gave her a wide smile back. "Some women do have associative smells when they enter subspace," he said. "Are you familiar with that word, subspace? Do you know what that is?"

Before Samantha could answer, Paul snapped. "Could we get on with things? Or are we just going to talk all day? Cause I didn't come here for an oral lesson."

Mr. Sinclaire's eyes cut back to him. "If we are agreed that Samantha's safeword is jasmine--" he looked at Samantha, who nodded-- "and since now I have some idea of her hard and soft limits, I guess we can get started."

"Good, because I've got some punishing to do," Paul growled. Samantha's face blanched. Mr. Sinclaire watched the couple, but said nothing. If this was the type of relationship they had, if this was what they both consented to, then it was not his place to judge or interfere, no matter how much it bothered him. But he would watch and supervise the scene in the activity room from beginning to end.

Calling the liaison to escort them down the hall, Mr. Sinclaire took them over to their designated activity room and showed the couple in. He took note of Samantha's face when she saw the St. Andrew's cross in the middle of the room: she looked surprised, and a little scared, but more than anything else, she looked fascinated--and aroused. Mr. Sinclaire caught her unclouded look of arousal and felt his balls tighten. He enjoyed working with women who got turned on by the sight of their own mechanisms of torture, and Samantha was clearly one of them.

Paul, on the other hand, looked over the cross, completely confused. It was as if he'd never seen a St. Andrew's Cross before, not even a picture, and had no idea what he was supposed to do with it. *This man is supposed to be a Dom?* Mr. Sinclaire thought. *A St. Andrew's Cross is as basic as you can get. Samantha clearly knows what it is. So why doesn't he?*

Mr. Sinclaire sighed and gritted his teeth again. It was his obligation to take control over what happened in his activity rooms, and if he needed to give Paul a lesson in the basics of dungeon furniture, he would. But he had a feeling he'd be having a lot more fun with Samantha if Paul wasn't in the room. The idea caught him off guard, and while pleasant, he had to push it away. It was not up to him to pick his guests, and certainly not his place to be jealous of a Dom's sub, no matter how much of a ignorant brute the Dom seemed to be.

Mr. Sinclaire began to roll up his sleeves. Time to get to work.

"Why don't we dive right in and start with the St. Andrew's Cross," he said. "Samantha, if you could please get undressed."

Samantha's eyes widened. "What, you mean take off all my clothes?"

"Yes, that usually is what 'get undressed' means," he replied.

"Take your clothes off, Samantha," Paul barked, looking at her with gleaming eyes. "A slut should be naked in the company of men."

Samantha looked down at the floor and licked her lips. Mr. Sinclaire waited to see what she would do.

Slowly, she began the process of removing her blouse, working the buttons with shaking fingers. But as she peeled the sleeves down her shoulders, she looked up and stared at Mr. Sinclaire. She held his eyes as the shirt dropped to the floor. Then she reached around her body and unhooked her bra. It was as if she was doing a little striptease act, but it was just for Mr. Sinclaire--she was ignoring Paul completely.

Mr. Sinclaire caught his breath. With any other submissive, he would have taken note of this small act of defiance and given a harsh scolding. He should have called her out for her cheeky sauciness, for snubbing her Dom; instead, he decided to play along with Samantha's little ruse.

He let his eyes do a silent mischievous dance with hers. Samantha continued the show, trailing her fingers down her body, slipping them under the hem of her skirt and peeling it slowly down. As she bent to lower it to the floor, she kept her eyes on her host, giving him a hint of a smile.

She bent again to strip out of her panties, this time squeezing her dainty tits together with her arms, letting him admire her cleavage. Her hair fell in her face, looking lush and disheveled, and she squinted at him through her tresses, looking at him like a seductive temptress.

Paul noticed the byplay going on between the woman and the host, and he tensed his whole body. It was obvious whatever was going on between the two other people in the room, he was being cut out of the action.

When Samantha was naked, she stood up straight, holding an expression of bland pride, and a gave a look of challenge to her host. It was clear she knew she had a luscious body. Pert, pink-tipped breasts cupped delicately above her lean torso and tight waist. Smooth thighs tapered out from compact, almost boyish hips. Her pussy, bared and denuded, was a thin line starting low between soft nether-lips. Mr. Sinclaire's mouth went dry, and he licked his lips, unable to hide his obvious attraction to her womanly charms.

"Turn around," he ordered before he could stop himself. He should not be the one ordering her around--her Dom was supposed to do that. But Samantha turned, and Mr. Sinclaire gazed at her lavish soft ass, surprisingly rounded considering her small size and overall narrow shape. There was not the slightest hint of ripple in the skin.

Paul noticed Mr. Sinclaire's obvious admiration, but instead of getting angry, he gloated.

"Yeah, she keeps herself in shape, Samantha does, like a good slut. Gotta keep the men's tongues wagging, gotta keep their cocks up. Isn't that right, Samantha? I *said*, isn't that *right,* Samantha?" Paul's voice grew louder when Samantha didn't answer right away.

"Yes," she said, keeping her focus on Mr. Sinclaire. She didn't seem scared by Paul's raised voice, and she didn't look at him. Paul scowled.

"How does this cross thing work?" He asked, walking around the heavy piece of dungeon furniture. Mr. Sinclaire looked at him, trying to remember his job was to instruct, not to judge--and certainly not to come between a Dom and his sub.

"I will cuff her in so she can't move, and then we'll get to work. Tell me, do you want her facing forward or back?"

"What difference will that make?"

Mr. Sinclaire tried to keep his voice calm. "Well, if you want to have access to her ass, she'll need to face back. If you want to work over her breasts first, she'll need to face forward."

Being presented with a choice of options in methods of Samantha's torture put Paul in a better mood--he felt more powerful, more in control.

"Put her face forward," he said with a twisted grin that showed too much teeth. "I want to work her breasts over first."

Mr. Sinclaire studied him for a moment. Paul didn't look so authoritative anymore: he looked almost giddy with excitement, like a sadistic school boy about to be let loose on a mangy dog.

"Very well," Mr. Sinclaire said. "Samantha, come here."

Samantha walked toward him slowly, keeping her arms folded in front of her. But she followed directions when Mr. Sinclaire told her to hold out her hands and feet against the X of the cross. He buckled her into the strong leather cuffs, already attached to all four posts.

Mr. Sinclaire stepped back and admired the picture she now presented. Stretched and bound to the St. Andrew's Cross, Samantha was a sight to behold. But Paul didn't take any time to admire her sleek lines and contoured body.

"Now what?" He asked. "What have you got for me?"

Samantha looked at Mr. Sinclaire with pleading eyes. She was trying to tell him something, he realized. But he had no idea what, and without her speaking up, it was impossible for him to figure it out. He decided to go very, very slowly.

"We'll start with a light flogger, and see how that goes. No reason to jump ahead," he said, keeping his voice even. He needed to tread carefully and see what would happen.

Retrieving the lightest, softest flogger he had from the wardrobe and handing it to Paul, he said, "Go ahead and let me see how you warm her up. I'll just watch for now."

"Oh, I'll warm her up, alright," Paul said under his breath. Mr. Sinclaire had a hard time letting go of the compact flogger, but he released it into Paul's hand. Paul slapped it against his thigh a couple times, looking at Samantha, his eyes bright and cruel.

"Here I come, Samantha," he said with a taunt, and raised the flogger high in the air.

The leather came down against Samantha's left breast with a stinging slap, and Samantha scrunched up her face in pain. Despite its worn-out straps and soft leather, it was still a flogger, and Paul was wielding it with force.

Paul flogged her left breast, then her right, and then worked indiscriminately between them, smiling as Samantha's cries of pain grew louder. Tears were spilling down her cheeks, and her breasts were mottling an angry red.

"Think you can embarrass me, Samantha?" Paul said when Samantha's cries grew into screams. Her tears smeared her makeup; her eyes were shadowy pits. Paul's voice spat pure venom. "Think you can contradict me like that in front of other people? Make me look like a chump? Think I'll let you get away with that?"

Changing the direction of his swing, Paul began to bring the flogger up and inside Samantha's spread pussy. Samantha shrieked, squeezing her eyes shut in agony. Mr. Sinclaire didn't stop him; Samantha had agreed to be whipped everywhere but the face and feet, and she had not safeworded. But he could feel the adrenaline rushing his blood like an open hydrant, and he kept his eyes open, alert, and focused on Paul.

Things were happening, now--something was going on inside Paul, something dark and menacing--and Mr. Sinclaire could feel his nerve endings standing on air.

"I saw the way you were looking at Sinclaire here," Paul continued, swinging the flogger with renewed vigor. "Horny for him, Samantha? Think he'll stuff your cunt up good? Hungry for his cock?"

His strikes came faster, harder, a blur of leather hitting skin, and Samantha's screams became frantic. Mr. Sinclaire took a step toward Paul without even realizing it.

"Nobody fills your slut cunt but me, Samantha! You hear me, you stupid little bitch? Nobody!"

Samantha's body twisted and struggled in the cuffs, her howls of pain ricocheting off the walls. Paul's face twisted into an evil grin, and his eyes glazed over with excitement. A particularly vicious hit struck her right between her pussy lips, slapping against the sensitive nerves of her clit, and Samantha let out a shrill cry.

"Jasmine! Jasmine!" She said, her voice high and desperate. "Please stop! Jasmine!"

Mr. Sinclaire raised his arm to take the flogger from Paul, assuming the scene was now over. Later, he would realize how relieved he had felt to hear her cry out her safeword--in his opinion, things had gone too far already.

But before he could do anything to stop it, Paul raised his hand and let fly the flogger once more, cutting it right into Samantha's pussy folds. Samantha's eyes rolled back, and she let out a sound like a wounded animal.

"Stop it, Paul," Mr. Sinclaire said loudly, grabbing Paul's arm as he held up the flogger again. Mr. Sinclaire wrested the flogger out of Paul's hand, pulling it out of his tight grip. "Samantha has safeworded. The scene is over."

For a second, Paul stared at him. He tried to focus and take a deep breath. But then his face became a vision of rage.

"I say when the scene is over, not this bitch," he whispered. Before Mr. Sinclaire knew what he was about, Paul stepped forward and backhanded Samantha across the face. Samantha's head snapped back from the force of the blow, and she cried out again. "She doesn't decide *anything*. She doesn't get to think. Not even *think*. She is nothing but a *slut*. She is a dirty stupid *slut*." He hit her across the face again, and a few drops of blood sprayed from Samantha's mouth.

Mr. Sinclaire forced his way in between Paul and Samantha and shoved Paul away, using all his strength. Paul didn't just move back; he fell back on his ass, skidding a little against the floor as he fell.

"The scene is *over*, Paul," Mr. Sinclaire said, pale with anger, his lips pressed into a hard line. "You don't get to touch her again."

To Mr. Sinclaire's surprise, Paul stood up and rushed at him. He raised his arm as he ran, closing his hand into a fist, ready to punch Mr. Sinclaire anywhere he could.

With Paul's arms looking like steel anvils, another man might have panicked and moved away. But Mr. Sinclaire easily deflected the punch, used Paul's momentum against him to swing him around, and landed his own punch across Paul's face, sending the wider man crashing down to the floor again.

As soon as Paul was down and a good few feet away from Samantha, Mr. Sinclaire realized he had limited options. Paul was acting psychotic, Samantha was bleeding...and he needed backup. He ran to door, found the button that would normally summon the liaison, and pressed it repeatedly in rapid succession: *poke poke poke poke*.

Unfortunately, the time it took Mr. Sinclaire to do this was just enough time for Paul to get up off the floor and cuff Samantha across the face again, this time splitting open her lip. Samantha screamed. A trickle of blood began to flow.

A wave of rage washed over Mr. Sinclaire like nothing he had ever felt before. He ran at Paul, keeping his head down, and rammed the man right in the side of his ribs. Then he turned and swung his arm into Paul's hard body like a blade hacking into flesh; the move would have cracked the ribs of a smaller man.

Paul folded in. He exercised a lot and looked strong, but it was obvious he was used to working with weights, not fighting, and he knew nothing of defending himself.

Mr. Sinclaire, who looked leaner but had years of experience in the boxing ring as well as martial arts training, punched him in the solar plexus, knocking the wind out of him. Then he went for Paul's face, punching him again and again, not giving the man one second of respite. Paul was completely outmatched, a fact he barely had time to register before realizing the other man was about to pummel him into oblivion.

It felt like the fight had gone on for a long time, but it was only a few seconds later that the door exploded open with a bang. About a dozen people rushed into the room. Taking in the scene quickly, they grabbed Mr. Sinclaire by the shoulders, pulled him off Paul's limp, lifeless body, and hauled him off to the side. Paul slumped to the floor.

"It's okay, Sinclaire, it's okay, we've got him, relax," one of the men said, an older gentleman with graying hair. He put his palms up in front of Mr. Sinclaire's face, trying to refocus him and calm him down. "You can stop now, we're handing this. Sinclaire...Brian, look at me. It's okay. Brian."

Finally, at the use of his first name, Mr. Sinclaire tore his eyes away from the crumpled, beaten Paul, and looked at the older man in front of him.

"Okay," he said, breathing hard but regaining his composure. "Okay. Okay." He looked wild, but his eyes told the older man what he needed to know, that Mr. Sinclaire wouldn't rush at Paul again. The older man put his hands down.

Mr. Sinclaire's eyes looked for Samantha: she was still cuffed into the St. Andrew's Cross. Her eyes were closed. She had not responded to the explosion of activity in the room; in fact, she looked asleep.

"How is she?" Mr. Sinclaire asked. Another woman had stepped in front of Samantha's lifeless form, and was now lightly slapping her face, trying to get her to come back from wherever it was her mind had gone. Samantha blinked her eyes and looked at the woman. Then she began to cry.

When the woman began to uncuff Samantha from the cross, Mr. Sinclaire rushed forward.

"Let me," he said. He worked as quickly as he could, uncuffing Samantha's feet first: he knew she would crumple as soon as her hands were freed. He was right.

Samantha fell forward as soon as she was freed from the cross, and Mr. Sinclaire caught her before she hit the floor. She continued to cry.

"It's alright, Samantha, it's alright," Mr. Sinclaire soothed, holding her close and caressing her face, keeping his hands away from her bleeding and swelling lip. The woman went to the wardrobe and retrieved a thin, satin blanket. It wouldn't serve to warm her, but it would hide her nakedness in the room full of people.

"What the hell happened here?"

The older man who had managed to restrain Mr. Sinclaire looked around the room before resting his eyes on the limp, befuddled Paul.

Paul was being held up by two other men, but only just. His knees were bent and his feet were dragging behind him, his toes scraping the floor. He was beginning to wake up a bit, but his head lolled back and forth; he was acting dopey and slow, like a wasted drunk. Mr. Sinclaire saw that one of the punches he'd delivered to Paul's face had opened up the man's nose. Blood was still trickling down and drying all over the man's chin. It made Mr. Sinclaire smile.

He would have loved to watch and see if Paul would choke on his own blood, but he had to focus on someone much more important: Samantha. Samantha was clutching the blanket to her chin and crying against his chest, sobbing softly. Mr. Sinclaire gathered her close.

"The bastard didn't honor her safeword," he said in answer to the older man's question, rubbing Samantha's back. "Or *any* of her consent rules. It was like he didn't even know what the word 'limits' *means*. He came at me when I told him the scene was over. I had to stop him."

The older man nodded in understanding. "She doesn't look like she got hurt badly enough to need a trip to the hospital," he said. "She just looks very traumatized. But am I wrong? Do we need to call an ambulance?"

"No, she got cuffed in the mouth a couple times, but I stopped that idiot before he could do anything worse. She'll need some help for her lip, though."

"Shern will bring the nurse," the older man replied, giving a nod to one of the other men in the room. The man nodded back, and left the room.

"The woman will be cared for here in the activity room before she is escorted back up to her own room," the older man said: a voice of authority. "I don't think it would be wise to drag her to First Aid looking the way she does. I don't want to embarrass her more than she already is. Mr. Sinclaire, you will stay with her until she feels ready to return to her own room upstairs."

"What about that scum?" Mr. Sinclaire bit out, motioning toward Paul.

"Oh, don't worry about him--we'll be handing him. Won't we, Marissa?"

Another woman standing nearby, who was staring at Paul's supported but restrained body with dispassionate interest, now turned her head. She smiled a wicked, ominous grin, and a cold chill seemed to enter the room of men.

"Oh, yes," she said, her voice soft and dripping venom. It sent shivers down the backs, and cocks, of all the males. They recognized her tone. Some of them glanced at Paul with varying looks of sympathy.

Paul was about to find himself delivered into the hands of a Hotel Bentmoore Dominatrix, one of the most respected and feared around, and God only knew what Marissa was going to do to him.

But Mr. Sinclaire had no pity for Paul. He looked at Marissa with a look of satisfied pleasure.

"Good," he said, giving her a brief nod.

"We'll leave you, then," the older man said. "Offer your guest what help you can, whatever she's willing to take. We'll let your other guests know there's been an emergency." His message was clear: Mr. Sinclaire's focus, from now until Samantha left the hotel, was to be on making this one guest happy. Mr. Sinclaire would be serving as host to her and her alone until she left the hotel.

Samantha had suffered through a horrible attack on hotel grounds, and it was up to the hotel to heal her, and help her, as best they could. They would do whatever it took to make sure she still left the hotel satisfied.

The older gentleman looked down at Samantha with compassion, his eyes tender and full of sympathy. Samantha didn't notice. Her eyes were pressed tight against her host's chest.

"Thank you, Mr. Bentmoore," Mr. Sinclaire said, hugging Samantha a little tighter. "For everything."

"No problem, Mr. Sinclaire," the man answered. Then, tight lipped, he turned to the men holding up Paul. "Get him down the hall to one of Marissa's rooms," he ordered. "We'll care for him there...and he'll be staying there for the remainder of his stay. Does that work for you, Marissa?"

"Oh, yes, that will work fine," she purred. "I will enjoy having a new pet, even if he does need some training."

With that, the men hoisted Paul up and dragged him out of the room, with Marissa following behind, looking almost gleeful.

Mr. Sinclaire could only hope Marissa would be able to teach Paul a few things, and give him the kind of instruction he deserved. But one thing was for sure: Paul would not be getting the kind of service he had been expecting from the Hotel Bentmoore.

***

Samantha held the cold compress to her lip as the nurse packed up her bag, getting ready to leave.

"It will be fine," the nurse said, giving Samantha a comforting smile. "No stitches required. Keep the ice on it if it helps, but the swelling's already almost gone. By tomorrow, with some makeup, you won't be able to even see it. You're lucky: your skin is in great shape."

The nurse was a tall woman wearing a slinky dress and high-heeled shoes. She looked nothing like a nurse. But she seemed to know her stuff, and Samantha looked at her with relief.

"Thank you," Samantha said. Her voice was low and hoarse. Her throat hurt.

Mr. Sinclaire walked over to her, holding a glass of water. "Here," he said. Samantha drank, and felt better.

"I think you can handle things from here," the nurse said, looking at Mr. Sinclaire. "I'm upstairs if you need me."

"Thanks, Marie."

"No problem. It's why I'm here. Take care of yourself, hon," she said to Samantha. Carrying her bag of medical supplies with her, she left the room.

Samantha held the compress to her lip, looking away from her host. Mr. Sinclaire had propped her up in the bed and wrapped her in a thin blanket, and now Samantha held it tightly around her. She felt tired, and overwhelmed, and her lip hurt...but mostly, she just felt embarrassed. She would not meet her host's eyes.

"Samantha, look at me." Mr. Sinclaire sat down on the bed next to her, forcing her eyes to look directly into his. "Talk to me," he said. "Tell me what that was all about, what happened with Paul."

"What do you want to know?"

"Well, for starters, how did a woman like you end up with--Paul?" He had wanted to say "that loser," but stopped himself.

Samantha sighed and put the compress down. "I met Paul a few months ago, at a club."

"A club. What kind of club?"

"You know, the kind you go to meet people who are into bondage, ropes, spankings...."

"You mean, a BDSM club? A dungeon club?"

"Yes, exactly. It was my first time there, and Paul was at the bar, getting a drink, and he struck up a conversation with me, and...." she waved her hand out, as if to say, *the rest is history*.

"How long ago was this?"

"About three months ago." Her brows went up as she said it. Had it been only three months? It felt to Samantha like three years. She sighed.

"And he's been behaving like this with you for three months?"

"No," she shook her head. "In the beginning, he was actually really nice. Swept me off my feet, really. He took me out, showed me off. But when he figured out what I wanted...I guess, what he could get away with... he began to change. He started trying to control me, and giving me orders. But--it's never gone as far as it did today." Her voice cracked.

"What do you mean?"

"He's never lost control like that before--he's never gone completely crazy on me, hitting me like that. But--" she stopped. Mr. Sinclaire waited while she found the words to continue.

"I think I always knew Paul had a dangerous side. I think...I think that's what attracted me to him. But I never thought he was *that* dangerous. I never thought he could hurt me like he did today. I thought...I thought he at least cared about me. Now I don't know."

"Well, I guess we're lucky you caught a glimpse of Paul's true character while you were here, in a safe place, and we could help you." Samantha looked miserable and heartbroken. It pulled at Mr. Sinclaire's heart, but it angered him, too. She clearly didn't realize how much danger she had been in.

"Samantha, do you understand what would have happened if Paul had changed like that in a place where the two of you were alone, where there was no one else to help you?"

"Yes." But she sounded unconvincing, so Mr. Sinclaire spelled it out for her.

"He would have beaten you senseless. He might have killed you, Samantha."

Samantha's eyes grew large, filling with realization, shame, and regret. Mr. Sinclaire sighed.

"Why did you even stay with him for that long? Even if he wasn't this bad in the beginning, even if he was nice *most* of the time, he must have, at some point or another, started to show signs of the kind of cruel person he really is. No one can hide that kind of uncontrollable rage for three whole months."

"I thought that kind of attitude from him was what I should expect from, you know, a Dominant man. I thought I just had to accept it, because of what I wanted from him."

"You thought you just had to accept his abuse? Why?"

Samantha looked taken aback. She had never thought of what Paul was doing to her as *abuse* before. "I met him at a BDSM club," she said again, trying to explain. "I was looking for someone to..." she couldn't finish the sentence.

Mr. Sinclaire quickly put two and two together. "You were looking for someone to give you pain," he whispered. "You wanted someone to hurt you, hurt your body, and you thought that meant you had to put up with what Paul was putting you through."

"Yes. I mean, if I *want* the pain, I can't really call it abuse, can I?"

Mr. Sinclaire made a sound of impatience. "Tell me something. This club you met him in, you said it was your first time there. Was it your first time in *any* BDSM club?"

"No. About a year ago I was visiting a friend in another town, and she took me to a club. *That* was my first time, being in a BDSM club and seeing that kind of thing first-hand. I volunteered to come up on stage and get worked over by a Dom. They told me he was a Master Sadist. He put me on a St. Andrew's Cross, too. It was the best night of my life. It changed me." Her eyes dilated and took on a dreamy look as she remembered.

That's why she recognized the cross and Paul didn't, Mr. Sinclaire thought.

"But the club you met Paul in three months ago--that night, you went alone? No friend came with you?"

"No, there was nobody to go with me. I don't really have any other friends close to me I could ask to go with me to a place like that."

"So there was no one to vouch for Paul, no one to tell you he was a good guy."

"No, I guess not."

"It could have been his first time there too you know, or he could have been there just to prey on unsuspecting women."

"I guess...But he was so sweet...."

"No, Samantha, he was not sweet. He saw an opportunity and he took it." He looked furious, but tried to tamp down his fury so he wouldn't scare her. He took her hand.

"I think I understand now what's really going on. You went to a BDSM club a year ago, and ended up under the skilled hands of a Master, but before that, you hadn't really known you would like that, had you? Like the pain. You didn't even know that about yourself. That night awakened something inside you." Samantha could only nod her head. "You went back to a new BDSM club near your own town, wanting a taste of it again. You were looking for someone to help you, guide you, teach you a few things." He cupped her cheek in his large, calloused hand. "Ahh, Samantha, you're nothing but a fresh-behind-the-ears newbie. Unfortunately, you got really, really unlucky." Samantha's mouth quivered; a tear fell from her eye and rolled down her cheek. Mr. Sinclaire gently wiped it away.

"Samantha, I want you to listen good. I'm going to tell you a couple basic rules. These are rules we follow at the Hotel Bentmoore, even if we don't always spell it out every time for every guest, and these are rules you should follow if you want to keep yourself safe, and out of the hands of people like Paul."

He leaned closer in, his voice growing stern. "One: there is a difference between sadism and abuse. I know that might confuse you, and it might take time for that to sink in, but--you need to learn the difference. A sadist will enjoy hurting you, he'll get off seeing your pain, *but he will only work within your rules of consent.* He will only do what you agree to let him do to you, what the two of you have agreed to in advance. A man who crosses your limits, who goes beyond what you consent to, is an abuser, plain and simple, and you should run from men like that as fast as you can. They will not stop what they are doing before they really hurt you, like you saw today."

Mr. Sinclaire took a breath. "Two: you're a masochist. That's obvious--" he stopped when he saw Samantha's look of surprise. "You didn't realize?"

"I...I knew I liked the pain I got from the Master, but I never really labelled myself *that* before." She looked upset.

"It's okay," he soothed her. "There's nothing wrong with being a masochist. Obviously a lot of women are, that's why there are Doms and Master Sadists at clubs, doing what they do. Sadism and Masochism, it's an integral part of the BDSM scene. Masochists are always looking for sadists to satisfy their own needs, just like you were when you met Paul. But here's rule number two: *being a masochist does not mean you have to put up with abuse*. It means you like pain, yes--but *you* get to decide on the kind of pain, and amount of pain, you can take. The choice is always yours, and must always remain yours. Anyone who tries to take the choice away from you, you should stay away from them. Understand?"

Samantha slowly nodded her head yes. Mr. Sinclaire leaned back, still holding her hand.

"Good. Now in a way, it's a good thing Paul showed his true colors for the first time here, so we could put a stop to it...out of curiosity, how did you two find out about the Hotel Bentmoore? What made you decide to come here in the first place?"

"My friend, the one who took me to the club in her home town, she called me. I told her about Paul, and how I wasn't always enjoying what he was doing to me. She told me about your hotel. She said maybe Paul could learn some new stuff."

Mr. Sinclaire looked at her shrewdly. "You didn't tell her everything Paul was doing to you, did you? You didn't tell her how Paul was making you feel, how he was turning into a controlling, manipulative bastard."

"No, I guess at that point I was too embarrassed," she said, realizing for the first time how deep down a spiral of self-loathing and shame she had gone. Paul had made her second-guess herself at every turn, had made her think she deserved the kind of "training" he was giving her, because of the pain she craved. But Mr. Sinclaire was right: she wasn't being given what she wanted. She had been exploited to satisfy Paul's twisted needs.

"Paul didn't want to come to the hotel at first," she said. "I told him to consider it a paid vacation." Mr. Sinclaire needed a moment to understand what she was saying.

"Wait a minute--*you* paid, for both of your stays at the hotel?" He asked. Hosts didn't usually discuss money and cost with their guests, but in this case, Mr. Sinclaire made an exception.

"Well, yeah," Samantha said reluctantly. "Paul doesn't make as much money as I do. I pay for pretty much everything." Her eyes darted away.

He had been starting to talk about moving in together, Samantha remembered. Luckily, she had always managed to push away that conversation, feeling a sick sense of dread every time Paul had brought it up. Now she knew why: inside, she must have known it would lead to her living with, and supporting, her own abuser. She shuddered.

"What's going to happen now? And--where is Paul?" She looked around, as if realizing for the first time he was no longer in the room.

"Paul is in very safe hands," Mr. Sinclaire said vaguely. "But he will not be with you anymore. The rest of your stay will be spent alone. We took the liberty of taking out all his things from your room."

"What? Where is he? Where have you put him?" She began to rise from the bed, and Mr. Sinclaire pushed her back down.

"I don't want you to think about Paul anymore. We're handling him. You won't be seeing him again unless we think there's a reason, so just put him out of your head. In fact, I want you to promise me here and now that when you leave the Hotel Bentmoore, you won't ever see Paul again. You and he are through, Samantha. Understand?"

"Yes," she agreed. "He and I are through. Just--just don't punish him on my account."

"Now that I can't promise." Samantha looked at him in alarm. "But let's talk about you," he said. "You've still got some days scheduled with us, and I'd be happy to keep working with you as your host. If you want me, that is. It's clear there's a lot I could teach you."

"You mean...you would still work with me? Do... things...." Her eyes darted back to the St. Andrew's Cross sitting in the middle of the room, and her breath caught. Mr. Sinclaire smiled.

"Oh yes, I would 'do things' to you. I am considered a Master Sadist too, you know. Samantha, I could make you feel things you didn't know possible. I could make you *fly*." His eyes became dark and liquid, deep endless pools full of hidden knowledge, and Samantha couldn't tear her eyes away.

"Yes, I would like that," she breathed. "Please."

"I'm warning you though. I will make you hurt. Afterwards, you will love it--love what I did to you, what I made you feel. My time with you may become the most erotic memories you ever have. But when I'm hurting you, while it's happening, you may not like it. In fact, I can guarantee you there will be many moments you won't like it at all."

Samantha swallowed hard. She knew she should be afraid of what he was saying, but instead, all she felt was aroused. The idea of putting herself in the hands of a trusted Master made her pelvis tighten and her breath catch. To feel again what she had felt that night...it felt so long ago....

"I'll have my, what did you call it? My safeword."

"Yes. You will always have your safeword, and when you give me your safeword, I will stop, immediately."

"And you won't try to do anything I told you not to. Like hurt my feet."

"No," Mr. Sinclaire smiled, "I won't touch your feet. I won't cross any hard limit you've given me."

"Then," she licked her lips, "then please, work on me, Mr. Sinclaire--"

"Sir," he corrected.

"Sir," she said breathlessly. "Sir, please do what you would to me. Make me hurt. Make me fly." She repeated his words back at him, almost swooning.

Mr. Sinclaire recognized her reaction and grinned. "Samantha, I will see you tomorrow morning. Eat a light breakfast, because when I get you back in that cross, I'm going to work you over but good."

***

When Samantha re-entered Mr. Sinclaire's activity room the next day, she felt like a different person. Some of her old sauciness had already returned, and she walked in with a spring to her step. She felt light, free, like a huge weight had been lifted off her shoulders and out of her life. It was a little scary to realize now how much Paul had managed to change her in only three months, turning her into a meek, frightened, cowering woman. She never wanted to be like that again.

True to Mr. Sinclaire's words, by the time she had returned to her room upstairs the night before, all of Paul's things had mysteriously vanished. It was as if he had never arrived to the hotel with her at all.

Samantha had curled up in the large bed and cried, letting the sobs go freely in the dark. It was the kind of crying that hits a person after an averted catastrophe, after everything is already fine, crisis averted, and they can face how close they had come to being seriously hurt. Her crying was cathartic, and when she was done, she felt clean, renewed, and ready to move on with her life.

Now, standing in the middle of the activity room and facing the St. Andrew's Cross once more, she hoped Mr. Sinclaire could help her make that move in the right direction.

"Hello, Samantha," he said. Samantha turned to look at him. He seemed different, too. The alert tension he had been cloaked in the day before was now gone. He seemed much more at ease, like he was looking forward to a playful scene with his new guest. A warm smile curved his mouth.

He still wore a pressed white shirt and tailored suit pants, but this time his shirt sleeves were rolled all the way up to his forearms, showing off his wide muscles. The shirt was open down the front, too. Samantha could see a tiny crease of tantalizing skin and flat stomach. Her mouth went dry.

"We're going to start like this is a brand new beginning, okay? It's just you and me now. A whole new scene, and a whole new set of rules--mine." He said this as he walked toward her, and put his hands gently on her shoulders. But his gentle touch was enough to make Samantha's senses go haywire; she closed her eyes and tried to breathe. They hadn't even started yet, and she already felt lightheaded.

"Easy," Mr. Sinclaire said, as if reading her thoughts. "Very soon you'll be off in subspace, but right now I need you here, focused on me."

Samantha tried to focus. "Subspace?"

Mr. Sinclaire smiled at her natural curiosity and innocence. *She really is so new to this,* he thought.

"Subspace is what we call the place where the mind goes when a sub or masochist starts to submit to the pain. The chemicals and endorphins hit your bloodstream, and it effects your mind. Thoughts start to drift, or just disappear. Often the senses also go haywire. Some women see colors, or fireworks, and others hear rushing noises--and some smell strong familiar scents, like you do your jasmine. Subspace is a kind of mental high. Women can experience multiple orgasms that way--I've been told an orgasm while in subspace is like no other."

Samantha made a sound of surprise, and her cheeks blushed crimson. Mr. Sinclaire looked at her shrewdly.

"When you were being worked over by the Master Sadist at the club that night, you came, didn't you?"

Samantha could feel her entire face grow hot. She had never admitted it to *anyone* before, but she had come twice on stage that night. It had seemed so perverted to her that she had enjoyed being tied up and beaten, to the point of orgasm. But Mr. Sinclaire didn't look at her in disgust. He looked at her in pleasure...and lust.

"A woman who can orgasm by pain alone is a lucky find," he said, his voice soft and hungry. "It opens up a whole world of opportunity. This day is going to be a turning point for you, Samantha. I feel honored to share it with you."

Samantha didn't know what to say to that. Mr. Sinclaire seemed so earnest, she wanted to kiss him, but at the same time, a part of her was wishing he would turn her around and start spanking her ass. "Thank you, Sir," she said.

"Your welcome," he said, walking to the cross. "Now get undressed."

"You first," she said. Mr. Sinclaire turned and looked at her in surprise.

Samantha put a hand on her mouth, looking just as shocked as he did by her insolence. She had no idea where *those* words had come from! More of her cheekiness had returned in full force, it seemed.

Mr. Sinclaire regarded her for a second, then sighed. He stepped forward to stand in front of her, raised his hands to her blouse, and began to unbutton it from the top down. Samantha made no move to stop him; she was too embarrassed by her outburst. Mr. Sinclaire gave her a stern look as he spoke.

"I realize it's your masochistic cravings we're delving into today, and not any predispositions you may have towards dominance or submission, but let's be clear: right now it's me giving the orders, Samantha. You will follow my instructions to the letter, and without argument. Is that clear?"

"Yes, Sir." She lowered her eyes in shame. Where *had* those impertinent words come from?

Mr. Sinclaire finished unbuttoning her blouse. He spread it wide. Samantha's nipples puckered under her bra, and her skin flushed under his heady gaze.

"Now, finish getting undressed," he ordered again, stepping away from her. He watched, and waited, and Samantha realized he would make a point of staring at her as she undressed. If it was to somehow teach her a lesson, he was mistaken. Samantha didn't mind if he wanted to watch her. She'd never had any qualms with undressing in front of a man, especially one who aroused her, and clearly desired her back.

When all her clothes were off and laying on the floor in a pool by her feet, she stood up straight and proud, looking Mr. Sinclaire in the eyes and giving him a look of pure haughtiness. Mr. Sinclaire noticed her brazen posture and narrowed his eyes.

"Put your clothes on the shelf over there and stand in front of the cross," he said, pointing to a narrow shelf by the bed. Samantha dutifully followed his instructions, feeling her nervousness begin to rise. She knew what was coming, and she was already so aroused her cunt was creaming. Her inner thighs felt slick.

She stepped up to the St. Andrew's Cross and turned around, facing out, the way she had the day before.

"No," Mr. Sinclaire said from behind the cross. "Face the other way. I'm going to work on your back and bottom today. That's what the Master did at the club that night, am I right?"

"Yes," Samantha said, her voice hoarse. "He had me lift up my skirt and lower my panties." The flood of memories hit her like a rush, making her whole body flood with tingling warmth.

Samantha suddenly felt a hand on her ass, and she jumped.

"I can understand why the Master wanted a taste of your ass," her host said. He caressed the mound of her bottom with a light touch, rubbing his hand up and down her soft curve, dipping it into her crease. "But it's not just your ass I'll be marking today." He lowered his hand down her leg, feeling her satiny flesh, then trailed his fingers up her slim back. His feather-soft touch sent goosebumps down her body, and she shivered.

"Turn around, hands and feet against the Cross. Spread 'em wide," he ordered now, lowering his voice into a no-nonsense tone. Samantha did as she was told, pressing her arms and legs against the Cross. Mr. Sinclaire worked quickly to cuff her in, making sure she would not be able to move away from it one bit.

Now Samantha was strapped against the Cross, at her host's mercy, and feeling incredibly horny. Her nervous anticipation began to get the better of her; she felt like she couldn't control her breathing at all anymore. She wanted to struggle against the cuffs, and stopped herself by shear force of will.

"Now then. Let's go over *my* rules," Mr. Sinclaire said calmly, moving to where Samantha could see him. "First of all: you're not on any kind of noise restriction. You can scream, cry, yell, curse, anything you want. In fact, I insist you don't hold back. I like it. Understand?"

Samantha nodded her head, surprised. It had not even occurred to her he might put her on some sort of noise restriction. How could a woman be cuffed into a St. Andrew's Cross, get her bottom spanked, and *not* make any noise?

"Next. If you need to come at any time, then come. You're not on any kind of restriction for that, either. Come as many times as you like, but let me know if you're about to. I want to know how many times you come tonight. Understand?"

Again, Samantha nodded, feeling out of her depths. She would ask him about the restrictions, and the lack of them, later.

"Next. I'll be giving you fair warning about what I'm about to do. I *might* even tell you how much to expect once I get started. But that doesn't mean you can argue with me about it. It's not up for discussion. It's just me going easier on you this first time. You've still got your safeword, but you don't get to negotiate with me. Understand?"

Samantha nodded silently, feeling her fear begin to overflow.

"Last thing." He paused. "I'm going to take you all the way to your edge, Samantha. But this is our first session together, and it might take me some time to learn how to straddle the edge. So: do you remember your safeword?"

"Jasmine."

"Yes. Use it if you feel like you have to--but only if you absolutely have to."

"How will I know I have to?"

"Oh, you'll know, believe me." When she gave him a dubious look, he leaned down and peered into her face, smoothing her brow with the pad of his thumb, like a soft caress. "Samantha, I am going to make you fly so high, you won't be able to see the ground. When you're so close to the edge you can feel yourself about to fly off into the abyss, that safeword will be the only thing stopping you. That's when you use it."

Samantha could feel herself melting inside. Mr. Sinclaire's voice was like a gentle flow of water, and she was already drifting away. Her body relaxed against her bonds.

As she stood there, her eyes closed, Mr. Sinclaire went to the back of the room, where a large, double-doored wardrobe sat closed. He opened it up, began pulling things out, and laid them on a large wheeled tray. When he was satisfied, he took his place once more behind Samantha's stretched and quivering form, pulling the tray behind him.

"Let's begin," he said. Samantha sensed he had grabbed something off the tray. Mr. Sinclaire gave her no time to ready herself: she had barely taken a deep breath before she felt the first searing smack against her soft skin.

Whap!

Whatever it was Mr. Sinclaire was using on her, he hit her right between the shoulder blades with a soft thud. What felt like a few dozen pin pricks dug into her back, stinging painfully.

"This is a braided bullhide flogger," Mr. Sinclaire explained as Samantha inhaled. He hit her with it again, using an easy, relaxed swing; Samantha winced as it came down, but otherwise made no noise. "It's not as mean as some of the other floggers. I thought we would start off slow."

Samantha was barely listening. As he spoke, he hit her again with the flogger, then again, aiming for the space between her shoulder blades, making her gasp and tense up her muscles. The pain was there, and it was bad, but at the same time it was a delicious kind of pain, exactly what she wanted. What she needed.

Soon, Mr. Sinclaire began to use heavier strokes, and Samantha pressed herself into the Cross, never wanting it to end.

He flogged her for a long time, and by the time he was done, Samantha's whole upper back was a beautiful, deep red. She was already off in subspace, feeling nothing but the pleasure in the pain. She was flying.

Mr. Sinclaire looked at her still form and smiled. "Time to move on," he said, knowing full well Samantha was barely listening. But still, he thought it important to talk to her as he worked, letting her know what he was doing and what he was using. She would remember it later, he knew.

He put the flogger on the tray behind him, and picked up a flat, wide-handled tool.

"This is a leather paddle, Samantha," he said. "I'm going to work that sweet little ass of yours now. Ahh, I can see how this is making you wet. Your pussy is dripping. Come when you need to, just let me know." He maneuvered himself next to her side and let the paddle wing, smacking it against the jutting rump of her derriere. This time, Samantha shrieked.

Smack! Smack! Smack! Smack!

He worked methodically, taking his time, alternating between ass cheeks as he paddled her. Samantha began to cry out with each stroke, feeling the sting of the paddle grow sharper.

Smack! Smack! Smack! Smack!

Samantha's tears flowed freely now. The pain was bad, much worse than the flogger had been. The paddle seemed to be biting into her flesh; Mr. Sinclaire was picking up his pace, giving her almost no time to recover between strokes. She couldn't get away from the sting, all she could do was cry out, and it hurt...but it was a *good* kind of hurt, it was *her* kind of hurt. Samantha could feel her pelvis tighten and her pussy clench, and she knew she was about to come. Then she remembered: she was supposed to tell him.

"I'm going to come, I'm going to --ohhh!" The orgasm hit, making her arch as far back as her restraints would allow. She cried out in ecstasy; Mr. Sinclaire continued to paddle her as she came, making her orgasm last even longer. Every time she thought she was coming down from the crest, the paddle would smack her again, and she would go right back up, convulsing against the cross. But after the third wave, she just couldn't do it anymore. She felt wrung out and limp.

Mr. Sinclaire stopped swinging the paddle. He was breathing hard behind her.

After a few moments, he leaned in to whisper in her ear. "It's going to get more intense now, Samantha," he said. Samantha couldn't articulate a reply; she was still high in subspace. But she could hear him, and inside, she shivered at the warm breath of his words, and steeled herself for what was to come.

"Get ready, Samantha. This is going to hurt, a lot. I'll do two at a time, and alternate between each cheek."

Samantha could hear a swish through the air, and then--impact. What felt like a few dozen wasp stingers pierced into her like needles. She screamed.

"It's a brush," Mr. Sinclaire said, his voice calm against her scream of pain. "Stings a lot more than you'd think, yes?" He swatted her again, and Samantha screamed again, desperate for one second, just one second, to compose herself. But Mr. Sinclaire didn't give it to her. True to his word, he swatted her twice on one side, and then did two quick swats on the other. They weren't even hard swats; Samantha could tell he wasn't putting a lot of force behind the blows. But the blunt bristles prickled her flesh like holy fire.

Samantha shook her head violently, twisting against the cross. The bristles began to feel like white-hot pokers against her flesh. Mr. Sinclaire began to put more force behind his blows, ignoring her screams.

He began pausing for a fraction of a second between each ass cheek. Samantha thought he was slowing down to go easier on her, but then she realized there was a secondary pain hitting her during that moment of respite, and Mr. Sinclaire just wanted to give her a chance to feel it. The bristles bit, and Samantha howled.

Swat, swat, pause. *Swat, swat,* pause.

The pain escalated until all thought was gone from Samantha's head and all that existed was her world of pain. Her breathing came fast and heavy. She could smell a sweetness in the air, the pungent odor of flowers: roses, lilacs, lilies, and above all else, the thick sweetness of jasmine...whole fields of them, overpowering her senses...the pain was shooting her up, and up, and up....

The smell of jasmine grew heavy and she couldn't bear the agony anymore. It was too much.

"Jas--oh! Oh, God!" Just as she was crying out her safeword, an orgasm exploded inside her, shocking her to her core. It burst from her center, slamming into her extremities, and then bounced right back. The force of it was intense; her head fell back, and her eyes rolled.

She must have blacked out for a few seconds, because when she came to, she was no longer cuffed to the cross. Mr. Sinclaire was carrying her like a baby over to the bed. His hands on her back and bottom hurt like rough sandpaper, but it felt comforting.

"That was...that was..." She couldn't finish the sentence. She rested her head against his chest, and then Mr. Sinclaire was putting her gently on the mattress.

"One more," he said, getting undressed. "Come for me one more time, Samantha." With half-hooded eyes, Samantha watched him take his clothes off, then gasped when she saw his stiffened cock. It was standing straight up against his belly, reaching high above his bellybutton. He had obviously gotten very aroused by what he had just been doing to her, but the man was *huge*.

He opened the drawer of the bedside table and pulled out nipple clamps, held together by a very long, thin chain.

"I didn't give enough attention to these today," he murmured, staring at her breasts.

Holding one of the nipple clamps open, he aimed it toward Samantha's left breast and fitted it right around the nipple. Then slowly, oh so slowly, he let go. The clamp bit into her nipple as it squeezed, and Samantha moaned.

Mr. Sinclaire did the right nipple next, staring in fascination as the rubbery nub of flesh swelled and bulged from the wicked metal mouth.

"It hurts, it hurts," Samantha cried, flailing.

"I know," Mr. Sinclaire answered, his voice soft. It was clear he was enjoying watching the way Samantha struggled with the pain of the clamps. "Do you need to safeword?"

"No," she whimpered. The pain was acute, making it hard for her to talk.

He pulled on the chain, just a bit, and Samantha shrieked. Her torso lifted off the bed. Tears spilled from her eyes as her face contorted with agony. Just when she began to panic from the pain, Mr. Sinclaire let go, and she came back down.

But before she could recover from his little stint, Mr. Sinclaire took the long loose chain and slipped it over his head. He moved himself directly over Samantha's wracked body, spread her legs wide with his own, and thrust his cock deep inside her cunt.

Samantha was very hot, and very wet after her multiple orgasms. But she was also very tight, and Mr. Sinclaire's large prick slamming into her caused her a different kind of pain. She cried out.

Supporting himself on his hands, Mr. Sinclaire pounded into her, thrusting hard. The chain around his neck kept her nipples high and erect. Every time he lifted his chest the slightest bit, the chain stretched, and the clamps pulled, tightening around her nipples even more. Samantha whimpered, and cried...and responded.

She widened her legs even more, lifting them high around her host's body. She held his shoulders, but didn't try to pull him down; she began to love the feel of the clamps pulling at her sensitive nipples, biting into them like tiny teeth, shocking her every time Mr. Sinclaire lifted himself up to slam into her cunt again with his ramming prick.

Her back hurt, and her ass hurt, her nipples were in agony, and her host was taking her brutally, pounding into her well-oiled cunt like a battering ram. Samantha could feel the orgasm building inside her, growing as big as before. But this time she knew what was coming, and got ready for it.

"Oh Jesus," Samantha had just enough time to say before the orgasm hit. Her muscles tightened, and her pussy clenched, squeezing around Mr. Sinclaire's thrusting cock like a glove. As her pussy spasmed around his length, Mr. Sinclaire came himself, groaning above her and shooting his cum deep into her sopping cunt. Once he was done, he collapsed on top of her, putting his head against her chest and breathing hard.

Samantha didn't notice. She was already out cold.

***

She woke up a while later to the feeling of someone smoothing the hair away from her face.

"Wake up," her host's voice came from above her. "Wake up, sleeping beauty."

Samantha opened her eyes and looked around. She was lying on her stomach on the bed, one arm draped over the side. Her back and ass hurt like hell.

"How long have I been out?" She asked, looking at Mr. Sinclaire standing above her. He smiled.

"About half an hour," he answered. "I took the liberty of coating your back and butt with some ointment we keep here at the hotel. It really helps with the pain and healing."

Samantha tried to get up, but when she pushed herself into a sitting position, she winced. The cream did seem to be helping, but she still hurt.

"How do you feel?"

She took a minute to really think about it. "Good," she said, grinning. "I'm sore, but I feel really, really good."

Mr. Sinclaire smiled at her answer, and Samantha's breath caught. He was so overwhelming to her senses. She had not felt this satisfied since that night at the club a year before, when the Master had taken her in hand.

"Do I need to feel rushed to get dressed?" She asked.

"No, take all the time you need." Mr. Sinclaire retrieved a short robe from the wardrobe, belted it loosely around his narrow waist, and sat back down on the edge of the bed next to her. Samantha fell back against the pillows with a thud, sighing in contentment. She felt very languid.

"So?" Mr. Sinclaire asked. "How was I compared to the Master you had at the club that night?" *How did he know I was just thinking about that?*

"Oh, I don't know," she answered, being flippant. "He was so good at what he did...but you were okay too. I guess." She tried to hide the grin curving her lips. Mr. Sinclaire scowled, rolled her onto her side, and started pinching her ass hard.

"Ow! Ow! Okay, you were amazing too," she cried, her voice full of laughter. Mr. Sinclaire growled but let her go.

"Samantha...Sam...I have a feeling you are going to live up to your name," he said, moving aside some stubborn stray hair in her face and patting it down behind her ear.

Samantha's eyes narrowed. "What do you mean?"

"I mean, you are a SAM. It's an acronym for Smart-Assed Masochist--which I have a feeling is exactly what you are."

"Is that a bad thing?"

"It depends. Smart-Assed Masochists tend to get themselves into trouble. They need a strong hand of a Dom, one usually wielding a heavy instrument, to keep them in line."

"I see." She batted her eyelashes at him. "And you think you have that heavy hand? You have what it takes to keep me in line?"

"Oh yes...at least, while you're staying at the Hotel Bentmoore," he said.

Samantha lowered her eyes. Mr. Sinclaire missed her fleeting look of sadness; he was already getting up from the bed.

"You want some water?" He asked, pouring himself a glass from a pitcher sitting on the opposite bedside table.

"No, thank you." Her voice was whisper-thin.

"We should talk about what you want to do tomorrow," he said, gulping the water down and returning the glass to the table. "Is there anything else specific you'd like to try? Or would you just rather leave things up to me to decide?"

"Sir, can I ask you some questions first, before we talk about tomorrow? You said some things that confused me, and it's not like I have anyone else I can ask."

"Sure, fire away," Mr. Sinclaire said.

"Well, you taught me about using a safeword, and told me to use it when I thought I couldn't take the pain anymore."

"Not just the pain, although that's most of it. Sometimes it's the fear that gets too much. Sometimes the whole scene just gets too psychologically overwhelming."

"But when I was on stage at the club that night, no one gave me a safeword."

"That's because the Master would have stopped immediately if you had told him to. You didn't need a safeword, you just had to say 'no' or 'stop,' and the scene would have been over. You didn't tell him to stop, did you?"

"No, I didn't. I...I really liked it, all the way up to the very end." She paused to think. "But the woman who went up after me, he was much harder on her than he was on me. She begged him to stop, and he didn't. If she had gone before me, I don't think I would have agreed to go on stage at all. I would've been too afraid, after seeing what he put her through."

Mr. Sinclaire thought for a moment. "Did she go on stage alone?"

"No, a man came up with her, but he stood to the side. I got the feeling they were together, like boyfriend and girlfriend. The guy watched the Master flog and whip her. He seemed to like it a lot."

"Sounds like they *were* together, but not as boyfriend and girlfriend. He was her Dom, and she was his sub, and he had ordered her to go up." When Samantha looked confused, he slowed down, trying to pick his words carefully. "She was following his orders. She had no choice."

"But you told me about rules of consent, and how the choice is always mine."

"Well...the choice to enter into a BDSM scene, to engage in that kind of play, is always yours. But sometimes, a person can also consent beforehand to give up their control completely while the scene is going on.

Rules are discussed in advance, but the details of what goes on once the scene starts is up to the Dom. Often in those cases, the sub will no longer have a safeword." When he realized he was only confusing her more, he sighed. "Samantha, it really depends on the relationship of the two people. The most extreme example I can think of is the Master/slave dynamic."

"Slave?" Samantha breathed, looking shocked.

"Yes. But there are different kinds of slaves, too. It all depends on what the couple has agreed on in advanced." He thought about Marissa and her collection of slaves, and wondered what was happening to Paul. He pushed the thought away. "Some Doms insist on having absolute control over their slaves all the time, night and day. But the slave always has Right of Last Refusal."

"Right of...?"

"Last Refusal. It means the ending of the relationship. The slave can sever all ties with her Master. It's hard, but the slave always has that choice, as painful as it is, to walk away."

Samantha took a minute to digest everything. "Mr. Sinclaire, Sir...do all your other, um, guests, have safewords?"

"No. Some of them have been coming to me for long enough that we don't use safewords anymore. I know their limits." He suddenly felt uncomfortable discussing his other clients with her, even vaguely, but didn't know why. "A scene with no safeword, it's...it's wild, and it's exciting, but it's exciting because it's dangerous. You can never really know how far things are going to go. It can get really, really intense."

"Then, that's what I want for tomorrow," Samantha said, her voice eager. "I want you to do a scene with me where I don't have a safeword."

"No."

"No? What do you mean, no?"

"I mean *no*. I will not do a scene like that with you." When she frowned, he said, "Samantha, you have just ended an abusive relationship. You are brand new to experiencing the pleasures of your own masochism--you don't even know your own limits. How can you expect me to agree to something like this, when you don't understand what it is you're asking for?"

"But I trust you. I know you'd never really hurt me."

"Then you're completely missing the point. No safeword means you *will* get hurt--more than you ever have before. What you felt today? That in *nothing* compared to what you'd go through with no safeword, even with me being the one working you over. Remember what I said before about being in subspace, straddling the abyss, and how you'd know when to use your safeword when you were about to go over the edge?"

Samantha nodded her head.

"No safeword means there is no straddling the edge," he said. "It means you get pushed over, stuck in that black zone of subspace, and it's up to me to get you to the other side. Once you start a scene like that, you have no choice but to finish it, no matter how badly you wish you could take it back and change your mind. The pain will feel like nothing you've ever felt before, and it won't stop until I decide to make it stop."

Samantha stared at him as he spoke, mesmerized. Her eyes grew wide.

"But that's what I want. To give up control completely to you, to see where the pain will take me."

"No, Samantha. It is simply too early for you to do this. I will not allow you to give up your safeword."

"Fine. I'll just find someone else who will." She jumped from the bed and grabbed her clothes from the shelf. "I'll be checking out of the hotel tomorrow morning. Thank you for all your help." She pulled her panties up her waist and began to put on her bra.

"Now hold on just a fucking second." Mr. Sinclaire grabbed her by the arm. "You're going to leave the hotel, and then what? Go to another BDSM club on your own, find another asshole like Paul to smack you around?"

"You told me I got unlucky. I shouldn't get unlucky twice," she quipped, yanking her arm back and lifting up her bra straps till they snapped over her shoulders. "Maybe I'll find another Master who can help me. And anyway, it's not like you're willing to give me what I want. So what choice do I have?"

Mr. Sinclaire gnashed his teeth together. It was obvious she had no idea what kind of predicament she was putting him in.

If he did this scene with her, and she became over-whelmed by the fear and the pain (and he knew, at some point, she would), he would have only two choices: keep going despite her cries and pleas to stop, or give in and stop the scene. If he stopped the scene, she would always wonder what could have happened, how far she could have gone with him, and whether she would have still enjoyed it in the end. She might even resent him for hon-oring her pleas to stop, when she'd specifically called for no safeword.

But if he kept going, and ignored her pleas, she may later come to hate what he had put her through, and feel like she'd been abused again.

He didn't want her to walk away unsatisfied. But he also didn't want to hurt her, at least not psychologically. He was a sexual sadist, not an emotional one. Mr. Sin-claire liked to seduce consent out of his guests, not ma-nipulate them into doing things they weren't ready for.

He'd called her a Smart-Assed Masochist, and he'd been right. She was goading him into doing what she wanted, manipulating him with her needs, and she was driving him crazy. And yet, the idea of having Samantha under his will, with no safeword...to have the freedom to take her as far as she could go, to see how high she could fly...could he really refuse such a demand? The sadist in him cried out *NO*.

And one thing was for sure: if he didn't agree to do this scene with her at all, and she left the hotel now, she would certainly get herself into trouble. Mr. Sinclaire had no doubts about that.

"Fine," he growled. "I'll do it." When Samantha's mouth widened into a huge, satisfied grin, he scowled even deeper. "I just hope we don't both end up regretting this. I'll give you until tomorrow to change your mind. I want you to really think about this, Samantha, because if I don't hear from the liaison that you've had a change of heart, once you walk through that door tomorrow, there will be no turning back."

"I understand," Samantha said. "Thank you, Sir."

"Wait and see if you'll be thanking me tomorrow," he answered, handing her the rest of her clothes. He knew one thing: he planned on punishing her long and hard for being the Smart-Assed Masochist she was.

***

The next evening, Samantha arrived to her activity room right on time. The liaison had escorted her from her room, to the elevator, and down the hallway, without once raising his eyebrows at her attire or giving her a single strange look.

Samantha, on Mr. Sinclaire's orders, had donned a loose, shapeless dress that he had sent up to her room. Samantha wore nothing underneath. Again, her host's orders.

Inside the activity room, Mr. Sinclaire was waiting for her. But this time, the room looked very different: the St. Andrew's Cross was gone, and another piece of furniture took its place. It looked wicked indeed, but Samantha tried not to imagine too hard what would be done to her on that piece of equipment. She would find out soon enough.

Mr. Sinclaire also looked different. He still wore the formal slacks, but no shirt, and his feet were bare. His contoured muscles shaped him into a fine specimen of a male, Samantha thought. She smiled.

"Hello, Samantha," he greeted her. "You had a good morning? Enjoyed the pool a little?"

"Yes, Sir," she replied. She lowered her eyes. "Sir, I saw Paul today, briefly, during my breakfast. He looked very...different." There was no word to describe the drastic change she had seen in Paul. He had been meek, subdued--almost frightened of her. The kind of person she had been a few days ago, she realized. But there had been no disguising the wide leather collar Paul had been wearing around his neck.

Mr. Sinclaire took on a worried frown. "Yes, I was informed he had been instructed to seek you out and apologize for his behavior. Did he? And to your satisfaction?"

"Yes. Very much." He had been desperate, in fact.

"Did you accept his apology?"

"Yes. It seemed very, um, heartfelt." Like his life depended on it.

"Did he say anything else to you?"

"Only that I wouldn't have to see him ever again, if that was my wish."

"Good."

"He was wearing a collar. Sir...what's happened to him?"

Mr. Sinclaire gave her a thin, twisted smile. "We have our own ways, here at the Hotel Bentmoore, of dealing with abusers. Marissa likes to call it her 'training camp.'"

"Marissa?"

"One of our Dominas." When he saw her look of confusion, he frowned again. "Put Paul out of your mind. He's fine--better than fine. He's going to walk out of here a new man." Samantha thought Mr. Sinclaire's tone quite ominous, but she decided to follow orders and drop it.

"Sir, what would you like me to do?"

"Before we start, I want to give you one last time to back out. I know I told you yesterday once you entered this room it would be too late, but I realized that might have come across as too harsh. We can still do a different scene, one where you have a safeword, and you'll feel just as good as you did yesterday, if you want."

She shook her head. "No. I want to see where this goes. You're the only one I trust to help me without violating my boundaries, and to keep control over the scene." She looked so earnest, in that moment, Mr. Sinclaire knew he could not refuse.

"Very well then," he said, taking control. "I have your consent to do as I wish, no matter how much you may beg me later to stop. And you will beg me, Samantha. You will beg and plead and cry and scream, and your cries will only press me on. Understand?"

Samantha nodded. Her mouth had gone too dry for her to speak.

"Get undressed."

There was no refusing him or getting smart-assed about it this time. Samantha only had to unbutton the first three buttons of the loose dress for the opening to be large enough for her to slip it down. In a matter of seconds, she was naked.

"Come here." Dutifully she obeyed, walking over to where he was standing next to the large, foreboding piece of furniture. Most of it was a long padded table, but there were two lower padded shelves protruding out the lower end, one on each side. "Get up," Mr. Sinclaire ordered. "On your stomach. Legs on the pads."

Samantha climbed on. She could rest most her body on the table; her hips, though, folded down and fell off the edge. She had to spread her legs wide to center them on the lower shelves. Her ass was thrust up, her pussy was fully presented and vulnerable, and her breasts were crushed beneath her. She felt akin to a rump roast being served on a silver platter.

Mr. Sinclaire began to strap her in, buckling her hips, waist, legs and ankles. Then he tucked her arms to her sides, and cuffed her wrists to the lower legs of the bench. Her hands were stuck to her sides now, useless. She instinctively began to fight her bonds, testing her restraints.

Ignoring her twists and jerks, Mr. Sinclaire tossed a long strap across her shoulder blades and cinched it down tight. Samantha kept her head to the side, her cheek pressed into the padding.

Fear was riding her hard now. It was not just how Mr. Sinclaire was restraining her--although that was most of it--it was the way his manner had changed while doing it. The intent expression on his face, the way he worked methodically, checking every buckle and strap twice to make sure it would hold her in place, made her think he wasn't even really seeing her anymore. Not as Samantha, anyway. She was his toy, to be used as he saw fit.

The thought aroused her, and frightened her to hell.

"Most of the same rules you had yesterday still apply," he said, stepping back once he was satisfied with his handiwork. "You can make as much noise as you want. You can come whenever you want, you don't even have to tell me beforehand. But there will be no safeword. I may, or may not, explain to you what I'm doing or what I have planned for you next." He didn't ask this time if she understood. It didn't really matter.

Samantha could feel her limbs begin to shake. She tried to close her eyes and take a deep, calming breath, but the straps around her shoulders and waist bit into her and she only managed to scare herself more.

The room became quiet, eerily so. She had no idea what her host was doing; she heard no footsteps, not even his breathing.

Minutes ticked by. Samantha could hear her heart beating in her chest. She was being induced to panic before they had even begun.

Finally, when she could take the silence no more and was about to call out, Mr. Sinclaire spoke.

"I will start with a flogger again," he said. Samantha wanted to groan in relief--at least she knew he was there and something was about to happen. "But this flogger is not the same as yesterday. I think you'll feel the difference immediately."

A second later, Samantha felt the flogger hit her ass, and he was right--she did feel the difference immediately. The straps of leather on this one were thinner, bendier... more *mean,* as had he called it before. The pain was intense: it felt like the strands were cutting into her skin like string through clay. Very quickly, she was crying in pain. The blows weren't hard, but they were hitting her at an angle, like Mr. Sinclaire was adding a flick to his wrist with each one.

Mr. Sinclaire fell into a rhythm, alternating between ass cheeks, and soon the pain wasn't so bad anymore.

It was still there, but Samantha wasn't stuck in its grip. She was somewhere far away. She was being lulled into subspace.

And then she felt something else smack across her ass, something much longer and stingier, and she screamed. It had whipped her right at the lower curve of her butt.

"This is a split-tongued tawse," Mr. Sinclaire said. Samantha could only gasp, trying to overcome the pain of that single blow. Her head came off the padding, and she panted, trying to breath through the pain.

"Head down, Samantha." When she didn't obey immediately, he whipped her once more with the tawse, harder than before. "I *said*, head down, Samantha!"

Slowly, Samantha lowered her head, burying her cheek into the padding. She began to sob. Mr. Sinclaire took no pity on her: he whipped her ass with the tawse, again and again, and all Samantha could do was twist against her restraints and cry out with each hit.

But soon she realized Mr. Sinclaire was adopting a rhythm with the tawse, just as he had with the flogger. He would whip her on the rising swell of her ass cheek, then on the sloping curve; then he would move around the table and do the other cheek the same way.

Samantha was crying, and panting, and tensing with anticipation, but pleasure was slowly starting to unfurl in her belly, until it was a huge ball of pain and pleasure all swirling into one big orgasm.

She yelled at she came, only this time they were yells of ecstasy, and it was clear Mr. Sinclaire could tell the difference. He whipped her ass back and forth as her orgasm went on and on, and when she was finally coming down from the ride, he stopped completely.

As her breathing returned to normal, Mr. Sinclaire came around and wiped her face with a cold wet cloth. It felt soothing, and helped to refocus her.

"Thank you," she said raggedly. Mr. Sinclaire didn't answer. When he decided she had recovered enough, he moved back behind her, and Samantha knew her ordeal was about to continue.

But she wasn't expecting to feel her ass cheeks being spread apart and something pressing against her asshole.

"What--what are you doing--wait--ahhh!" Something cold, meaty, and slightly juicy was being pushed through her sphincter. There had been no warning and no let-up to the pressure. Her tight ring of muscle was forced to yield, quickly and painfully.

"Please, you didn't say you would put things in my--"

"We did talk about your limits, Samantha. Your ass-hole was not one of them."

"But--but--ohhhh," she groaned as the thing being stuffed up inside her grew wider, stretching her muscles apart. Mr. Sinclaire was telling the truth: during his questioning, she had admitted to being fucked in the ass before, and not minding it. She had not put it as one of her hard, or even soft limits, because she had not envi-sioned being violated in this way. Now it was too late to try to protest.

But the thing being shoved rudely up her ass was clearly not his dick or a dildo; it was something else, something much more menacing. It was too wide, and too long, and Samantha felt like she was being impaled.

"Just give me--a minute--to get used to it--"

"No." He pressed harder, and Samantha was crying all over again.

"Please! Please!"

"No." He pushed it in hard, and Samantha thought her skin would surely rip apart. But then it stopped, and Mr. Sinclaire let go. Her ass cheeks snapped back. Whatever it was, it was in, and there to stay until her host removed it.

"We have a few seconds," he said. Samantha didn't understand. Why did they have only a few seconds?

"This is the where things get hard, Samantha," he said. "I'm going to use a crop next. Every thirty second, you'll get a swipe of the crop. When five minutes is up, I'll use a vibrator on your clit, and you'll come. That's ten swipes every five minutes."

Samantha was trying to pay attention to what he was saying, but something was going on inside the rim of her ass...a stinging sensation...whatever it was her host had put inside her, it was starting to burn.

"Oh," she gasped. The burn was growing worse.

"I see you're starting to feel it," Mr. Sinclaire said. "What you have inside you is a ginger root. It won't cause you physical damage, but it will feel like the fires of hell are licking your asshole. You'll try to relax your muscles against the pain, but it won't help--and every thirty seconds I'll be coming at you with the crop, and you'll clench that root right up your insides." His voice was calm but eager with anticipation.

The burn was growing like fire, and Samantha's eyes were tearing.

"Please," she whispered. "Please, I don't know if I can take this."

"You'll take it. There's no going back now. I'm setting a timer for the crop. You'll feel the first hit, and then a secondary pain as your flesh bounces back."

He backed away, and Samantha started to cry in earnest. If she could have, she would have safeworded right then. But she could not.

A hiss came through the air, and then the crop hit. Mr. Sinclaire had aimed it across her upper thighs, and Samantha had not been expecting that.

If felt like a branding iron pressed into her flesh...but that was nothing compared to the secondary pain he had warned her about. That pain was indescribable.

Samantha's whole body stiffened with the pain, and in doing so, her asshole squeezed around the ginger. She let out an ear-piercing scream.

"Thirty seconds," Mr. Sinclaire said.

"Oh, GOD." Samantha tried to relax her asshole around the root; it seemed to lessen the pain somewhat. But the root was huge, and there was no releasing it completely. She even tried to push it out; it was well planted and not budging, and her efforts only hurt her more.

There was a couple of short beeps, followed by a long beep: the timer was going off. The crop came down again.

Samantha screamed until she had no voice left. Her head came off the padding; her body strained against her bonds. And her asshole clenched.

Ten times the crop came down, and ten times Samantha took it. She tried to escape into subspace as much as she could, but the timer did a good job of warning her before the crop came down again, just enough time to pull her out of subspace but not enough time for her to prepare for the impact.

Finally, the first five minutes were up.

"Time to come," Mr. Sinclaire announced. Samantha could hear a buzzing noise behind her. Mr. Sinclaire put a wide vibrator against her cunt lips, just kissing her clit.

Samantha didn't know how Mr. Sinclaire thought she would be able to come. She was still crying in pain. But as soon as the vibrator started to work its magic, she could feel the orgasm growing. Pleasure fought with the pain, doing a short, erotic dance inside her groin and head, and then she was coming hard, tensing against the ginger, and the burn mixed with her pleasure until she couldn't tell the difference.

But all too soon the wave of the orgasm had washed away, and all she felt was the fire raging inside her asshole, worse than before.

As soon as Mr. Sinclaire was sure the orgasm was gone along with any tiny aftershocks that had rippled her body, he came at her with the crop again. Samantha cried out in shock and dismay. She had to try to safeword. She had to. She couldn't do this.

"Jasmine, please Sir, jasmine, I can't--"

"Thirty seconds," he reminded her.

"Sir, PLEASE--"

But he ignored her.

Samantha began to sob, this time with desperation. Mr. Sinclaire had tried to warn her what this would be like, but she had stubbornly refused to listen. *Oh, God, how could I have been so stupid?* She thought. She would have given anything to take it all back, anything. But there was no changing course now.

Three sets left. God help her.

Beep. Beep. Beeeep!

The crop came down again, and Samantha barely had any voice left to scream. She fought the bonds violently, rocking the table, but it didn't help. Nothing helped. She was breaking inside.

Beep. Beep. Beeeep!

Another hiss through the air, another swat, another agonizing cut, and then the secondary pain. Samantha sobbed.

When the five minutes were up, all she could do was sigh in blessed relief when the vibrator hit her pussy, not because it felt good, but because it meant she would get a break from the crop, however short it was.

She actively tried this time not to come. She wanted to enjoy the soothing comfort of the vibrator for as long as she could. The fire in her ass was like a volcano, but at least with the vibrator, she could push that aside just a little bit.

But what Samantha didn't know was that the ginger was turning her body's natural reactions against her. Blood was engorging her entire pelvic area, turning her clit a deep pinkish hue. Her pussy was dripping juices. All her nerves were going haywire, reacting to the slightest touch. She was being primed to come, whether she wanted to or not.

"Oh, oh no, oh please," she begged. But she came, long and hard, and when she was done she began to cry again, because she knew the crop would soon resume its assault on her thighs and ass and there was nothing she could do to stop it.

She was not wrong.

Swipe!

Thirty seconds later, again.

And thirty seconds later, again.

And again. And again.

The ginger burned like molten lava against the sensitive tissues of her anal sphincter. The crop was a steady, relentless meter of torture.

She couldn't live through this. She couldn't.

Samantha's mind began to break down. She could smell the spicy aroma of jasmine, filling her consciousness and drowning her with its sickening scent. It was all her mind could register, the only thing that existed for her now. The smell of jasmine...and the pain.

She wasn't in subspace anymore. She was somewhere in a black and endless void, utterly lost.

The vibrator returned; she could feel her host nestling it against her clit, deep inside her swollen pussy lips. This time, the orgasm broke out of her like crystal hitting concrete. It didn't feel good; it felt like she was being torn into pieces. Another assault of her body's reactions that she had no control over.

"Five more minutes, Samantha," Mr. Sinclaire's voice came from far away. "You can get through this."

Despite her despair and pain, Samantha wanted to laugh. What choice did she have *but* to get through this? He wasn't going to stop now. All she could do was lay there and take it and hope she didn't end up broken, inside and out, by the time it was all over.

The crop didn't come down as she was expecting it to, but Samantha didn't hold her breath waiting for it. There was no use; there was no place safe for her mind to go to fly away from the pain.

She felt a gentle hand brush against her cheek, and when she opened her eyes, Mr. Sinclaire was looking down at her.

"You are so beautiful, Samantha," he whispered, piercing her eyes with his own. "You are so strong." Samantha held his stare for a moment. Something deep and powerful passed between them.

Mr. Sinclaire nodded. Samantha nodded back. Then her host disappeared behind her, and took his place to whip her once more with the crop. But it felt different now: Samantha could take it. She knew it. She would not break.

Even the ginger didn't burn as before. It was still bad, but the heat was coming down, leaving a strange, tingling warmth.

Nine last smacks with the crop, and Samantha cried, but she knew the end was near, and some of her cries were in relief. *Three more, three more, I can take three more...two more, just two more...one more...OH GOD!*

The last hit was the worst. Mr. Sinclaire put his full force behind the blow, and Samantha let out a noise that was shrill and completely inhuman. But by the time she was done, Mr. Sinclaire was already putting down the crop and turning off the timer. He pulled the ginger root out of her ass smoothly, with one slow pull, and Samantha felt like crying all over again. It was finally over.

"Come with me this time, Samantha," Mr. Sinclaire said. He entered her pussy from behind, filling her cunt with hard, demanding cock. He pumped into her gently, using deep but slow thrusts.

At first, Samantha was in heaven, enjoying the gentle and easy fucking he was offering her. The cropping was over, the ginger was out, and now he would just fuck her until they both came.

But somehow his slow, gentle thrusts soon weren't enough. Her ass felt tingly all over, inside and out. It was a new and strange sensation, and she didn't know how to handle it. Her asshole throbbed, and tingled...she needed...she needed...

"Fuck my ass," she begged. She had no idea where the words had come from, but once they were out, they felt exactly right. "Please Sir, fuck my ass."

"Samantha, I'm too big," Mr. Sinclaire grunted, still pumping into her from behind. "You won't--"

"Please!" She said, barely rasping out the words. "Please, Sir--my ass."

Mr. Sinclaire was about to say he didn't want to hurt her, but then he stopped himself. *What the hell am I thinking?* He thought. *She* wants *the pain*. With that, he pulled his entire length out of her sopping cunt, and pressed the helmeted head of his prick right against the cringing gate of her asshole. He lunged.

Samantha cried out. She couldn't scream, she had no voice left to scream, but her lungs released until she had no breath and her diaphragm froze. It was a stabbing assault, and Samantha felt skewered.

Mr. Sinclaire began to pump into her ass just as he had her cunt, with steady, even strokes, and Samantha moaned. Her engorged and highly-sensitive asshole spasmed and pulled; the feel of his huge cock sliding and rubbing against her tight hole was exquisite, a perfect balance of pleasure and pain, and Samantha closed her eyes and let herself just feel it.

She couldn't move her body, she couldn't rock back against him, but Mr. Sinclaire seemed to know what she needed, and began to thrust faster, pumping into her hard. Samantha gasped with each thrust, taken by surprise by the increasing pleasure. It felt so good, *so good...*

Mr. Sinclaire reached around, nestled the vibrator against her clit, and turned it on. The orgasm that had been building inside Samantha exploded, and she came with a screech, desperately trying to grind her ass against her host. Mr. Sinclaire moved in kind, grinding in, savoring the feel of her soft mounds slapping against his groin. He kept pumping in and out of her asshole, and for the first time that night, completely lost control of himself. Her asshole was clenching and throbbing around his cock, trying to swallow him up whole. He couldn't hold on.

He didn't have to.

As Samantha came down from her intense orgasm, tiny aftershocks still racking her body, Mr. Sinclaire came too, shooting his cum straight up her warm, delicious ass. He collapsed on top of her as he finished. Samantha could feel his cock shrinking inside her, but he didn't pull out.

Only when his body was done shuddering with his own aftershocks, his cock limp within her depths, did he ease out slowly, trying not to hurt her further. The scene was over, and he knew her asshole would be very sensitive for a while, possibly even sore. Smug satisfaction filled him with the thought.

She watched with hooded eyes as he walked around the table to release her, one buckle at a time, but she didn't react. She didn't say anything: she only lay there, flaccid, watching. Only when he picked her up from the table and gently lifted her into his arms did she finally react.

"What?" she said. Her eyes darted; her head fell back against his arm, then snapped up. She looked dazed, almost drunk. "So sweet. Too much. Why?"

"You're okay, Samantha," Mr. Sinclaire reassured her. He walked over to the bed and carefully put her down onto it. "You're okay."

She looked at him wildly; then she started smacking his chest. "Please," she cried, starting to sob. "Too much. Jasmine--too sweet. Oh God. The smell. Too much. Please."

"Shh, sweetheart, shh," Mr. Sinclaire said softly. He wrapped the blanket around her like a mummy so she wouldn't hurt herself, then lay her down next to her and held her.

Women would often act loopy after their drop from subspace, he knew well. They would sometimes say insane things, cry for no reason, or just generally act highly charged and emotional. Mr. Sinclaire had been expecting it from Samantha, and was ready for it. He would give her responsible aftercare for as long as she needed it, and make sure she came to no harm.

So he held her close, making soothing noises as she babbled and cried. For a while, Samantha fought the blanket and his strong hold, but then she gave up and simply keened.

Finally, she fell into a light sleep.

Mr. Sinclaire continued to hold her.

***

This time when Samantha woke up, she did so on her own. Mr. Sinclaire was laying next to her, watching her as she slept, a smug smile on his face.

"Hello," she said.

"Hello," he said back. "How do you feel?"

"Give me a few minutes to answer that." Her voice was gone; she couldn't talk above a hoarse whisper. She tried to sit up.

"Slowly," Mr. Sinclaire instructed. "Here, let me help." He unwrapped her from the blanket, then carefully pulled her up by her hands. Samantha cried out in pain.

"Oh Jesus, my legs," she gasped. They felt like they had been cooked on a barbecue.

"They'll be sore for a while. Here, drink some water." He poured her some water from the pitcher and helped steady the glass in her hand as she tipped it to drink. She felt very shaky.

"Thank you," she rasped. The water helped; her throat felt a fraction better. But she doubted it would be back to normal anytime soon.

"I want you to lie down until you feel okay to get up. Take your time; there's no rush. I don't want you getting up too soon."

"Thank you," she repeated. He had just flogged, cropped, and violated her ass, and all she could do was thank him. The thought made her smile.

"You're smiling, so you must be recovering," Mr. Sinclaire said with a grin. "That's good. Are you still feeling emotional, or are you calming down? Does the room still smell strange to you?"

It took a minute for Samantha to understand what he was talking about. "I was pretty out of it there for a while, wasn't I?" She was horribly embarrassed.

"Don't feel bad. Hey." He leaned in to catch her eyes; she was too busy looking down at the bed to first notice. "Don't be embarrassed, okay? A lot of women act the way you did after a scene like that. It's the 'drop' after subspace. Some women do even crazier stuff than you did, believe me."

"Really?"

"Yeah, but those are guest secrets, so you'll just have to take my word for it," he said with a laugh. He lay down next to her and snuggled her into the crook of his arm.

Samantha took stock of herself. Her ass cheeks hurt, but nothing really bad. Her thighs hurt worse. But she realized the pain was well above her knees. Mr. Sinclaire had kept the worst of the welts on her upper legs and the swells of her bottom. They would not show under a skirt. Even while cropping her, Mr. Sinclaire had been thoughtful of her needs. And her asshole no longer hurt at all. He had told the truth, there would be no lasting damage.

His lips brushed against her forehead. "You okay?"

"Yeah, I'm...okay," she decided. "What you just did to me...it was...intense. More than I thought it would be. You tried to warn me, but there was no way for me to imagine that."

"I know. And now that you've gone through it, and you're on the other side?"

"I feel like I've gone through a religious experience," she said, trying to find the right words to describe how she felt. "Like a whole new level of understanding has opened up inside me. It'll take me some time to let it settle, though."

"That's true. But you don't have any bad feelings?"

"Bad feelings?"

Mr. Sinclaire suddenly looked uncomfortable. "You're not angry at me?"

"Why would I be angry at you?"

"Because I'm the one who did all this to you." He looked nervous, like he was sorely afraid she would be furious with him for what he had done to her, and too scared to say so.

"No," she said, her voice final. "I'm not angry. I wanted you to do all that to me. Well, maybe not like *that*...it was really, really hard. But I wanted the pain. I wanted to experience what it would be like, to be under the complete mercy of a Master Sadist, one who would still honor my limits and stay in control. You showed me." She was thoughtful for a moment. "While it was happening, I think for a while there I was just lost in the pain, and I wanted it to be over, because it hurt so bad... but now that it's all over, I'm glad I did it. It was an experience I'll never forget."

Mr. Sinclaire looked relieved. "Thank you." He kissed her forehead again. "Thank you for trusting me, Samantha. It was an experience I'll never forget, either."

She moved away so she could look into his face, really look at him. She was surprised by his gentle tone and softened expression. It seemed she wasn't the only one who had felt the intensity of their shared experience.

"It was my pleasure, Sir," she said.

"Was it really?"

"Well, no. But you know what I mean."

***

They snuggled on the bed for a while, and then Mr. Sinclaire helped her dress to return to her room. She understood now why he had instructed her to wear the loose dress: it barely touched her legs or ass as she walked. Samantha didn't think she'd be able to handle panties or jeans right now.

She checked out of the hotel the next day, as scheduled.

She only saw her host once more, when it was time to say goodbye. The liaison didn't bring her to the activity room this time, or even to one of the meeting rooms. He brought her to Mr. Sinclaire's private office.

"It's small," she said, looking around the square room.

"We don't generally spend a lot of time in our offices," Mr. Sinclaire smiled. Samantha smiled back.

"Samantha, I know this goes against propriety, and you don't have to answer if you don't want to, but...can you tell me the name of your city?"

"Phoenix," she answered without hesitation. "I live in Phoenix. Why?"

Mr. Sinclaire swiveled around to his filing cabinet and rummaged through some files. When he found what he was looking for, he pulled it out. It was a small black business card.

"This is the name of a reputable Master who works in your city," he said, handing her the card. "He does occasional work at BDSM clubs, but mostly he does private functions, working through referrals. If you call him and tell him I sent you, he will connect you with other people in the BDSM scene who are trustworthy, and can help you move forward in whatever direction you decide to go."

"Thank you so much." She tried to focus on putting the small card inside her purse. The tears were threatening.

"I want you to know, Samantha, that I'll never forget what we did together. I hope you'll come back to the Hotel Bentmoore and let me be your host again. It would be my honor."

"Thank you Sir."

"Good luck, Samantha."

"You too, Sir. Goodbye." She quickly rose and left the room before the tears could escape.

Mr. Sinclaire was not her boyfriend, or her Dom; and she was only his guest, one of many. He had changed her in ways it would take a long time for her to work through, but in the end, there was no lasting bond tying them together. He would move on to the next guest, and she would go home and go on with her life. Her new life. Her new self.

She left so quickly, she didn't catch Mr. Sinclaire's expression. If she had, she would have recognized all the longing and desire she was going through herself.

But she didn't see, and Mr. Sinclaire, by sheer force of will, kept himself from running after her and giving her one last, yearning kiss goodbye. Hosts of the Hotel Bentmoore simply didn't do things like that.

***

"You wanted to see me Sir?" Mr. Sinclaire took a seat across Mr. Bentmoore's desk. The older man looked up and leaned back in his chair.

"Sinclaire, yes," he said. "I take it you and Samantha got along well?"

"Yes, very well." His tone was wistful.

"But you're ready to move on with your other guests? Lauren has been waiting for you."

"Yes, I'm ready," Mr. Sinclaire said. It was time to get back to work, put his mind to other thoughts. "By the way...where's Paul?"

"Ah. Paul has requested a chance to stay on here at the hotel, and work as Marissa's assistant."

"By assistant, you mean slave."

"Yes, but let's not worry about semantics."

"Of course not, Sir. You are ready to give him this chance?"

"I'm thinking about it. Paul is not the same person he was when he walked in here, same as your guest. He is quite the changed man."

"I'm sure he is." Mr. Sinclaire and Mr. Bentmoore both looked at each other, and shuddered.

"If that is all then, Sir...?"

"Yes, that's all. I'm glad you were able to help that young lady, Sinclaire. You did good work."

"Thank you Sir." He left the room and shut the door quietly behind him.

His time with Samantha would be forever etched into his memory, scenes never to be forgotten. But he was a host of the Hotel Bentmoore, a Master, and it was time to get below and put his talents to good use.

Lauren would be first. She had a thing for clothing clips....

Also by Shelby Cross

Short stories:

Tales from the Hotel Bentmoore: Alice
Tales from the Hotel Bentmoore: Deborah
Tales from the Hotel Bentmoore: Mark and Audra
Tales from the Hotel Bentmoore: Elizabeth

Compilation:

Tales of the Hotel Bentmoore: The Complete Collection

Coming Soon:

The Taming of Red Riding
The Edge of Jasmine